COME for ME

C.J. SWEET

Copyright © 2024 by C.J. Sweet.

All rights reserved. This book or any portion thereof may not be reproduced or used in any manner whatsoever without the express written permission of the publisher except for the use of brief quotations in a book review.

Printed by Broken Spine Publishing, LLC, in the United States of America [2024].

Broken Spine Publishing, LLC

405 E Laburnum Ave Ste 3

Richmond, Virginia, 23222

ISBN: 979-8-9909120-1-4

Cover Design: Jaqueline Kropmann

Formatting: Samantha Pico

First Edition: 2024

This book is dedicated to the good little readers that beg for me to fuck with their feelings...
Come for me.

IMPORTANT NOTE

This book was created by a mental health professional who has taken what they know about human desires, needs, and trauma, and put them into words to foster feelings as close to real experiences as possible as listed in the trigger page. Please practice self-care.

Reading is a beautiful coping skill and temporary escape from a reality we must all return to. A friendly reminder that avoidance is an involuntary trauma response which can overtime lead to other mental health issues. Please consult a mental health professional as needed.

Happy to provide a temporary safe space as well as wishing future healing from any battles you might be going through.

MENU

C.J. Sweet, the sweetest seductress of all, invites you into her dark, fantastical world. C.J. encourages you to get a taste of her books, as each of her stories come with a menu to appeal to your personal and most intimate palette. With C.J.'s books, you can embrace your darkest desires, while also discovering new kinks along the way. A sweet tease of a book awaits you. All you have to do is lie back and open it for me.

This book contains tropes, microtropes, kinks, and dynamics best described as:

Praise
Powers
Begging
Pet Play
One bed
Collaring
Dirty Talk
Dark Past

Zelophilia
Public Sex
Breath play
Fated Mates
Degradation
Odaxelagnia
Face Fucking
Predator/prey
Electrocution
Exhibitionism
Hybristophilia
Imprisonment
Brat Tamer/brat
Royal Monarchy
Touch Her and Die
Age Gap (5+ years)
Double Penetration
Sadism/masochism
Breast/Nipple Torture
Impact Play/Spanking
Dominance/submission
Cunnilingus and Fellatio
Loveable Side Characters
Restraints and Vincilagnia
Edging and Orgasm Denial
Morally Grey and Unhinged MMC
Stubborn, Sassy, and Strong FMC
Werewolves, Vampires, and Witches
Funishments, Punishments, and Other Forms of Discipline

CONTENT WARNINGS

I recognize anything could be a trigger to a person's trauma/mental health. It is important to be self-aware of what those are. Some aspects in this book that could potentially be triggering include but are not limited to:

Death and Dying
Blood and Murder
Domestic Violence
Grief and Loss
Foul and Degrading Language
Consensual Force
Appearance of Cheating
Parental Abandonment and Death
Discussion of and Use of Substances
Religious Themes
Suicidal and Homicidal Thoughts/Plan

PART I

CHAPTER ONE
Alaina

The crowd erupts in laughter and excitement. Music fills the clearing before us, alight with movement and energy in anticipation of the annual Hunt.

I've been dreading the day. As the embers floating upward toward the stars fade, so do my dreams of knowing who I am. My packmates pray they'll find their fated mate in two days' time, while I pray mine doesn't exist.

With the mate bond comes the threat of my departure from the only home and family I've ever known, severing any ties from my mother.

My best friend, Taya, appears beside me with her hands full, awkwardly passing me a beer with a bottle of Moscato tucked under her arm and a glass in the other hand. She plops in the lawn chair next to me, pouring herself a cup.

I scrunch my nose at her beverage choice.

"I don't know how you drink that. It's too sweet." I take a swig of my beer, the hoppy flavor a welcome distraction from my racing thoughts.

Taya sets the bottle down, exhaling as she leans back. Her wavy blonde hair rests over the ridge of her breasts. Her rosy cheeks, stunning red lips, and curves deem her instantly hated by insecure bitches.

Taya's teeth smacking fills the silence as she savors her wine. "I happen to like juice. Besides, I don't like the taste of alcohol."

"Aw, baby doesn't like the taste of alcohol."

Taya laughs, giving me the finger.

She knows I love her.

The truth is, I envy her. Taya doesn't turn twenty-one until the fall, making her ineligible to participate in the Hunt until next year.

The Hunt is a decreed spring tradition, in which every unmated werewolf in the kingdom gather in search of their fated mate. Wolves who haven't found their mate after their twenty-first birthday are required by imperial law to attend. Mated werewolves, especially fated mates, strengthen us and, therefore, the pack, making it our unfortunate duty to participate.

All unmated, fresh twenty-one-year-old males will be led by their alpha to the castle at Crescent pack, while the females will be led by their luna. In the misogynistic tradition, men play the role of hunter, while she-wolves are considered prey.

According to those who've gone before, the men, arriving before the women, are securely caged in jail-like holding cells until hunting begins in the woods. Once confined, a witch casts a spell on the male wolves so the female wolves can't sense them.

Once in the woods, the female wolves shift and run when instructed, allowing for a head start. It is customary for them to run so their mates could prove their prowess and power.

Given the signal, the witch lifts her spell so she-wolves can sense the males. Then the chase commences at the alphas' howls, signaling the release of the "hunters." Afterward, the male wolves are uncaged. In the forest, the men capture and mark their new mate before the Moon Goddess.

Ugh. How barbaric.

Most will mark each other immediately, while others may decide to wait. For those who don't find their mate, they can take a chosen mate. Others may continue to search for their mate outside the Hunt.

Over time, we become weaker with each passing year without a mate, making us more vulnerable to attacks.

With the Hunt in two days, our pack is throwing a bachelor/bachelorette party to celebrate what may be one of our last nights single. Others are saying goodbye, as it's likely this'll be the last time all of us are together. Tradition dictates female mates move to their mate's pack. Many females here tonight may never return home.

That is the last thing I want.

Unfortunately, I turned twenty-one last summer and didn't find my mate among the pack, so my participation is mandatory this year.

I take another swig of my beer, thinking about having to leave my home.

High-pitched squelching followed by moans and heavy breathing snap me out of my thoughts.

"The fuck?" I say, catching the dribble from my mouth.

Following the noise, I spot Tyler and some redheaded she-wolf moaning as they sloppily make out on the log beside me. Cradling her in his arms, he leans his partner back enough that her hair is invading my space.

I don't recognize her. Knowing Tyler, he probably picked this girl up at a bar out of town. Goddess help whoever is Tyler's mate. I've never seen him commit to much of anything except a pissing contest with every male.

Ignoring them, I glance around at what looks more like a college party. She-wolves are crying over their boyfriends breaking up with them. Individuals are making out and sneaking off into the woods to hook up.

That's why Taya and I brought the chairs. We knew there would be drama.

I smile at the chaos, admiring the ultimate people-watching spectacles, thankful to have avoided ever getting too emotionally involved with anyone.

The couple's make-out session has escalated. They're shamelessly using my armrest to steady Tyler's recent conquest as she straddles him.

Annoyed, I scoff and scoot my chair closer to Taya.

"That could be you and your mate tomorrow." Taya giggles at my misfortune.

I roll my eyes. "Not gonna happen."

"You don't know that. By this time, in a couple days, you could be at another pack . . ." Taya looks over at the redhead sucking on Tyler's finger. "Doing whatever it is *they're* doing."

Taya and I laugh, but sadness fills the air as the reality of her words set in.

I've lived here my whole life, and because some old tradition says so, I may have to leave everything behind. *Wolves are only required to participate in the Hunt the first year they're eligible,* I remind myself.

I'm hoping I don't find my mate.

Jemma would be disappointed, though.

Though we aren't related by blood, Jemma was practically a sister to my late mother, and it was my mother's dying wish for Jemma to raise me. Having never met my father, I understand she's the only family I've ever known.

Whenever I ask Jemma about my mother, she tells me the same story of some pregnant she-wolf who showed up on her cabin doorstep seeking refuge. The pack took her in, and she lived with Jemma throughout her pregnancy.

My mother never told anyone who my father was, but one day, Jemma finally asked her. When she saw my mother panic for the first time, she didn't pry further. When I asked Jemma who she thought my father could be, she told me she didn't know but figured it should probably stay that way.

Jemma said my mother always seemed to be in deep thought. Always climbing and sitting in trees for hours, probably thinking about my father.

That is, until she died giving birth to me.

What kind of mother would she have been? What advice would she give me as I faced the Hunt? I yearn for her wisdom and voice to guide me.

Dread filled my heart as the reality of not recognizing a mate among the pack, including Alpha Jack Waller's son, Caleb Waller, sank in over the past year. I couldn't fathom a time I wouldn't have Jemma tie me to my mother's memory. All I knew of her—all I had of her—was this pack.

Once I complete the mate bond, my tie to the Bloodhound pack's mindlink would sever as my bond with my mate's pack forms. By losing my connection to them, it'd be like losing her again.

Jemma explained to me once that, when my mother came to the pack seeking refuge, the alpha had taken her for interrogations. All of which were documented, giving me hope for video, audio, and even notes to provide insight into who she was. Answers to questions about my family history I didn't think to ask may be in those records.

I remember how thrilled I was when Jemma told me and how disappointed I was to find out that only the alphas and their lunas have access to these records, meaning Caleb couldn't tell me, either.

I'm shaken out of my thoughts by shattering glass and roaring flames.

Caleb and his buddies laugh as they throw alcohol into the fire. He catches me staring at him, his eyes flashing gold, followed by a smirk. Maintaining eye contact, he tells his friends he'll "be right back" and walks toward me.

COME FOR ME

Not immune to his charm and stunning looks after all these years, my eyes wander over his daunting frame. As the heir to our pack, Caleb's genes are pure alpha. From his confident stride to his unyielding service to our people with his caring hands, he radiates masculinity and desire.

Somehow, he has it all—he dominates all his fights yet is still so gentle and loving to pups. Caleb's stern, compassionate gaze could hold anyone's attention. His broad, strong shoulders will carry great responsibility one day and, frankly, also look great with my legs dangling over them. He's built of muscle and testosterone, from his arms wrapped around my waist to the sturdy thighs holding us against various structures.

His speed and agility are unmatched, yet he takes his sweet time closing the gap between us. Caleb's stride brings him closer, the details of his blue eyes shining in the bonfire light. Caleb, undeniably the most handsome male, takes after his father but receives his softness from his mother.

The Moon Goddess had determined our fate; the man standing before me is just as unmated as I am. Seeking solace and excitement in the pleasure, our bodies could soothe the disappointment that we weren't mates after all. As the alpha's son, Caleb has higher stakes to find a mate than everyone else, as it certifies his ability to take his father's place.

The Hunt is meant to mark a time of hope and blessings to our packs, but to Caleb and me, it marks grave realities. We stand to lose everything: he, his Goddess-chosen mate, and I, my family.

Judging by his expression, he's thinking exactly what I am.

"Alaina." He holds out his hand.

With no explanation needed, I take it, and he leads me into the woods.

* * *

Minutes later, I scan the area for my shirt while trying to tug my jeans over my ass, retracing our steps.

Okay, we were making out by that tree, where I took his shirt off...

"My father says I have to take a mate this Hunt, no matter what."

I snort. "You don't say."

I'm not surprised he's expected to bring home a mate. He told me an alpha is weakest without a mate and would, therefore, deem him not quite ready to rule.

Having heard this from him before, I search for my shirt.

...And then I was bent over here.

"If I can't find my mate tomorrow, I plan to mark you as mine."

My breath catches in my throat.

The forest stirs, birds flapping their wings as if they, too, feel the uncertainty. The moment stretches into an eternity as his words settle in. His declaration has taken me—and nature—by surprise.

Caleb's pecs contract as he tightens his belt, and I tear my gaze away, biting my lip, thinking over his proposal.

Mating with Caleb could be a win-win for us. I could stay here, which he knows I want. Being his luna would also mean access to confidential pack records, where I could learn more about where I come from and who my mother was. Caleb's a nice man, not bad to look at, and I'm comfortable with him.

Saying yes would mean Caleb could appease his father and rank up to an alpha. If I don't say yes, I risk getting weaker, and if my Goddess-chosen mate finds me one day, I'll have to leave. The only downside is I would be expected to work toward my luna duties, gaining heirs to ensure the future of the pack.

"And what if *my* true mate is there?" I ask, resuming the search for my shirt.

Even I can't resist the mate bond. The Moon Goddess chose our fated pairs. To decide against Her and mark another requires a balancing of the scales. By tempting the Moon Goddess, we would cause the ultimate demise of our intended mates.

He comes into view, holding my shirt with a knowing smile.

Caleb always was one of the best trackers and hunters in the pack.

Smiling, I take the shirt from him.

As I dress, he steps back and leans on a tree, crossing his muscular arms. We stare at each other, communicating silently. His face relaxes upon the awaited arrival of my realization.

Everyone knows how mate bonds are severed: either the true mate is killed or a wolf is claimed by another before the fated mate can. Once marked, I would quickly lose my ability to recognize my mate, and he would eventually die of a broken heart.

Would I rather my mate be killed than live somewhere else? Would I choose his agony over my own?

My silence is a response Caleb picks up on.

My soon-to-be mate pushes off the tree, smiling.

CHAPTER TWO
18-year-old Alaina

The natural waterfall roars, cascading into a rippling pool. Butterflies flutter in and out of hazy beams of light where the sun peeks through over the rock dome hiding this oasis. The water sparkles even brighter under the crepuscular rays.

Hidden in the depths of the forest, this little sanctuary has become one of my favorite spots. Caleb showed me this place when we were kids. Only the Wallers knew about it; it was their secret getaway where they could be a normal family of three rather than our pack leaders. He made me promise never to tell anyone, so I didn't.

Caleb uses this place to take a break from responsibilities, while I use it to escape from prying eyes to doodle. Although no matter how many paint mixtures I try, I can never get the colors of this place quite right.

"What're you drawing?"

A voice startles me.

Instinctively, I cover my notepad, turning to Caleb, who's standing over me.

"Nothing," I lie.

My cheeks become hot.

Please, just drop it. No way was I letting him see it. I'd be mortified.

A grin spreads across his face. "Nothing, huh?" *He's not buying this; he knows me too well.* "Let's see . . ."

He rips the pad from my grasp.

"Caleb, don't," I whine. "Stop. Give it back!" I claw at him, desperately trying to snatch it.

A lift of his eyebrows and a low chuckle tells me I'm too late.

Humiliated, I bury my face in my hands, groaning.

"What is that?" Caleb rolls on the ground, laughing.

He points to my X-rated drawing of a male and female with their arms wrapped around each other, naked. His penis is straight out, erect, against where women pee and bleed, as she's sitting on it like a seesaw.

Lately, I've had a lot of pent-up . . . sexual energy. Sketching out my desires helps me deal without *dealing* with it.

"I don't know, okay?"

This is half true. I don't know what I'm really drawing, but I know what I was *trying* to draw. I don't know the layout or where things go.

Clearly, I've never had sex before, let alone a mother or older siblings, to ask about this stuff. I asked Jemma, and all she said was my first time should be with my mate, and I'll know what to do when the moment comes.

I find that hard to believe.

Jemma is super religious and preaches abstaining before mating, as she believes the Moon Goddess intended.

I don't subscribe to that, although it's been a good excuse when people ask why I'm an adult and haven't had sex yet.

Caleb rotates the notepad, viewing it from multiple angles. His forehead scrunches. "That's not how it works."

I snatch my notebook. "There are multiple ways to do it, Caleb!"

He snorts. "Well, that's not one of them."

I wish he'd stop talking, but he continues.

"Actually, if some girl bounced on my dick like that, it'd hurt. I don't think it would do anything for the girl, either... Not unless—"

"Oh my goddess, stop."

"Are you blushing?"

Oh dear goddess, please make him go away.

"No," I lie again. I cross and uncross my arms, trying to find a natural, more convincing way to stand.

"You are... Alaina, are you...?"

I avert my eyes.

"Has no one ever...?"

I look at the ground, trying to think of *anything* to say to change the topic.

"Alaina..."

"No! Okay? No, I haven't... I don't know..."

I don't even know why I'm embarrassed. I thought being a virgin is supposed to be a good thing in the spirit of double standards and everything, right? Then, why did it seem like admitting I've never had sex was like saying I was less than desirable?

Caleb's eyes widen, running a hand through his hair. "Jemma never . . . ?"

I shoot him a look. "Are you sure we're talking about the same Jemma?" I snort.

Caleb stares at me, perplexed. Taking a breath in, holding it, before audibly exhaling.

Goddess only knows what he must be thinking of me. As a girl growing up, you're taught that guys are after one thing, yet, somehow, here I was, the weird eighteen-year-old virgin.

Of course the future alpha has had sex before, along with everyone else I know.

So, what is wrong with me?

"I guess that makes sense."

I punch his arm, causing him to yelp. "Asshole."

"No, I don't mean it like that," he assures me, running a hand through his hair.

I cross my arms, waiting for an explanation.

"You're beautiful."

I'm what?

"But I know you, and I know this pack."

The future alpha thinks I'm beautiful?

I can't pay attention to anything else he's saying.

"There's not a guy here worthy of touching you."

What is happening?

COME FOR ME

"It's drugs, right? You're on drugs," I rationalize, turning away from him.

Grabbing my arm, he spins me to face him. Minutes pass as he holds me close, our breaths in sync. His tongue quickly darts out, peeking between his full lips.

He stares at mine before finally leaning in. The kiss deepens, and I open my mouth, welcoming his exploration.

Something awakens inside me.

I break the kiss. "I don't want to be eighteen and a virgin anymore," I blurt, cringing.

Idiot.

He searches my face. "Are you sure this is what you want?"

I nod.

Yes.

* * *

Right before midnight of Alaina's 21st

Scratching shakes me out of slumber—not that I was sleeping well. It's hard to sleep when there's so much pressure on my shoulders.

Rolling over to find Caleb perched on the ledge of my window, I furrow my brow. Tossing the covers, I pull myself out of bed. I quickly shuffle toward the window, unlatch it, and push it outward.

"What're you doing here?" I whisper.

Caleb climbs in, not even bothering to ask, knocking over my paint brushes as he swings his feet inside.

"Shh, you'll wake Jemma."

A cupcake with pink frosting appears from behind his back. The whites of his teeth in his boyish smile shine brighter than the flame flickering on a single candle.

"I didn't want to miss the moment my wolf might recognize yours."

My heart melts. There isn't any point in denying it. We're drawn to each other. Whether it's teenage lust or early signs of a mate bond calling, we aren't sure, but there's *something* between us.

It's seconds from the clock striking midnight when Caleb tells me to close my eyes and make a wish.

I wish for Caleb to be my fated mate.

* * *

The day of Alaina's 21st

I'm curled up in bed when there's a knock at my door.

Midnight had come, and Caleb and I felt nothing more than we already had. After I found out Caleb wasn't my mate, I scoured the pack grounds until sunrise, sniffing, hoping someone—anyone—from our pack would be my mate. I came up with nothing. Which meant my mate didn't belong to this pack.

I'm physically and emotionally spent from the search. I've been sulking since, but I find the strength to sit up, my back propped against the pillow. The door creaks as it's pushed open.

"Happy Birthday, 'Laina." Jemma enters, smiling.

Despite what most people might think, 'Laina isn't a nickname. Jemma's thick Southern accent makes it sound like she skips over the "A" in my name. She doesn't enunciate the *uh* in "Alaina."

"Goddess, I remember when you were six years old and you got so mad at me for how I say your name." I smile. She loves to tell this story. "You put your hand on your hip and pointed your little finger at me with the most serious face and said, 'Jemma, it's uh-lane-uh, not lane-uh.'" Jemma clasps her hands together, laughing as she reminisces.

I shake my head and laugh.

I'm glad she finds this story humorous now because I remember it not being funny to her when it happened.

The part she leaves out is how I didn't stop there at critiquing her accent. I made fun of the way she says "wash," which sounds like "wersh." Then I imitated what it's like when she's mad, when her voice pitches up and makes her accent more prominent. If we weren't in front of people, she might not have been as embarrassed. But we were, and she turned red as I laughed at her.

That's enough, she would warn. When I didn't listen, she would grab my hand, rush me home, and spank me. Hard.

She never spanked me again.

I think she omits that, not because of how I acted but how she responded. It wasn't easy raising a kid, let alone one as stubborn as I was . . . *am*.

Jemma gently pinches my cheek. "Today's the day you could find your mate. Are you excited?"

I nod.

I want to tell her Caleb isn't my mate, but I don't want her to be disappointed; she loves Caleb like a son. She practically raised us. Jemma would watch Caleb at our house while his parents attended meetings or performed their other duties.

Growing up, Jemma apologized to his parents plenty of times on my behalf. I say on my behalf because I flat out refused to apologize. I wasn't sorry for biting him after he stole my animal crackers, then ate them in front of me. Or when he yanked my pigtails and I pushed him in the dirt.

Jemma is old school, but I never agreed with justifying the notion of when a boy likes you that it's okay if they show it by picking on you.

In the words of Jemma, six-year-old me showed Caleb "he gon' learn today to act right." Kids need to be taught to process and express big feelings in a prosocial way, or they'll end up with a mouthful of dirt like Caleb did.

I stand by younger-me's decision not to apologize. If anything, I might've prevented Caleb from becoming a domestic abuser.

Honestly, his parents should thank me. I laugh to myself.

Jemma's high-pitched voice drags me out of my thoughts.

"'Laina?"

"Huh?"

"You're smiling . . . Are you thinking about Caleb?"

Jemma's eyes sparkle with hope, and tears spring from my eyes.

"What, honey?" She pets my hair, concerned. "What's wrong?"

"Caleb's not my mate," I finally say after breathing through my tears.

Jemma clicks her teeth. "You don't know that."

"Yes, I do. He was here last night, and once it hit midnight, we felt nothing."

Jemma raises her eyebrow and points to my bedroom floor. "Here?"

I nod.

"You mean to tell me he snuck into your room in the middle of the night? In my house?"

Jemma's flabbergasted.

"Ugh, that's not the point!"

I just told her Caleb isn't my mate, and that's what she got out of the conversation? Unbelievable. She forgets I'm twenty-one, not sixteen.

"It's my point," Jemma mutters but relents, sighing. "I'm sorry, honey. You'll find your mate one day."

"My mate isn't here, though. Which means he belongs to some other pack," I whine. "I don't want to go to another pack."

Jemma frowns.

She knows my ties to our pack grounds are deeply rooted in my identity.

"I don't have anything of hers but this place"—I gesture to the space—"and old stories I've heard hundreds of times."

When my mother showed up on Jemma's doorstep, she came with nothing.

Jemma takes hold of my hand, giving me the best smile she can muster. She was also wanting my mate to be someone from this pack. Even more so, she was hoping it was Caleb.

We all were.

Jemma pats my hand. "I have something for you." She pulls out an ornate box.

At her silent instruction, I open the box, revealing an uncut violet stone looped in silver thread. The stone matches my wolf's eyes, unlike my pack members', whose glow gold.

I clasp the necklace into place. My fingers graze the spectacular stone.

It's flawless.

"It belonged to your mother."

CHAPTER THREE

Alaina

The next morning, I primp myself in the mirror for our celebratory brunch. I detangle my brown locks and golden highlights with my fingers. My hands smooth over the front of my silk knee-length plum dress. The dainty straps rest on my shoulders, while the V-neck shows off the curves of my breasts. By some miracle, the bodice contains their size within the delicate fabric.

Caleb loves how the silk contrasts against his rough hands and how the color complements my wolf's eyes.

If I'm to be his mate, I guess I should start dressing the part for him.

I grin at the thought that, come tomorrow morning, the Bloodhound pack will be my home forever if I choose Caleb and his true mate isn't there.

Alpha Jack mindlinks for the pack to come to the Hunter's Quarters, a designated meeting spot at the center of our civilization.

All kinds of important speeches, festivals, and celebrations have been held there, such as our annual feast before the winter months to give thanks to the Moon Goddess for our good fortune of fuel.

Thanks to Alpha Jack's hunting and tracking mastery, our pack is notorious for its resources to survive the harsh weather, as opposed to others, making us an ally in high demand. This lethal combination offers our pack disproportionate protection against our foes.

No one wants to bite the hand that feeds unless you are prepared to flee for the rest of your life.

We have allies from all over, near and far, and not just of the werewolf species. Witches from various covens request favors in search of herbs and other plants for their potions and spells. Vampires also visit from clans in the far East. They burn in the sun but no more so than Taya when she sits in the sun for too long with her fair, freckled skin. Because of this, the vampire population mainly resides in the darkest depths of the forest. There, stone-colored fortresses blend into the mountains, making them inconspicuous to humans.

Unlike witches, they don't often seek the tracking assistance we can offer. Needing human blood to survive, vampires prefer to minimize problems of world hunger and food insecurity among the human population.

When a vampire is made through an eternal bond, their initial eye color is replaced with infinite red eyes, making it impossible for them to blend in among humans. We pass as mortals, able to outsource food to the human world without arousing suspicion. In exchange, vampires don't hunt on our lands. Since they don't care for a stroll in the nice weather, we seldom see them. Our species coexist with mutual indifference.

Today, the Hunter's Quarters serve as the venue for the brunch. Circular tables dressed in white tablecloths are scattered across the cobblestone. Champagne flutes and gilded cutlery surround floral centerpieces.

Alpha Jack stands at the front of the vast space, with Luna Kathy by his side. The entire pack is here today, as it's tradition to dine together one last time to prepare for departures and additions to the Hunt.

Luna Kathy clinks her knife against her glass. "Everyone, please be seated."

Once seated, Alpha Jack steps forward.

Caleb is a harmonious mix of his parents. From their charismatic smiles to the toffee crown of hair, their piercing eyes, he is a spitting image of his father, but I owe Caleb's sweet and sensitive side to his mother. Her charm, lighthearted demeanor, and grace have been woven into his father's fierceness, forming the man who will soon be our pack's leader.

Alpha Jack gives a speech about his son coming of age to take on the role of alpha.

Luna Kathy leads the pack in prayer that her son's fated mate is among the Hunt, that she is healthy, strong, and contains all the traits of a leader, and, if we're lucky, generational powers.

Caleb and I lock eyes. He winks, and I blush.

Unable to help herself, Luna Kathy throws in a tidbit about fertility.

"Jeez, Mom," Caleb mutters, arousing a laugh from the gathered pack. He shakes his head, palm covering his face.

Luna Kathy smiles and shrugs. She lifts her mimosa, and everyone follows.

"To the Hunt."

"To the Hunt," the pack repeats, clinking glasses with their neighbors.

From my flute, I spot Taya scurrying and excusing herself as she weaves through the throng until she makes it over to our table. The white tablecloth gets caught on a jewel on her dress as she hangs her purse on the back of her chair. I unhook it from her before she accidentally takes everything with her.

Taya's typically poised and graceful except when she's late.

She finally sits, scooting her chair in, whispering, "Hey, what'd I miss?"

"Luna Kathy making a toast about wanting an heir," I snicker. I take another sip of my beverage.

"Gross."

"He's not that bad."

Caleb's been my designated friend with benefits since we were barely eighteen. In the beginning, Caleb was a pleasurable distraction from life, a way to scratch an itch and enjoy my fill. At the time, his boyish charm still lingered, slowly evolving into his manly charisma. Long gone were the stumbling attempts to remove my bra, replaced with skilled motions and calculated ease as we found our release in each other.

Staring at Caleb, I try to imagine what our pups would look like.

He catches me and winks.

I lift my glass to him but regret it when I spot who's sitting next to him.

Aw, shit.

"Incoming," I warn, hiding my face with my hand.

"Where?" Taya looks around frantically until she spots him, who's gotten up from his table to make his way toward us.

Tyler.

"Ugh, he's the worst. Why is he coming over here?"

"I don't know. He must've thought I was staring at him."

"Why would he think that?"

"Because he was sitting next to Caleb . . . Oh, shh. Here he comes."

Tyler towers over Caleb, with his dark hair and pale blue eyes. His good looks make him likable, but it isn't long before everyone grows up to realize pretty is common, and substance is rare.

Tyler peaked in high school. His insecurity shows up in a pathetic way—mainly cockiness. Otherwise, he gets really uncomfortable in large groups. Tyler can't engage in conversations not centered around himself and has no interest in any activity if it doesn't involve nailing the hottest bitch or getting hammered.

"Ladies." He stops when he sees my best friend. "And Taya."

She meets his insult with an obvious fake smile.

Their history is . . . complicated. Taya is the only one who's been successful in beating Tyler at his own game, making her his number one enemy and vice versa. She slept with him and made it clear she wasn't impressed. Tyler retaliated, telling everyone how awful she was. Taya, the posh woman she is, said nothing and paid him no mind, making her more credible and Tyler an ass.

They've hated each other ever since.

And insistent on trying to get me to sleep with him to spite her.

"You look good."

"Thanks." I force a smile, trying my best not to gag.

Tyler has never actually possessed any game, solely relying on his looks. Because when Tyler doesn't say anything else, his presence plagues our table with awkward silence.

"Well, I'll let you get back to your meal. Alaina, let me know if you want someone to keep you company for your last night."

"Barf," Taya says.

I fucking love her.

CHAPTER FOUR
Alaina

Standing in the Hunter's Quarters, the alpha and this year's bachelors prepare for their journey to the royal castle for the Hunt. It's the morning of, and I can't stop picking at my cuticles. *Am I making the right decision?*

Alpha Jack stands in front of Caleb and shifts. Alpha Jack's wolf—with deeper reddish-brown fur than Caleb's—is graying. Caleb and the rest of the male suitors in the pack follow. Caleb's wolf is larger than the others, his size intimidating.

His wolf looks at me and mindlinks, *"I'll see you soon."*

I nod at him.

My pulse quickens in anxious anticipation of the Hunt. Mating Caleb solidifies my future, erases the unknown, and opens the door to unravel the mystery of who I am. I take a breath, squaring my shoulders, nearly imperceivable, as I hold the gaze of Caleb's wolf.

He notices the correction of stance with a flicker of a brighter gold in his eyes.

Alpha Jack howls and races off in the direction of the Crescent pack.

Caleb takes off after his father, his bounding strides creating distance between us. The other males follow him close.

Luna Kathy clears her throat and claps. "Everyone, while we wait for the men to reach the Crescent pack and get set up, please eat and enjoy yourselves. I will let you know when it's time for the ladies to start their journey."

A few she-wolves indulge in the feast before us, gathering energy for their mating. Others graze, giddy with the prospect of a new life and adventure.

"Your mother would be so proud of the woman you have become," Jemma says to me through the mindlink.

Her attempt to comfort me only solidifies my decision.

Caleb will be my mate.

* * *

The castle oozes with authority when we arrive in the Crescent pack's territory. The grounds vibrate with energy. Its powerful aura emphasizes the medieval structure before us—thick stone walls defending the pack. The fortress warns any passerby with a silent threat of danger to any who dream of attacking.

The stone was carved from massive boulders that lay throughout the grounds. It was forged from the land and, therefore, appeared as if it arose from the whisper of the

COME FOR ME

Goddess's command to be centered beneath Her in the night sky. The strength and will needed to create such a masterpiece are evident in its masonry. Though built centuries ago, the building adorns lights, which illuminates the windows and torches guiding our path to our fated mates. My gaze travels up the castle walls and finds an arched balcony with French double doors I imagine overlooks the kingdom.

Our luna leads us through the castle gate to the front entrance, toward the oak doors adorned with iron sigils for protection and carved with wolf emblems. As we enter, she instructs us to line up, to parade past the caged wolves like lambs presented to the wolves for their devouring and through the royal courtyard before we're released into the forest.

The witch, a tall and slender woman, floats into the courtyard. She carries wisdom, her forty-some years on this earth having carved lines above her brows and softened her smile. Her long, silver hair twists around her shoulders with such a design only achieved by enchantment. It moves as she greets and ushers each pack's unmated she-wolves through the doors.

As is custom, our packs wait in anticipation. It's our turn to be greeted by the witch. She approaches Luna Kathy with a smile, grasping her hand.

I stare into her piercing, electric eyes as they reach mine, their depths seeming to know unspoken truths.

The witch grasps my arm but jerks her hand away and rubs her palm, wide-eyed. "You burned me."

What?

"I didn't even touch you."

Why bother defending myself? I shouldn't be surprised; witches are quirky due to their lack of socialization. Although overall good-natured, dabbling in healing and balancing the elements, they're more in-tune with their spiritual wellness than their social wellness. Witches also make up a small population compared to the vampire and werewolf kingdoms, so it isn't often you run into one.

The witch holds her hand out, flipping it over to expose a raw pink patch on her brown complexion.

With my mouth open, I gape at her, not sure what to say.

She smiles wide and squeals with glee.

Oh, she's messing with me.

I shake my head, pointing at her. "You got me."

"Bloodhound pack, it's time for the Moon Goddess's blessings."

The witch soothes us with enchantments, stripping our abilities to sense our mates.

She leads Luna Kathy to the doors. "This way, ladies."

One by one, we file into a line again. As I walk over the threshold, the scent of leather and spice wafts in my direction. My wolf feels restless and calm at the aroma.

Only for panic to burrow deep as I register what this means...

Mate!

All the male wolves' scents are covered... Then how is my wolf sensing our mate? Unless the witch missed the enchantment of one lone male. *Unlikely.*

Whoever I'm smelling must be someone who isn't participating in the Hunt but was here recently, which would explain why their scent is so strong. My guess is, it's someone from the Crescent pack who's been inside the castle walls before. The smell makes my wolf want to roll over and spread her legs.

I lose myself basking in his pure dominance, finding empowerment in his strength, until my anxiety ruins the moment.

If I can smell him, can he smell me?

My breathing hitches as I think of what I could lose if my mate finds me: *home. Taya. Jemma. Mom. Me.*

My mind fogs over from the overwhelmingly delicious scent, and I picture what he must look like. *Who is he?*

As I follow my luna and fellow she-wolves through the castle, I try to distract myself with its interior. The grand staircase before us rise to the floors above, winding toward a stained glass ceiling.

Did my mate caress the banister when he left for the ceremony?

I shake my head of its thoughts and shift my focus to the corridor. Great care and skill went into the castle's construction. Each detail appears purposeful, designed to celebrate the royal pack. Near the ceremonial hall, the craftsmanship of the crown moulding showcases the delicate intricacies of wolves running through the forest.

My mate's scent has become more potent, making my wolf drunk off the full-bodied essence.

My wolf urges me to find him and make him ours. I imagine basking in his aroma as he fills me with his seed, sinking his teeth into my neck. In excitement, my body buzzes, the promise of my mate's claim pooling delicious heat between my thighs. The thought of his tongue tasting me and his scent on mine.

Focus, I bark at myself.

The bond is already clouding my judgment and getting in the way of my future. It's a threat to my plan, holding onto who I am and everything I've known and loved my entire life. It dissolves the sheer tether to my mother and severs my chance at finding my origin. Despite what I'm feeling, I can't want him. But the ache and need settling in my pussy has claimed otherwise.

Caleb will just have to kill him.

Immediate pain and rage boils inside me. I try to shake the feeling by reasoning with logic. *My mate could be an awful person who kills without purpose and commits heinous crimes.*

I try to hold my breath to avoid inhaling his heady incense.

Turning the corner, I startle at an eruption of growls and shouting as bodies slam against cage walls.

The wolves sense we're approaching and can hear our heartbeats quicken at the sounds of their fever echoing in the corridor. Snarls and gnashing teeth interweave with the howls and desperate threats of wolves separated from their fated.

If not for the silver and steel surrounding the wolves, strewn across the space would be a bloody mess of fur and bone as they tear apart their competition. Restraints madden the wolves and propel their desire to hunt their prey. They are beasts demanding freedom, demanding their mates.

The instinct to mark and claim fated mates is heightened by the presence of other viable males who threatened their bond and, therefore, their existence.

The white marble floor and silver-coated steel bars of the wolves' cages are a striking shift from the medieval interior from before.

We are led through the large white hallway with multiple steel doors on each side where the male wolves are. As we walk down the hall, the word *mate* echoes through the mindlink of my pack along with threats to destroy if they're not let out of the cell soon.

I try to listen for Caleb, but too many members are talking through the link. My heart races as I think about what might happen if Caleb finds his mate and my mate finds me. Everything I could lose.

Home. Taya. Jemma. Mom. Me.

The words repeat like a mantra.

Each echoing clip of my heels on the marble floor takes me farther away from them and toward the unknown.

I push away the thought.

Pure sounds of chaos surge. Snarling, growling, howling, and whimpering permeates the room.

Over to my left is the redhead from last night, who is biting on her nails and staring straight ahead, clearly trying to dissociate.

Gasps from other she-wolves emit as wolves thrash against the steel doors. The ethereal shimmer, caused by the witch's glamour on the castle interior, illuminates the white hallway and dances around our feet on our passage to the royal grounds.

My wolf's fur threatens to burst through my skin with each step.

The witch stops, looks at us, and says foreign words. Our group of she-wolves sniff around.

"Mate" bursts from the females in our pack. A sudden need to shift and run vibrates within us, likely the witch messing with the elements, enhancing our instinctual urges.

Giving in, I dash into the woods when Caleb mindlinks, *"I'm coming for you, mate."*

CHAPTER FIVE
Dax

"That's the last of them, boss," my beta, Sam, informs me as he drops the last of the vampires.

At his feet lies the corpse, bruised and bloody where he'd slain it.

Bodies of rogues and vampires alike lie in the area surrounding my men. These attacks have become increasingly frequent. Our strength and training are tested as the vampires and rogues become more brazen, pushing closer toward our territory.

What did they want?

I rack my brain for the thousandth time. They kill anyone and everyone who crosses their path. And it's fucking frustrating.

None of my warriors are seriously injured, but that isn't a surprise. Our bodies will fully heal by the time we reach pack grounds, as if the gruesome scene never happened.

Glancing down at the forest floor, I examine the ringed hand beneath my foot.

Iron burns my nose.

I'll sever the heads and carve out the hearts of every vampire and rogue if it uncovers their intentions. *What's the point of having a Goddess-given power if it doesn't lead me to answers?* Now more than ever, I need the answer.

My men are depending on me to know. Their lives are my responsibility, and I'm failing to maintain the upper hand.

Never in the history of werewolves have rogues teamed up with new vampires, and it doesn't make sense why they would start now. We've dealt with rogues before, but for the most part, they keep to themselves, not wanting trouble.

My men have been training specifically to combat these new attacks—to protect and destroy our enemies at my command with precision and without hesitation. My warriors are trained assassins, instructed to kill without emotion or regard.

The eyes of the rogues who had fought against their own kind were glazed over and lifeless.

No, *soulless.*

One had to be soulless to fight against fellow werewolves. We're meant to be a civilized species; we have evolved. But those massacred at my feet are a sign of the true nature of rogues and vampires, preferring to perish than parlay.

Being in a clan is important for a vampire's survival and easier access to human blood. This hardship brings uncertainty and instability, not to mention *hunger*. Like anyone, when hungry, it can be impossible to focus, but for vampires, it's deadly. It makes them crazed, their careless mistakes inevitable. This detriment leads to their quick beheading under my pack's canines.

Let tonight serve as a reminder.

"Let's move out," I instruct my men.

Any warrior mated will join me tonight except for Sam. Sam and I participated in the Hunt ourselves after we turned twenty-one, hoping to find our mate. Neither of us had, and the constant disappointment was exhausting. Other alphas and betas could take a mate, but being king came with different rules.

I told Sam he had my permission to choose a mate. He wasn't held to the royal council's same standards, but Sam didn't mind not being tied down, allowing him to sleep around. It'd probably take finding his fated mate for him to stop.

Between the increasing rogue attacks and the pressure the council has put on me to find a mate, I've never been more stressed. Ever since my parents died and I became king, the privy council has been pushing me more.

Up until now, I've dodged their matchmaking efforts and refused to mate if she wasn't my fated. But at twenty-eight, I'm the oldest alpha without a luna, and my strength has been dwindling. If I want to be strong for my pack, I must take a chosen mate, or we'll all suffer.

That's why a marriage has been arranged for me—to a vampire who has a claim to the vampire throne. The intention is to join forces against a common enemy, in hopes the attacks will subside.

Once I mark her as mine and bond myself to her, our combined species will be lethal. Aside from this, mating with a living corpse is comical and far from something I want.

The trek back to my pack is tiring. Normally, I'm relieved to return, but my home is currently overrun by the festivities of the Hunt. I can't wait until it's over. The idea of horny males and she-wolves overrunning my castle doesn't appeal to me.

It's the same thing every season, yet the futile attempts of unmated she-wolves throwing themselves at me become more obnoxious and pathetic. It never fails. Bitches stray from the Hunt to try and capture my eye. Hoping this would be the year I grow tired of waiting for my mate and choose them, in a desperate effort, they would hand their pussy to me on a platter.

Sometimes, I indulge in their desires to serve their king, but no bitch could fuck me into oblivion and make me stupid enough to mark a chosen over a fated. *If only they knew just how patient I can be.*

If it weren't for the council, I'd wait forever for her. But they're right; my kingdom can't afford to hold out for their queen much longer.

I'm irritated and exhausted. I don't have the patience to be a "good host" to greedy she-wolves who await me. They aren't the release I need. I've failed my people by not getting answers.

I don't want their pleasure. I want their pain.

Normally, when I feel this way, I break in new prisoners to take the tension off. But with attacks happening almost every day, my collection of captives have grown at an impressive rate.

Unfortunately, I've broken them all into submission. They're conditioned to quiver when my boots thump past their cells. When my laughter booms through the dark corners of my dungeon, panic sets in, and they can't tell from the echoes where I'm coming from or who I'm coming for. The stench of centuries-old piss and sweat follows in response to the terror I instill.

Long gone is the bravery they encompassed when they first entered my lair. The smart mouths I enjoyed smacking learned not to speak unless spoken to and never questioned whether I made good on my threats. I always follow through—an innocent's life means nothing if my kingdom is at stake.

I can't relieve myself by breaking in new prisoners. Now I have no choice but to find solace in a naive she-wolf with the first one stupid enough to rub themselves against me.

I won't just test their limits. I'll break them.

Unlike the Hunt, I won't have to chase my prey. They'll come to me. My power and ability to command will lure them to me, like a moth drawn to a flame.

"Oh, King Dax, I'll do whatever you want."

Of course she will, and I always grin. What can I say? I like it when my prey steps into their own trap. It makes for a sweeter kill knowing they did this to themselves.

They don't make me work for it, but I damn sure make them work for me. They tell themselves they crave my torturous ways to justify not using their safe word. Of course, they always consent to this—I'm sadistic, not a rapist. They're told they can stop. They have the power to end their suffering. They just never do.

And that's what makes their willful sacrifice so fucking savory. The chance to be at my side isn't something they want to forfeit, and in the end, I always chuckle, impressed with how far the next is willing to go. The last one, I had lick my cum off the floor with a leash in hand. Their desperation to climb the social ladder is astounding.

With my attention on them and a smile, they're caught with no chance of escaping. My facade as a pleasure lord elicits moans and promises to do whatever I want. The man behind the smile is revealed when my true sadistic, defiant nature sets in.

"Whatever I want?" I coo.

In truth, I count on their determination to please their king. I know they will—that's what makes this game so fun. By the time my canines break their skin enough to have blood trickling down their neck, they're won over by false promises of pleasure.

They think I'm going to mark them, claim them as mine with my bite.

It gets them every time. I never say I'll please them, but their fear pleases me.

"Yes, whatever you want!"

Oh, this part's good, too. Because, by this point, they're clawing at me, begging for their pleasure god, and I've barely touched them. From the moment they tempt me, their soul no longer belongs to a god but the devil himself.

COME FOR ME

When the test of their willingness begins, I drink in their fear and regret like a lifeline. I enjoy seeing how far they go to make excuses as to why there are tears running down their face. I ask them sweetly if they want me to stop, patronizing them, followed by taunts about how my future queen should handle adventure. Petting their messed-up hair, I tell them it's okay, that we can stop after all, that not everyone is fit for a king.

As horrid as my behavior sounds, I can't allow myself to feel bad. They don't want me. Look at how far they're willing to go to make me think otherwise. And for what? They're power hungry. Greedy. And worst of all, *selfish*.

My patronization instills a second wind, and they pick up their pieces and hand me the same metaphorical hammer, begging me to break them.

The poor women have no idea what they promise, as my teeth grazing their neck prevents them from making sound decisions, thrusting them right into my dangerous grasp.

They shouldn't feel bad, though. I have a knack for playing against weaknesses. The moment they pursue me with their intention for power and materialistic things is their end. And all it takes is a smile against their neck to capture them. My teeth scrape their skin, and their knees falter. The promise of my mark and wealth is all too enticing for a greedy bitch. While I won't give it to them, I know they can't handle it or me all the same.

Not like my mate is destined to.

Nonetheless, I persist in playing with my scared little prey. I can't resist. I love it when they scream.

The ones who don't seem fearful and rather appear to welcome my sadistic nature quickly bore me. I'm not interested in pleasing anyone other than my mate. I'm only after their pain, their slow break, and, inevitably, their destruction. Their sunken expressions as they realize they've reduced themselves to this power-hungry whore, willing to do anything for something I didn't promise to them, for a man they can never have.

With pleasure reserved for my mate, I let my men have a turn, tossing her to the wolves. Their disappointment in my absence and disinterest is fleeting, though, as their vaginas, just as greedy as them, get railed and filled by my men. They all seem to make the same inference, too, that I'm into watching others satisfying my mate. So, once again, they consensually participate.

As if I would ever share my actual mate.

By the time my men are done with them, the Hunt is over, and their Goddess-chosen mate has likely picked someone else, one who didn't give into greed and has pure intentions. They're better off without someone who doesn't value the mate bond.

But I don't feel bad for them. This was their choice, and they were rejected. They could have been happy to be picked in the Hunt or, even better, could have discovered the one destined for them. Instead, they gave into greed. They chose me. I just don't choose them. The she-wolves who throw themselves at me are so ungrateful for this chance to find the one.

COME FOR ME

As we near the castle grounds, my plans to take advantage of a willing subject are sabotaged by the sweetest smell of black raspberry and vanilla. Her scent infiltrates my plan and overcomes my darkest intentions. This dark lord's storm is calmed by her aroma as I inhale further. As I drink in this newfound heaven, my cock hardens. Her natural fragrance alone, whoever she is, has caught this demon's attention, and I won't be satisfied until I've possessed her very soul.

Tension and the weight of my duty to the throne rolls off me like sand recedes with the waves—for the first time in eight years. All because of *her*.

"*Mate*," I mindlink to my beta.

Like a meerkat, Sam's head pops up, wide-eyed and alert. "*What?*"

He never thought he'd ever hear the word. None of us did.

Animalistic instinct takes its form, pinpointing her scent and darting off after her. My wolf snatches control as we search for our queen, the woman to bring this man to his knees.

She doesn't yet know what power she has over me, but she'll find out soon enough.

Hope radiates through me, leveling me up to new speeds. The brawn her presence inspires within me threatens to destroy the mountains until I have her at my side, her sweet aroma throwing my world off kilter. These vampires and rogues would be a flicker of annoyance upon our mating.

My world is already better with her existence.

No other pairing—vampire or otherwise—is more sacred or formidable than the power of a fated bond. Especially one of royal pairing.

Eagerness quickly overturns my pride. Warmth spreads through me, and I chuckle when I register these emotions aren't mine but hers, as she's able to sense me.

If I were in my wolf, it'd be faster, but I don't want to scare her away with my nakedness upon first meeting her.

That will come later.

"I'm coming, baby. Hold on."

Thrilled she's just as ready to meet me as I am her, I snicker at my mate's impatience.

I pump my arms harder, and Sam comes panting beside me.

"Are you sure it's her?"

"I'm sure. I can feel her."

Crunching leaves, panting, and thudding footfalls are the only prominent sounds between us as we dodge branches and jump over rocks. My miles-long lawn, stretching out in front of my castle, comes into view.

I never thought I would hate having so many acres of land until now, when it stands between me and uniting with my mate. Her scent gets stronger as I draw near my home, with Sam still on my tail.

I'm too busy getting high off her that I almost forget what day it is.

"Shit!"

My heart races.

"You think she's in the Hunt?"

I stopped visiting other packs a few years into my reign and sent liaisons. I lost hope I could find my mate among them, convinced this was the Moon Goddess punishing me for my sins.

Most people didn't go through the Hunt five times like I did, in hopes of finding their mate, only to emerge unmated and question if the Moon Goddess has forsaken you. Once was disappointing enough to come out of, which is why the majority of those only participate in their first eligible year.

Even though I haven't participated in the past few years, I would've known she was here. My mate would've come into my home to be paraded among the wolves—males drooling over what they wish they could have, not knowing they're in the presence of royalty.

"She has to be," I conclude before Sam could answer.

With that, I know two things to be true about my mate.

One, she's twenty-one.

Two, she's participating in the Hunt.

With a roar, I shift. Fear and adrenaline have me charging, causing Sam to fall farther and farther behind.

Sam yells to my men guarding the castle, "Open the fucking door!" He shifts.

I sense her again. Only, this time, she's in pain, confused, and scared. My heart races from the rush pumping through me.

The whiff I pick up on leads to the woods in my backyard, confirming my suspicion, but I didn't expect to receive her fear.

My wolf whimpers, knowing what this means.

"She's being hunted. Someone's chosen her."

Sam growls, ready to spring into action at the news that my queen is in trouble. Already a protective beta to her.

"You'll get to her in time, Dax. Don't worry." Silence passes between us. Then Sam simply adds, "And if you do not, you'll kill him."

Damn right I will.

It takes everything in me to push away the intrusive thought of someone trying to force a bond on what's mine. Rage hits like a tidal wave, and my claws rip through the earth. Picking up the pace, I fantasize all the ways whoever is causing my mate pain will suffer.

He's mine to torture. Mine to kill. And I will enjoy every moment of it.

Hang on, darling. I'm coming.

CHAPTER SIX

Alaina

Our plan's working. Caleb hasn't sensed his mate this Hunt if he's choosing to pursue me. Soon, he'll mark me, making him eligible to assume his birthright as the pack's alpha to appease his parents. Jemma will be happy I found someone to start a family with, and Taya and I can still see each other.

Everything is falling into place. I pick up the pace when Caleb's paws pound behind me, instinct taking over. I've always been the fastest in the pack, and I like reminding the future alpha of this any chance I could get.

There was never any indication from Jemma of my mother being unnaturally fast for a wolf, and I don't sense my abnormal speed as a power. Chalk it up to my small size, I guess.

I weave through the trees to lose him. The low branches up ahead spark an idea: let Caleb get close enough to let him think he almost has me. He nips at my tail. When we get closer, I dodge to the side, causing Caleb to get a branch to the snout.

Caleb chuckles. *"You'll pay for that."*

"Oooh, I'm soooo scared."

"Come on, babe. Why delay the inevitable?"

With his question, the flight response subsides, allowing me to slow my pace as the logic returns. The sooner he marks me, the sooner I can access pack records. Another thought crosses my mind, invoking panic that my mate may soon realize I'm here and come for me before Caleb does.

My decision whether to end the cat-and-mouse game is quickly made for me as a boulder comes into view. I skid to a stop. Caleb's pattering paws tells me he's too close behind to run in the opposite direction.

Turning, I see Caleb's wolf licking his chops and stalking closer to me while baring his teeth.

"Shift," Caleb demands.

Giving into his command, I change into my human form. Caleb does as well, leaving us naked and vulnerable.

His reddish-brown fur recedes into his muscles, his tall frame rising. Everything about him is hard and powerful. He'll be a good mate, an honorable alpha, and I'll be his luna.

I raise my eyes to his and lift my brow in a challenge. *It stops now.*

Caleb is on me in an instant, one hand pulling me to him by the waist, the other caressing my cheek. His touch attempts to soothe me and my wolf. However, when his skin touches mine, it burns and crawls.

My wolf howls, raging a war inside of me, knowing our mate is here. She's revolting against the idea. But I will be stronger.

His touch is a transgression. My wolf's howls and threats to take over my body cause my human form to shake. I clench my teeth as I fight against my wolf.

We can't lose our home and my family. The chance to know who we are. Don't you want that?

My wolf growls, *We can't lose mate.*

Once we mark each other, my wolf will stop fighting me, and his touch will elicit pleasure through our bond. I have grown to love him, and with the mate bond in place, I will fall *in* love with him.

But as his hand glides over my hips, encircling my waist, things are changing. His fingers linger above my ass, pulling my soft curves and large breasts against him, no longer eliciting moans from my lips.

I think about last night, when his embrace thrilled me. Now, in the same position, my nipples harden against his chest. Caleb is familiar, his hands having explored every inch of my body. Yet his touch feels like a violation. Only my mate can bring me such pleasures until the bond is erased and until Caleb's mark claims me.

"Alaina," he whispers, nuzzling himself into my neck.

Ignoring my unease, I tilt my head to allow him more access to my sensitive spot.

His toffee hair and hot breath tickles my ear, hands grasping my curves and pulling me into his hard form. His large erection throbbing against my lower abdomen stirs heat and pleasure.

Growling in appreciation, he says, "My luna."

My gut churns at his words.

When I gasp in realization, Caleb misinterprets it as encouragement. As his wolf revels in the idea of claiming me against this boulder, his cock jerks against my stomach.

As he sucks the spot between my neck and shoulders, softening the skin in preparation for his mark, trepidation washes over me. The pressure would likely form a hickey, as if we were love-drunk teenagers. His lips coax moans from mine before he kisses me deeply. Just like he will in our future. I want this, but my heart aches thinking of another marking me.

Shaking the thought from my mind, I force my hands up his arms and caress his biceps. I hold still, keeping command of my wolf as Caleb prepares my flesh for his taking.

Caleb's canines descend, settling on my sweet spot. They puncture my skin with searing pain as they cut through sensitive flesh.

This is supposed to be euphoric; the claiming of your mate is meant to start a lifetime of pleasure and connection. Nothing of that nature is true. It's as if I'm being stabbed with silver as my heart is ripped open. Claiming of a chosen signified the loss of our fated, while pleasure from the bond of your chosen only occurs after severing ties with your fated.

My wolf alternates between whimpering and growling. My head and heart are split in two. I'm frozen, fighting the compulsion to push Caleb away and run to my mate. All the while, my heart breaks in my choice to end my fated bond. The struggle coursing through my brain is showing the world my wavering conviction. I whimper from the pang of betraying my mate and the Moon Goddess Herself.

My wolf attempts to pull my neck from Caleb's embrace. Claws dig into Caleb's biceps in torment instead of scratching in bliss. Once again, I try to persuade my wolf of what's best for us, promising a happy ending with the wolf in front of me. Silent pleas fill my head as I beg my wolf to hold claim to Caleb, our family, our home.

Caleb notes my hesitation and extracts his canines from my neck. My blood drips onto his tongue, quickly licked and savored by his wolf. My wolf sneers at his display of pleasure at our taste.

He looks at me as if to ask if he should proceed. A flicker of emotion swirls in his eyes and settles in his pupils: love and concern. To try to make this as painless as possible, he's going slow, but we don't have time to be gentle.

Despite my wolf, I *want* to be his luna, and once we claim each other, my wolf will, too.

"Babe, we don't have to. We can wait," Caleb says.

His sincerity proves that statement is true, but time is running out.

I shake my head, not wanting to wait another minute in case my mate discovers me, his smell never wavering.

"No, I want this."

Caleb continues to stare at me, not convinced.

"It's fine, really. I'm just nervous. Please, just do it quickly."

Caleb furrows his brow at my impatience, pausing as he gauges my request. Finally, he sighs and gives in. His canines protrude once more as he leans into my neck and pierces the sensitive skin. Careful not to hurt me, he stops again, allowing me to adjust to the pain. He moves his thumb in caressing circles to distract and console my mind. His claws puncture my hip to hold me in place, doing little to numb the pain radiating through my body. His knee finds its way between my thighs, friction threatening to build as fire spreads through my veins, and my breath ceases.

This isn't what I imagined. As pups, we were told marking is beautiful, a declaration of love and commitment. It's pleasurable. As young adults, we were even told marking was erotic. Mating comes with inevitable pain as our animalistic nature declares another. But the bite shifts to pleasure and ecstasy. Like the first time one experiences sex, the scary, unknown, painful entry is replaced with pleasure, joy, and love.

This feels nothing like that. This hurts like hell. As agony spreads through my body, I remind myself why I have to do this. *The sex is always good. He's undeniably handsome, is the pack's future alpha, and has many qualities of a great father. He's an ideal match, and I believe we can be happy. The pain will be worth it then.*

The smell of spice and leather hits my nose more than it ever has, and fury mixed with fear envelops me. These are not my emotions but his.

Mate has found us. Mate is close.

I panic.

"Hurry," I mindlink Caleb.

I close my eyes in anticipation for him to go deeper into my neck, but he doesn't.

A growl permeates the air.

My heart stops, and a chill travels up my spine. Caleb's weight is lifted off me.

A snarling wolf, dark as midnight and the size of a horse, throws Caleb against a tree, cracking wood and bone.

Caleb shifts into his wolf, and I panic once more as his form doesn't even compare to this wolf. Caleb lunges at him, and the tussle is a blur until he has Caleb pinned under him. The wolf's paw rises, ready to strike.

"No! Please!" I beg just before his massive paw guts Caleb.

The wolf looks at me. His caramel eyes stare into my own, his downturned muzzle painted into a sinister grin. He's the big bad wolf, ready to devour his enemy whole. My human and wolf are dwarfed by his frame before me.

"Run!" Caleb urges.

The wolf's aura exudes a power unlike any alpha I've ever encountered. Fire dances in those eyes as his energy imposes the surrounding clearing, threatening to bring me to my feet. He demands submission from my wolf and me. We had planned his undoing by letting Caleb attempt to mate me. To him, Caleb was just as guilty as I, almost taking what belongs to my mate.

Carefully, I approach the black wolf and stare directly into his eyes, my hands raised. "Please, let him go."

The black wolf stares at me and exhales hard through his nose, as if contemplating. Finally, he lowers his paw and looks back at Caleb. He growls a warning at Caleb, rises, and shifts into his human form in an instant.

My jaw hits the floor.

He stands before me, a massive wall of muscle and power. Basking in the sight of him, I notice his aura brings clarity that he distinctively surpasses all in the kingdom by size and strength. Caleb is in high regard with his physique, but this man is outmatched. *The Moon Goddess Herself carved his body from stone.* My wolf howls and wags her tail in approval.

His sun-kissed skin is reminiscent of the high cliffs surrounding the land. His shoulders are as expansive as a mountain, providing a protective shade to anyone who stands in his shadow. Pecs form powerful hills on his chest that rise and fall with each breath. The six-pack chiseling his torso paints peaks and valleys that taunt my eyes lower. My mouth yearns to lick the beads of sweat rolling to the black tendrils surrounding his package.

"Mate," I say instinctually.

My tongue darts to lick my lips, my wolf craving to close the distance between us and devour the man before me. My wolf's recognition of him conjures a sensation that I've been missing him for a lifetime.

The man in front of me smiles, confirming my discernment. His appraisal of my soft curves soften his fierce gaze into a slow savor as he explores my naked form, the murderous gleam in his eyes transforming into devious intent.

"You don't know how long I've waited for you."

He breathes silk.

Muscles flex as his piercing stare travels down my navel and loiters over my sex. His fixation holds before exploring my thighs and coming to rest at my feet. Caramel eyes swirl a fiery storm as they've settled to my own once again. He hasn't even touched my body, and it's as though he's explored every inch.

My wolf writhes under his attention, longing for him.

"Worth it," he says.

"Who are you?" I ask.

My hair blows in the wind, the ends teasing my breasts as if he's willed them to linger and caress my skin for him.

"King Dax, I—" Caleb stumbles back, eyes wide.

King Dax snatches his throat and growls at him, baring his teeth.

"King?!" I parrot. Shocked, I gaze between Caleb and the man before me.

This can't be happening. The king will *never* let his fated mate get away, and I can't imagine Caleb could kill him so that he can mark me instead. Especially not if everything I've heard about King Dax is true. He's known to be intimidating, dark, and ruthless. The king of torture.

This is a disaster. *He* is a disaster.

Mate is tall, dark, handsome, and powerful, a perfect masterpiece.

And potentially a murderer, I remind my wolf.

My wolf shrugs. *Mate probably had his reasons.*

My wolf and I don't always see eye to eye. Although part of me, she sees things as an animal would. While I see a murderer, she sees an apex predator, an ideal mate to breed with.

Mate can murder this—

Absolutely not, I respond.

When a wolf's parent dies, the power lives on in their first born, so when King Dax's parents died—or, like others say, when he killed them—he inherited his father's ability to see people's plans. Because of this, King Dax is the best fighter in the kingdom. While he can anticipate everyone else's intentions, he is anything but predictable. Deranged and unhinged.

Some days, he kills unnecessarily, as if he can't be bothered by inconvenience. Other times, he enjoys himself while he tortures his prey. I've heard of the women he breaks during the Hunt, ruining their chances of being with their mate after luring them into his twisted lair. He is a selfish prick. A collector of women.

The Hunt was created centuries ago to give alphas and royals the best chance to find their mate. Pack law states an alpha's offspring couldn't inherit the throne until they are mated. However, his parents' death escalated the situation, making him a young king at twenty years old. The council had high hopes he'd find his true mate the following year, making him and the pack stronger. That was eight years ago. Now that he's found me, he'll never let me go.

Fuck my life.

"Leave," he seethes at Caleb without taking his eyes off me.

Caleb scrambles to his feet and dashes toward the royal pack house.

The king looks extremely pissed as his hard chest heaves. His shoulders rise and fall as he stares into my soul.

COME FOR ME

He moves toward me, eyeing me like a predator stalking his prey, focus unwavering.

I fight back tears at the thought of never seeing my home again, and I immediately resent him for existing. My blood runs cold with the realization that everything will be taken from me with his bite. I swallow hard, and my breathing quickens.

Panic, excitement, and arousal swirl inside me at the thought of him marking me, while I step back until my back presses into the same boulder. The cool stone does little to calm my racing nerves and leaves me with no escape. He will devour me like meek prey and leave only a carcass of who I once was.

"I can't believe you're here."

He speaks as though I am the answer to all his prayers.

As he gets closer, his muscles contract, veins bulging in his arms. The two ragged claw marks slicing from his left eyebrow to his nose shine in the moonlight. Pack-inspired tattoos decorate his right pec, traveling across his shoulder and down his biceps into a full sleeve on his right arm. They dance with each expression of power he displays, like wolves on the prowl. Immense skill is required for such intricacies, and I long to explore and map out these details with my fingers and tongue.

His scent makes it hard for me to think clearly. All I want is to get as far away from him as possible, but my body hums in anticipation of his touch, my feet bolted to the ground.

Stupid wolf, resist him. Run!

As if he can read my mind, King Dax closes the distance between us in the blink of an eye, resting one hand beside my head, grabbing my chin with the other. His fingers dig into my cheeks.

Looking directly into my eyes, he challenges, "You think you can run from me, darling?" Inspecting me, he swivels my head.

I swoon at the way the pet name rolls off his tongue. His voice is rough and taunting, a gravelly growl.

Engorged, hairless pecs rise as he breathes me in and out. As his nostrils flare, his hold on my chin tightens.

Does Caleb's scent linger on me?

Unable to fight my wolf's urge to ease my mate's angst, I rest my hand on his heaving chest, and electrical sparks tickle my palm. The lines between his brows appear, and he blinks slowly.

When he opens his eyes, they're no longer caramel but a glowing gold with jealousy, lust, and longing hitting me at full force. His eyes flicker with emotion and a hint of danger. The power emulating from him is immense and weakens my knees. Having my mate this close is skewing my priorities. I crave his touch and imagine him overpowering me with his strength.

I squeeze my thighs together as my sex takes notice of him, cursing myself for being turned on by his ferocity. The friction ignites a fire instead of suppressing the sensations. My body desires nothing more than for him to take the intense feelings he's having out on me.

What's wrong with me? He just hurt Caleb, and I'm still lusting over this guy I met mere seconds ago?

Come on, Alaina, get it together. You're better than this!

He looks down at my thighs, trails his eyes back up my body, and smirks. His eyes flash gold, sensing my arousal, before returning to brown. A hand trails sparks from my chin, down the center of my chest, palming my lower back, pulling me into him.

Okay, maybe I'm not better than this.

"The *mutt*," he says.

His dangerously calm tone sends chills down my spine. It's a question posed as a statement. But he's not asking. He's demanding. Anger simmers beneath his surface as he stares down at me.

"Caleb?"

He chuckles. "I know who he is, darling."

Then, why ask?

Removing his hand from my back, he takes his knuckles and nudges my head to the side, exposing my neck. He inspects the spot Caleb was intending to mark. A hint of relief and fury rolls off him.

I swallow the lump in my throat as he emits more waves of anger, and I try my best not to move, not wanting to find out what happens when he loses control.

At least not under these circumstances, my wolf purrs.

I blink the thought away. *You can't want him*, I tell myself.

"You begged for his life. So, what I want to know is . . ." He moves his hand from my face and grabs a fistful of hair.

I gasp at his force, force that should be drawing me away from him but is only making the need inside me stir more. My scalp stings as he tugs and tilts my head toward his.

Glaring at him, I suck in through my teeth.

"Who is he to you?" he says, staring intently, searching my face for answers.

He stalks forward, his voice calm, while his aura screams danger. His massive form crushes me into the cool boulder. Sharp rock protrudes into my back as his touch ignites my skin. He's impossibly hard, muscles flexing to control his wolf, which is visible with feral power and immense control shimmering under the surface.

Everything about this man screams predator—his gaze, the way his eyes glow when he's angry, his muscular frame, how he towers over me, not to mention his scent.

The night air taunts my wolf and me. The breeze kisses my skin, cooling my burning flesh and permeating his scent. It's overwhelming having him so close, as he has lit a fire under my skin, deep in my core, stealing my resolve.

His spiced, leathery scent swirls through my nose and places its mark upon my wolf, who's dying to bury herself within him, to bask in him until he covers every inch of us. My nipples harden in the chilly breeze, aching for the warmth of his mouth and the roughness of his touch.

I inhale the intoxicating combination as my betraying body pools wetness between my legs. No doubt he can smell what his proximity and dominant nature is doing to me.

I'm reminded of our nakedness when his hardened member presses against my stomach, and I wonder what it would be like to have him thrusting inside me. Desire floods my system as I register his size. He'll stretch and fill me until pleasure and pain mix into delicious torture. I'll die, impaled and entirely satisfied, destroyed by his claim devouring my body and soul.

His eyes flash gold at my acknowledgment, expression relaxing from a death stare to a knowing smile. He hums, and it comes out as a soft rumble from his chest. The deep vibrations emanating from his wolf settle into my core and heighten my desire.

Looking into my eyes, he grabs the back of my neck, pulling my ear to his lips as he dips his head. "There are ways I can make you tell me."

Through his devious grin, his breath tickles my ear, the warmth a stark contrast to the cool breeze. Shivers run down my spine at his promise of endless torture. Moving his hand from my neck, he rubs his thumb over the spot where Caleb's mark should have been. He seems to wish to erase Caleb's touch, and I yearn for the same. Sparks of static electricity lick my skin under his caress. Where Caleb induced fire and pain with his touch, King Dax raises insurmountable pleasure within me. Desire and need surge through my senses. My body shivers in anticipation of his next move.

He trails soft, open-mouthed kisses from my jawline to the spot, his canines gently scraping a path between each. His hand travels up to my chest, skimming my curves and squeezing my large breast as he presses into me closer. It spills over his fingers as his thumb and index finger rolls and tweaks my nipples, eliciting moans from my lips. Slipping his touch lower, he palms my ass and lifts me.

He lays another kiss where his mark would be, and I shiver again. Once more, I can feel him smiling at my response. I'm brought to my tiptoes as he takes handfuls of my soft curves, handprints scorching my skin as he crushes between me and the boulder. Urgency and feral desire seeps from him, evident by his fierce touch. Hints of pain from the stone, his canines, and the trail of pleasure from his lingering indulgence dissipate as he floods my system with his evocative fragrance. It's all too much and not enough. It will never be enough.

I need more of him.

My sex pulses at the need for my mate, and my body lights up with his skillful coaxing and teasing. While my wolf fights for control, pleas and moans escape my lips in mews and gasps as he takes what he wants.

His hand travels down to my throbbing clit and parts my folds. As he spreads me open, his index and middle fingers circle my swollen flesh. They tease, tiny circles increasing in pressure until my breaths hitch at his touch, my hands clawing at his shoulders to steady my shaking legs. I grind against his palm, trying to increase the pressure and speed of his slow strokes against my area of need, greed taking over as I try to take more from him.

My back arches to him as I moan. Pleasure builds to undiscovered levels as he continues his steady assault on my bud. A groan of ecstasy escapes my lips, echoing around the clearing, as my drenched pussy begs for release. I can hear how wet he makes me, my juices slickening his fingers, betraying my resolve and resistance.

I'm engrossed and overwhelmed when he sucks on the sensitive spot on my neck. Practically combusting at the feeling, I completely forget what would happen if he marks me. My wolf takes control as his fingers bring me to higher levels of pleasure threatening to shatter my soul. It feels as if it will consume me, as he surely will. But my wolf seeks to dive off the deep end into the arms of her mate. She's winning, her vibrating presence under my skin ablaze with fire. The carnal pleasure is blinding.

"He's nobody," I say, out of breath, the surmounting orgasm rasping my voice.

He pulls his attention away from my neck, fingers still stroking my sensitive clit. Watching me intently as I try to keep it together, he narrows his eyes and cocks his head. His wolf teeters on control, yet caramel eyes meet my own.

"Tell me . . ." Dax plunges a finger into my wet, needy sex, a smirk forming on his lips. His finger curls inside my inner walls, finding my g-spot, and applies gentle pressure. He coaxes my orgasm higher, his thumb circling my clit with increased pressure, teetering me on the edge. "Do you always bare your neck to nobodies?" he growls into my ear.

I bite my lip to stifle a moan. My nails break skin as I fight against my omission and the orgasm he is threatening to release. *No one could withstand his torture.*

He chuckles.

Damn him, his skilled fingers, and this stupid mate bond.

"Did you fuck him?" he asks in a calm but accusatory tone.

While I don't suspect judgment will follow, danger lurks beneath his question. His wolf is speaking to me more than the man is. His wolf is staking his predatory claim over me—his mate—and my body.

As I'm about to tell him to mind his own fucking business, he inserts another finger, stroking the walls of my inner most self, silencing me with his skilled pursuit. Words choke in my throat as the sensations flood my mind.

"Did that *mutt* touch what belongs to me?"

His fingers rub my cervix, moving between caressing my walls and rubbing my clit. He means to mark and claim me, both outside and in. There will be no question I am his, then. It's evident he intends to mark my neck with his bite and claim my cunt with his seed.

My wolf is eager to be his.

He sucks the sensitive crevice between my neck and shoulder hard enough to tug the skin, then slurps me up when he unlatches from me, rubbing the juices over my slit.

"You're so wet." He continues his taunting circles. "Were you this wet for him?"

My juices lubricate his pursuit of my pleasure and soak his fingers.

Never.

I'm so close. I can't fight it any longer. It's too much.

Sensing my intention to come, he increases the speed.

My chest rises and falls as the orgasm builds, breaths uneven and hitched, as I whimper at the need to come.

"Come for me, darling."

At the sound of his voice, my body tenses in one last attempt to fight against the pleasure. The urge to deny him my release burns in my heart.

Darling. Something so simple and sweet coming from such a demented individual makes it that much hotter.

His lips twitch over my throat as he inserts another finger into my greedy cunt, the pressure against my neck heightening. My resolve shatters in uncontrollable spasms with the curve of his fingers against my g-spot.

"It's so fucking beautiful seeing you come undone for me," he growls in my ear.

Body shaking, I come around his fingers. An explosion of fireworks sets me ablaze and radiates heat throughout my body. Inside and out, I'm on fire—the source, my king. My mouth opens in an "O" as I gasp for air. I quickly bite my lip as I attempt to barricade the screams attempting to break free from my lips.

"Let it out. I want to hear you scream."

Unable to resist his command, a cry of pleasure pours past my lips and echoes through the forest. And his fingers don't relent as I come down from my climb, mercy seemingly unfamiliar to him. Yet something tells me this *is* him being merciless. The potential for his savagery ignites me once more. My body has a mind of its own, rolling like a wanton whore against him. It's as if my body no longer obeys me and, instead, belongs to him, following his commands.

Despite how sensitive my bud is, my hips tell me to suck it up as they attempt to handle more of his torture. Screams of pleasure and pain from the sensitivity escape my lungs at his continued pursuit. His engorged cock throbs and twitches against my curves, begging to be buried deep inside me, just where he belongs. Slick release glistens down my thighs as he pumps his fingers in and out of my throbbing cunt.

"Rub your clit."

"Please," I say as my hands reluctantly move from my stomach down to my sensitive flesh.

I'm helpless to his commands. And I no longer know if I'm begging for my body to resist him or for him to stop.

His words coax like enchanting music that makes my body dance to his every command. My fingertips encircle my clit as I only listen to his hypnotic voice. I'm completely under his spell.

He licks my tears that have fallen onto my collar bone, a low groan from the taste of me vibrating against my skin as his eyes roll back into his head. Lapping up my mating mark, he sends pleasure from his tongue.

I pant as the orgasm rolls through my body, my walls clenching and milking Dax's fingers as I quicken the circles around my clit. My wolf is begging for more of my mate. I'm a slick mess, wet and needy for every orgasm he can give. I need him inside me, stretching and filling me with his cock, taking me.

"I like the sound you make when you scream for me, darling. I can't wait to feel those screams when I'm fucking your throat."

My eyes bug out at his promise.

"You look so fucking beautiful when you cry for me," he says.

He kisses and nips at my clavicle, but I'm high off his promise to make my throat raw in more ways than one.

I want his taste on my tongue, craving to take him deep in my throat and taste him . . . *Maybe I will.*

COME FOR ME

Before I can make my move, Dax hums deeply in approval at my intent. "Soon."

While he can't hear my thoughts, my intentions are bare to him, and I curse myself for forgetting that.

I submit to his thrusting fingers. He's rolling my orgasm into multiples, increasing my pleasure to unknown heights. My wolf bends to his desires, sending astonished moans from my lips as he takes over and tweaks my sensitive clit.

It's as if he's studied some secret manual on all the ways to elicit intense pleasure from my body. He's astonishingly skilled.

He's made for us.

Even I haven't forged the pleasures he easily inspires from within me. It was as if he's studied all his life, learning how to make me implode.

Perhaps this is your torture for keeping him waiting for so long, my wolf muses.

That thought is met with an onslaught of sensation only he knows how to produce.

He circles his thumb over my bud, applying maddening pressure before inserting his fingers deep again and curving against my g-spot.

If his fingers feel this amazing, how good will his cock feel? My wolf howls at the thought as I moan.

"You're incredibly sexy when you're coming for your king," he breathes.

I need his body on mine more than I need the air I suck into my lungs. My body responds to him like a siren's call. It's impossible to deny the attraction and magnetism in his orbit.

He draws me to him, and, like an addict, I need my next fix—even then, it'll never be enough.

Only he can forge an orgasm within me, and I need it. Need the release. Need him.

It's inevitable and impossible to fight against the passion he ignites. I have no control over the sensations he elicits from me. *I crave them.*

His hand travels from my ass to my nape, fisting handfuls of my brown hair as he holds my head still. The pain from the pull on my hair coaxes mews from me as my leg hooks around his hip. My wolf, no longer able to withstand the distance, has me almost climbing his frame. I need him deeper, more than just his fingers fucking me. I need *him.*

For a moment, the thought scares me but then the weight of his erection throbbing against my stomach distracts me. The heat from his dick is maddening as his tongue laps from my shoulder to my ear. My body craves for his cock to stretch and fill me, claiming me as his.

I strain on tiptoes toward his touch, my hand free from my clit's demands clawing at his neck, trying to grab ahold and claim what is mine. His teeth graze the spot between my shoulder and neck. The hint of pain hits like a bolt of lightning, bringing me back to my senses. My path to blissful oblivion is halted by the pressure of his canines. Panic registers as I realize he's going to mark me.

No!

Against my better judgment, I push him away. My wolf whimpers, instantly missing his touch.

COME FOR ME

I almost lost everything. *He almost took everything.* One bite and I would have been taken away from my home, my family, friends, and what's left of my parents. I'd lose myself.

I use that fear and my pent-up sexual frustration to fuel my anger so I can muster the strength to tear myself away from him. *I can't think when he's this close to me.*

"Get away from me."

CHAPTER SEVEN
Dax

My canines retract back into my gums, as I'm dumbfounded at her rejection. I roll my neck out of frustration, having been so close to marking her, and my cock is still rock hard.

This little wolf is testing my control tonight. Twice, she has denied me, and she was at my limit the first time. It takes all my strength to hold back my wolf from claiming her, biting her neck, and burying my cock to the hilt inside her.

If I couldn't smell her desire, her words would've gutted me. She can feel the pull of the bond as much as I can. My dick twitches as I think about the sparks emanating between us, her little moans as I touch her sensitive bud, and how her body is wet with need at my mere presence.

Wanting nothing more than for me to claim her, she was ready to be spread open for me and scream for her king. Her wolf begs for it. *For me.*

COME FOR ME

Chills roil through me as I think about how she shivered as I sucked on the spot where I intended to mark her.

Where that mutt tried to take what belongs to me.

Correction, where she almost *let him* take what belongs to only me.

The thought of her giving herself to another enrages me. *Does she love him? Or did she think I wasn't coming for her?* I had grounds to kill him, but her pleas were hard to ignore.

I create distance between us by leaning back against a tree, my dick still hard from the sight of her unraveling under my control. I cross my arms and stare at her, fighting my wolf's need to be near her.

I need answers.

My wolf struggles for control, lacking patience for this song and dance, the shift threatening beneath my skin. He wants to rut our cock deep into her and sink our teeth into her neck.

Think about how spectacular she would be as she implodes around our cock, my wolf taunts, growling at how beautiful she looked unraveling for me on my hands.

Fuck, my wolf isn't being fair.

I adjust my crotch. I felt how tiny her frame was against my own, her curves molding into my hard form. My cock would stretch her, fill her to the brim, and ruin her for all others.

She'd be mine.

The violet in her eyes would waltz through her blue iris seas as I would grasp her massive breasts with my claws, thrusting over and over into her tight sex, beckoning her orgasming pussy to clench around my length.

She would run her hands through her hair, mumbling, while asking herself what she is doing. She'd be conflicted—of course, this is all new to her, having found out her mate is the king. But I didn't expect her to push me away.

"Is this about the mutt?" I spit.

If she was conflicted before, she's not anymore.

"Caleb."

Clear irritation is directed at me and written all over her face as she corrects me.

Interesting. So, she does care about him.

"Are you in love with the little alpha pup?" I tease.

Her next words will hold gravity. My tone may indicate I'm joking, attempting to ease her guard down. Thinking of that mutt holding her love while I get her hatred sparks unfamiliar jealousy in me. *Hmph, jealousy. That's new for me. Only I should have her love, not some insolent mutt.*

That upsets her. Sparks light up in her eyes. Violet storms meet mine, as fury courses through her veins and mesmerizes me. She's infuriated with me, and it's magnificent. My cock twitches again with her rage.

Unaware of whether a lie or the truth will save him, she stays silent, intending to protect him.

Smart. Little does she know neither answer will save him.

Staring at me with those blue eyes, her nipples still taut, she says, "What happens between me and my alpha is none of your business."

Her long chocolate-colored hair with golden highlights sways down her back as she crosses her arms and turns her back to me like a brat throwing a tantrum, a behavior I note to fuck out of her later.

I need to make sure she knows *exactly* who her alpha really is.

Pushing off the tree with my shoulder, moving toward her like a predator stalking its prey, I wrap one hand around her waist, grabbing the front of her throat with my other.

She sucks in her breath as my stiff cock presses into her perfectly round ass.

"That *mutt*"—I bite her ear—"is *not* your alpha," I whisper-growl into her neck, brushing my lips over that sensitive spot.

Her heavenly black raspberry vanilla aroma fusing with her arousal kisses my nose. Leaning her head back onto my shoulder, she relaxes, her skin smooth.

And in need of some color.

She gasps as I spank her but doesn't protest. Instead, she arches her back, pushing her ass farther into me.

A low growl of approval leaves my throat at how her body responds to me.

Laying claim to my mate and decorating her neck with my mark places her at as much risk as leaving her bare does. Her hesitation and resistance are an unexpected concern. Most she-wolves throw themselves at my feet, yet this little one fights me, pushing me away and denying our bond. Yet she would have let the mutt mark her. I need to understand why.

My little mate is not ready to be claimed. She's young. I've had years to contemplate her existence and our mating. But that does little to ease my decision. I have many enemies in our world. With vampires and rogues teaming up, the kingdom is in uncharted territory. I still don't know their intentions. I could be throwing her directly into their path by signaling who she is. There's too much risk, too many unknown factors and hidden intentions to unearth. As my mate, she is a target but, left unmarked, she's vulnerable. There's no easy option.

The little wolf before me is the source of my strength, but she is also my greatest weakness. I can't afford to hand over such a tantalizing pawn to use against me. I stand behind her, bound by duty to the throne and kingdom.

She can keep her secrets. For now, I'll just have to mark her in other ways.

"Put your hands on the rock. Ass out for me."

Her lips part and eyes widen in astonishment at my command. I stand back, stroking my length to the sight of her perfect hourglass body. It's enthralling watching her do as I say, her obedience sweeter than the thousands of others who would bow before me with a lift of my brow. While they bowed to their king's orders, she stands against them. She challenges me—the only one to defy me.

The Moon Goddess created a match for me, and a match, she is. Both her bold defiance *and* submission have my cock hard.

Feet shoulder-width apart, back arched, and her pink lips on display for me makes me practically combust at the sight.

Fucking beautiful.

"Good girl."

I reach between her thighs, and my fingers are instantly coated.

COME FOR ME

"So fucking wet for your king," I praise. I take my fingers soaked with her juices and press them to her mouth. "Open." My fingers trace those plump, soft lips I want to sink my teeth into.

They part for me, granting me access to another one of her pretty little holes I plan to fill. Her tongue tickles my fingertips as it laps and sucks up her essence. The tease of what she desires to do to me is maddening.

It takes every fiber of my being to keep myself from pouncing on her. It's not in my nature to go slow.

A slow death. Goddess, is it fucking killing me.

I growl, my wolf flashing thoughts of her lips around our cock. My wolf fights to mark her.

I remind my wolf the delay will be worth our torture.

Massaging the length of my fingers with her velvety tongue, she increases the pressure as I pull them from her lips, resulting in a pop of her mouth.

I trail my fingers between her breasts and over her soft curves. Delicately, I make my way down her mound and tease slow circles over her clit, and she releases her stifled breath. I concentrate on her throbbing bud. She breathes out once more, her body arching toward my touch.

Feeling her clit getting harder, my attention shifts to her neglected breasts. *Such a shame they haven't yet been properly worshipped.* They deserve to be marked and tortured by my mouth and hands.

Leaning forward, my weight presses against her back, my free hand snaking between her form and the cool stone. My touch traces a path back over her hip and roams across to grab her breast. I palm her large bust with my hand, the soft, heaving flesh spilling over my fingers. Her breasts are larger than I can hold, and it's erotically irritating when my large hands can't grasp all of her.

I squeeze and knead, stopping only to roll and tug her nipples. Her head falls, and her hair cascades along the sides of her face like a waterfall. My fingers dig into her flesh, feeling the weight of her tit and how those perky bulbs heave with her moans.

Trailing my touch to the other, I palm and tweak her other nipple. The agitation amps me up further, causing me to be rougher. I draw moans from her lips, her hips wiggling back against my grip. Her hair swings as she rocks herself against my touch, trying to obtain more friction, submitting to the pleasure.

"Mm, yes, roll your hips for me like that, darling," I moan. "Fuck," I hiss at the sight of her rubbing her clit against my fingers.

My wolf is clawing at the surface, threatening to take control and rut her needy pussy to his fill.

I almost want to let her come as a thank-you for the private show, but my naughty little vixen needs a lesson from her new teacher.

"Now..."

My fingers slow to a torturous rhythm, enough to keep her right on the edge but not enough to send her over.

She whimpers and increases the rhythm of her hips.

Needy little thing.

COME FOR ME

Her inner walls contract around my fingers as she teeters on the edge of orgasm.

"Who did you say your alpha was?"

Softly, she whispers, "You."

I pull my fingers away, and she groans. Her hand starts traveling down her body to remedy her starvation.

Growling, I snatch it before she can serve her needy center without my say-so, my one and only warning.

She whimpers and continues rolling those fucking hips to hold on to the build inside her.

I scoff in amusement as her body begs for my attention. *My personal little whore.*

"You what?" I ask innocently.

I want her like this all the time, panting while her pussy pulses for me.

She whines, sounding like she's about to cry when she isn't sure what answer I'm looking for. Then she's silent, realizing her pleas aren't wearing me down like it would on some pathetic omega.

Although pleas from her filthy mouth have probably made even the strongest of alphas bend to her will in the past.

But that won't be me, darling. I own you. You'll get used to that. I'll have that defiant mouth begging to please me.

Her lips tremble as she tries to figure out how to greet me. Her lips part, yet no words come out. Even her silence is music to my ears.

Her uncertainty is adorable.

Part of the devil inside me wants to see what she'll come up with and laugh at all the flattering names she showers me with. Her cheeks would get red as she refers to me in high regards, and I'd pinch her clit when she'd get it wrong. *Would she cry pretty tears for me? Goddess, I'd fucking hope so.*

But my wolf urges me to throw her a bone this time.

"In public, it's Dax." I reach between her thighs, gathering her juices to stroke my cock at her entrance. "In private, you'll refer to me as my king." The tip of my cock strokes her slit, sliding down to tease her bud before returning to her entrance.

"Yeah, I'm not calling you that," she scoffs.

Her laughter rolls through her curves beneath me.

I grab her throat. "What was that?"

Her breath is ragged, but her eyes dance at my force.

My mate likes it rough.

Squeezing her delicate neck, I dare her to push me further, to give me reason to punish her bratty mouth.

For a moment, I think she's going to, but instead...

"My king," she says, and I moan.

Those words have never been sweeter. If her moans were music, her proclamation of my honorific was a drug. It's scorchingly hot, hearing her submission, her declaration of what I am to her, of who she is to me.

Mine.

I lean into her ear and rasp, "That's right." I rub my coated hand over her face sloppily.

She shakes her head and grunts in disgust, and I laugh.

My dick slams into her, buried to the hilt in her convulsing sex.

She feels fucking magnificent. No other pussy has felt this wonderful. No food, no drink, no comfort has been found that could ever compare. With no remorse, I'll consume her until there is nothing left.

I snatch her hips, my fingers digging into flesh as I hold her still, angling her to take my dick perfectly with each stroke. Deeper and deeper, I drive into her tight pussy, the tip of my cock hitting her cervix. My hand soothes up her back and fists her hair as I hold her in place. My wolf works in unison with hers, chasing the orgasm building between us.

We've turned to wild animals rutting in heat, claiming her as desperately as she needs me to take her.

Sam tries to nudge me through the mindlink.

Whatever it is, Sam can handle it while I mate with their queen.

My focus returns to the beauty beneath me, who's growling, moaning, and gasping from my cock. Like a siren, her music fills the clearing with a devious symphony, our slapping bodies syncing with the tempo of her song as our orgasms build to a crescendo.

I hear footsteps behind me and smell Sam.

"Sir," Sam says.

Fucking hell.

At the sound of his voice, my mate stills. Her embarrassment surfaces as she realizes we're not alone.

When she tries to stand, I yank a fistful of her hair, my cock still buried inside her. She winces, sucking in a breath, and places a hand over my fist.

I dip my head and growl into her ear, "I don't remember dismissing you. Make no mistake, I will make this whole kingdom watch you submit to me if there is any confusion as to who you belong to."

Her eyes widen at the promise. Then she giggles.

Mate thinks we make idle threats. Seems she's in need of another lesson.

My eyes darken, and she's no longer giggling.

"You learn fast." I reward her with a sharp smack to her ass. "Good girl."

My attention returns to the mating spot where my surface-level bite marks lie. Flat against her skin, my tongue licks her clavicle to her shoulder. My teeth find their indentations and bite.

Careful to not sink myself too far yet, I hold them there, applying pressure as my hands cup her breasts, their weight dropping in a bounce as my palm slides over her clavicle. My fingers wrap around her neck, my thumb applying pressure to her carotid artery.

An added thrill washes over me, as I could easily cause delicious destruction and pain with the right amount of pressure in mere moments. Her blooming blush rejuvenates her fragrance in my mouth, and I suck in her flesh. Hard. Blood pools beneath my lips, my canines descending to nick her sweet skin.

"Does it feel like I'm done with you?" I twitch my cock inside her, and she bites her plump lip, shaking her head. I bend her back down by her hair. Choked whimpers escape her lips, her scent permeating as her cheeks blush further.

I continue thrusting into her.

"Talk fast, Sam," I say over my shoulder.

Picking up the pace, I relish in her moans as they fill the air once again.

Sam averts his eyes.

If she were some she-wolf, he wouldn't have bothered. My discretions never fazed him in the past, but this is no she-wolf but rather his future queen. No one will lay eyes on her naked body unless I say so.

"Yes, Your Majesty. It's Alpha Jack of the Bloodhound pack and his son, Caleb. They're requesting an audience with you."

I stop thrusting at his name, and I can sense her panic.

Growling in annoyance, I sigh when my hard-on softens. I pull out of her and face Sam.

My wolf is surfacing, fighting for control.

Sam's making a habit out of popping up at the worst time, cockblocking me every chance he can. If he can't take a hint, I'll have to teach him a lesson.

"About?"

Sam looks in her direction, and she covers herself.

"Is it about me?" she asks through quickened breaths, darting her gaze between us.

Even though he's only curious about who will reign queen after waiting so many years, he'll have to wait until she's decent.

I growl, stepping in front of her, blocking Sam's view of her. While I meant what I said about fucking her in front of the pack as a reminder of who owns her, that would be on my terms.

"Get her some clothes and then take her to my room."

Sam hands her my white T-shirt, keeping his head down.

My shirt is practically a dress on her. At the sight of her in it and her roughed-up hair, I bite my lip. My mate is darling.

I step in the direction of the castle.

"Where are you going?"

I peer over my shoulder and shrug. "To kill the mutt."

CHAPTER EIGHT
Dax

Alpha Jack and his insignificant offspring are standing in my study when my guards open the doors.

Looks like the moonlight isn't the only thing creeping into my office.

The two dark-blue chairs in front of my desk are empty, with Jack and the mutt behind them. The mutt's father is tall and proud, like an alpha should be, especially in the presence of royalty. Meanwhile, his son paces the room, his nervous energy and determination reeking up the place.

For the love of Goddess, stop moving.

The mutt is stupid to show his face here. He might not have known before that she's my mate, but now he knows I've decided to claim her. Yet here he is, about to make foot-sized holes in my hardwood flooring if he doesn't fucking stand still.

My powers play out like a movie in my mind, lending me the foresight that the mutt has brought his daddy to talk her hand out of mine. *Pathetic.* Daddy won't save him and would only serve as an audience to witness his inevitable end.

I watched Jack work for my father growing up. He saw firsthand how harsh my father was toward those who would die for him.

Meanwhile, Jack had the pleasure of watching my father use his cruel methods to train me as the future king, which involved humiliation and barbaric conditioning. I respected Jack and how he took my father's leadership in stride and lived, not letting his pride get in the way of survival. My father could have rubbed Jack's face in piss like a dog, and he would find the peace to wipe his face, bow before his king, and walk away without letting anyone know he was bothered. Jack never showed weakness.

It's clear he carries that same respect for me—or if not, he'd never let me think otherwise.

Jack's offspring, on the other hand, seems to miss that trait. To be fair, Jack watched me turn into the force of nature I am now, one who won't hesitate to eliminate any threat to the kingdom. The mutt, however, seems to need a lesson on who I am and exactly what I'm capable of.

Jack's intent flashes before my eyes.

Jack is dwarfed by my bookcases and my desk rimmed with a stoic sense of duty to protect the mutt from the death that awaits him. He's bound by familial responsibility and love for his son.

Jack isn't here to manipulate me into using our history together to sway my decision. Jack has integrity.

He survived my father's tyranny, which meant he knew what a king could do and, in turn, intended to approach me diplomatically. After the mutt's transgression and the threat to the kingdom he has created, he's lucky to still be alive. It would bode him well not to aggravate me further.

I'm confused why someone with as much experience as Jack, who has worked under my family line, would be so stupid as to support his son's actions to contest my claim to my Goddess-given mate and demand an audience with his king.

Even if she weren't my mate but rather some she-wolf, does he really think he could take her from me? He knows the rules. If the mutt wants her, he'll have to fight me for her. That's how the Hunt and our very nature works. The mutt knows he can't physically beat me, yet here he is, ready to die for someone made for me.

Unless Jack doesn't realize she's my mate.

I study Jack to understand why he cares for my mate so much. I note a paternal sense of responsibility Jack has toward her.

A vibration under his form becomes noticeable with the impatient tapping of his fingers at his side.

Fear and apprehension linger in the air, a sour taste for the task at hand.

He means to protect my mate from me.

My wolf stirs.

Although a strong, impressive alpha in his own right, Jack and his son can't compare to my height, strength, speed, or knowledge of the kingdom. I've lived and fought for those under my responsibility. But my mate? I would destroy the world for her. My responsibilities to anyone else would be damned to hell. None were nor will ever be above her.

My mate's presence radiates strength within me as she enters the study moments after I step through the doorway.

Stubborn girl.

These men weren't welcome to begin with, but they're important to my mate.

With that, I mindlink my men, and the door shuts behind us. Locking it is solely for dramatic effect and sadistic enjoyment. It's not like they could escape me, even if they tried.

Jack swallows at the sight of me but doesn't waver, while the mutt sweats at my dramatic act.

They're both scared. *Good.* Scared people don't want to die.

Their eyes fall to my mate.

Instinctively, I sidestep, blocking her from the mutt's view. My muscles contract with tension surging through my wolf and me.

The two divert their gazes, and my wolf's temper reduces to a simmer.

Jack clears his throat. "Pardon the interruption, Your Majesty, but I feel there's been a misunderstanding."

Plopping myself in the brown leather desk chair, I fold my hands in my lap. I lift an eyebrow, waiting for further explanation.

I can assure him I've misunderstood nothing.

Sam guards my mate at my side, his hands behind his back, feet planted shoulder-width apart, head high. Already, my beta is ready to die for his queen.

Another trusted guard stands at my side, who's skilled in his dissection of enemy strategy and torture.

What's his name again? Shit, I've killed a few before him who didn't quite fit the bill and stopped learning their names. If he keeps it up, I might bother to remember his name.

My mate side-eyes Sam and what's-his-name, appearing confused at their proximity but not uncomfortable.

They're protecting you, darling. Get used to it.

Jack clears his throat. "My son, Caleb Waller, the soon-to-be alpha of Bloodhound pack, has chosen Alaina Grove—" He gestures toward my mate.

Alaina. Her name sears my brain, crashes into my soul, and lays claim to me. Beautiful syllables form a heavenly title for my gorgeous mate.

Queen Alaina.

The honorific will roll off my tongue and taste divine. I'd gladly worship her in every way and pay tribute with my tongue. The thought excites my wolf.

Alaina Taylor. Even better.

"—as his chosen mate. I can assure you that what you saw was consensual and within the rules of the Hunt."

So, Jack doesn't know that she's my mate. And with that realization, the dots are connecting. He thinks I was intervening because I thought she was a damsel in distress, not because he was about to mark what's mine. It's with that I entertain the idea of letting them live. At least for now.

That may change tomorrow.

I stand and watch as the mutt walks to her and makes the grave mistake of grabbing her hand and smiling at her. His father's words have emboldened him, made the mutt believe he was well within his rights. His gesture meant to prove to me that this was all innocent and out of love.

Well. Fuck. That.

I'm on him before he can register I've reached him, pinning his hand against the wall. My forearm is cutting off his airway. "No one touches my mate." *No one gets to even entertain the idea that her heart could belong to anyone else but me.*

Rage consumes me at the sight of the mutt's hands on my mate, coloring my vision as the wolf inside me erupts with a possessive claim. The frame of a painting cracks as glass shatters with the force and falls to the floor.

The mutt grunts from the breath leaving his body as he's slammed into the wall. It'd be so easy to kill him. His pack wouldn't even bother to retaliate. They don't have the numbers to take on my pack. If it weren't for her, I would've killed him earlier when this mutt tried to claim her for himself. Blind rage hits me again when I recall the memory. I press my forearm harder against his throat, restricting his airway.

My wolf has been ready to mark her, and he won't rest until we've claimed her. Surely, this mutt isn't the only one after my mate. It's dangerous for her to walk around unmarked if threats like him walk around. I've waited seven years for my mate to come along, eight if you include when I became king before becoming eligible to participate in the Hunt—I'll be damned if anyone thinks they can take her from me now.

COME FOR ME

Alaina sobs.

Fucking hell. I don't like when she cries.

That annoying thought dawns on me that killing him could mean losing her respect. After grappling with it, I decide her favor outweighs all my reasons for killing him.

I'll protect her from anyone. She'll learn that. But I don't want her believing she needs protection from me. At least not in this context.

"Stay. Away. From. My. Mate," I grit before easing my weight off him.

The mutt stares at me with dead eyes, not at all remorseful.

I don't know whether my power is a blessing or a curse. Because the mutt's eyes project no intention of following my orders. Far from it. He wants what's mine and thinks no threat will deter him from pursuing her.

But force will.

I could show force, starting with ripping out his canines so he can't mark anyone. To be chosen but never able to choose from any future mate, having someone but never able to give himself to her fully. A fate worse than any torture I could elicit.

Alaina's sobs confuse the wolf within me, stopping me from doing so. My wolf desires to rip the tears from her—if not for me, as they serve no purpose. She still holds a candle for this monstrosity, cares for him more than her mate.

Who is he to her? What happened between them that she would risk his life again? What hold does he have over my mate? She'd rather shed sweet tears for him than mate with me and taste sweet oblivion. Her tears were designed for my pleasure and enjoyment, not for his pity and pain.

If she wants to cry for him, cry for him, she will.

"Was I not clear, mutt?" I spit, my voice gravelly as I cock my head.

Sorry, darling. He's given me no choice. I have to protect you.

I break his hand in one swift motion. The mutt collapses to one knee, while I crush his hand in grip. Not at all bothering to stifle his screams, showing how pathetic and weak he is to everyone within earshot. I roll my eyes at his outburst as I drop his hand. *Some alpha. What does she see in this guy?*

My peripherals find her as she gasps, fear and fury fusing with her black raspberry and vanilla scent.

Staring at the pathetic, sobbing mutt, she balls her fists.

"Did that clear up any misunderstandings, Jack?" I look over to Jack, who doesn't react, despite how much he wants to.

Void of emotion, he holds his head high as he looks me in the eye and regards me with a nod. He moves to tend to his sniffling son, who is clutching his broken hand to his chest.

Jack's lack of reaction to my show of force doesn't surprise me. If my father were still alive and Jack had said anything other than "thank you" to this merciful lesson I have bestowed on his son, he would have killed them both, deeming them unfit to lead their pack. I'm sure Jack believes me to be like him.

But he'd be wrong. I'm far worse.

My father was an awful parent, a tyrant king, and took to torturing prisoners and enemies for the sake of information.

COME FOR ME

He was feared—never loved. But it wasn't his torture or teaching methods that instilled fear but rather his paranoia. He didn't believe his powers—telepathic predictions I've been possessing since his passing—when they showed people's intentions.

My father always thought someone was after him, which is what made him so unpredictable. I almost couldn't blame him for being the way he was, as he was clearly sick.

It was after his brain injury that he was convinced his powers were damaged, resulting in the killing of innocents. Even worse, he would doubt his powers and think a truly ill-intended person was innocent and let them go free. I had to clean up behind him a lot.

But me? I'm in control. I'm not plagued with paranoia. My power to see someone's intent and anticipate someone's next move never fails me. I know the difference between purity and pollution.

What makes me unpredictable is that I don't always care what someone's intent is. Doesn't mean I won't kill you for something as minor as an inconvenience or whether I just feel like it. Sometimes, it's not the intentions but the impact that matters. My father's lessons on how to rule our kingdom stirred a darkness within me that even he couldn't comprehend.

Where my father was a tyrant king, he had forged me into the ruthless overlord I am now. His paranoia made him thorough in his torturous ways. The torture transcended its purpose to discover enemy plans into my pleasure and expertise.

Guards required desensitization to handle my sessions with the prisoners, while some required orders to swallow their bile and control their composure. Where they winced and feared, I reveled and feasted upon the screams, spilled blood, and demise of my victims.

My enemies fared worse, and the she-wolves I've encountered were never the same once I had dealt with them. Whispers of my shocking little games had made me so renowned that few dared wish to experience it firsthand. I had a fearless reputation to uphold.

Once a true intent is unearthed, their fate is sealed. They'd die by my hand if they posed a threat to me or my kingdom. Emotion and reasoning did little to sway me. I never hesitated to kill potential threats before they actualized and spilled innocent blood.

At least I didn't until . . . *her*.

My beta escorts Jack and his mutt of a son out of my office.

I look at Alaina, who appears shocked at my show of force, then sit in my office chair and pat my thigh with an eyebrow raised.

Alaina listens like a good girl and sits on my lap. I bury my face in her neck, taking a whiff of her hair. Her scent and proximity soothe my frustrations. A sense of calm puts out the fire in me as I breathe into her neck.

"Go near him again, and I will mark you whether you want to be marked or not. Am I understood?" I exhale out of my nose, followed by a hum from my throat.

She gulps and nods slowly.

"Good girl," I say, hypnotically drawn to her lips.

CHAPTER NINE
Alaina

I still. The claim of his lips holds promise of mass destruction, yet I melt into the kiss, allowing him to take possession of me. My mind whirls with the thrill of danger from kissing the devil himself. I'm gasping and struggling to breathe with his tongue drawing my soul out of me, as if the devil is tricking me into replacing my need for oxygen with his lips.

I was raised to run from danger, yet here I am, kissing him.

Alpha Jack and Caleb had only one side to the story: they didn't know I am Dax's mate. A clear misunderstanding, yet Dax wouldn't hear them out. If Dax had just mentioned that, Caleb wouldn't have touched me. It was almost as if Dax *wanted* to be provoked to put Caleb in his place. It was all so unnecessary.

But the devil loves to play games. Meaning none of us are safe.

I should've been deterred when Dax broke Caleb's hand so easily. Instead, my wolf purred over Dax's display of dominance. This act of violence is considered sinful. But I'm not immune to how seductive sin looks on Dax.

Dax had shown restraint because Caleb wasn't a serious threat to him. The idea of what it'd be like if Dax didn't hold back terrifies and excites me at the same time. My wolf feels proud to have such a strong, powerful mate.

Great, my wolf seems to be both horny and stupid.

Our kiss deepens. His tongue caresses mine in longer strokes. My pussy aching, I roll my hips against him and moan into his mouth as the friction further fuels my need. I wrap my legs around Dax's waist as he stands. Dax lays me down on his desk, his mouth still covering mine.

Consumed by him tugging my nipples through my shirt and his kisses, I turn my head, granting him more access.

A pair of boots come into view, revealing a man I didn't know was here. I tilt my head back as far as I can and take in the rest of my surroundings.

Two other men stand guard at the door. Their eyes stare straight ahead, giving the illusion of privacy. But I am very much aware of their presence.

Their black leather boots connect to sleek black pants. As my eyes travel up their frames, I notice white shirts within their blazers. His men seethe danger and skill. They may look the part for a royal pack, but they are assessing threat and danger, guarding and protecting the king while his attention is focused elsewhere.

Their tall, massive frames are muscular, their strength evident with large biceps, pecs that stretch their shirts, and thick columns of thighs. They are tan, likely from their hours of training.

Dax stops kissing my neck, sensing I'm no longer mentally present. Hovering inches above my face, he studies me carefully. Confused as to what took me away from the moment, he follows my gaze's direction. It doesn't take him but a second for him to catch on and looks back to me with a knowing grin.

"Eyes on her," he says.

His men shift their focus to us.

His warning from before echoes in my mind. *Make no mistake, I will make this whole kingdom watch you submit to me if there is any confusion as to who you belong to.*

Goose bumps dot my skin as their eyes travel to my body, creating heat within me. Their gaze roams over my curves as he caresses my mound and exposes me to their observation. My hands flex, the desire to cover myself fighting with the excitement stirring in my veins. Their attention thrills my wolf, knowing I'm desirable and an object of envy for my mate.

It's intoxicating having Dax above me, touching me as they look. It emboldens me.

Smiling, I lick my lips as Dax's hands roam over me, caressing my curves for their viewing under my shirt. It feels as if I'm bare before them, my hips grinding wildly against his cock.

I can sense their longing and desire to join. To use me to fulfill their sexual frustration. *To fuck a queen.* I know his men can smell the arousal pooling between my legs.

Dax hums in approval before kissing my neck to my chest. My sadistic mate appreciates the torture I'm able to elicit among his men.

The thin fabric of my shirt is torn away as he pins me to his desk.

Cool air greets me as Dax sits up. I groan at the loss of his touch. He grips my thighs, his fingers leaving indentations as he pulls my hips to the edge of the wooden surface. The zipper cages his member in a striking coolness against my hot mound excited by his manhandling. He leans forward, and the friction increases against my clit as I grind.

His frame covers my stomach, revealing my breasts to the guards. The thrill hardens my nipples as he spreads my thighs wider with his, exposing me to his men.

His lips trail to my nipple, biting and pulling. Clasped between his teeth is my hardened nipple, his hand pinching the other. A moan escapes from me, and my back arches off his desk. I let out a hiss from the pain, the wood cool and hard against my shoulder blades.

His hands firmly travel up my breasts, as he watches them rise and fall with my every breath. Dax's hands spread my arms wide, sliding up my limbs before spreading me open and leaving me helpless beneath him. My hands stretch open, mimicking the motion of a cat's paws before they make biscuits into a blanket, then ball into a fist as he squeezes my wrists, pinning me down again.

The hard surface is unyielding under his hold. Glimmers of mischief in his eyes dare me to move, yet he commands me to obey with a smirk. His movements increase pressure on my clit and awaken my sex, resulting in my juices gathering the fabric stretched over his lap. I could come just from grinding against him like this.

The guards' presence, their gaze on my body, and their enjoyment in my pleasure, are edging me closer toward release. My hips have a mind of their own as they grind against his cock, moans escaping from my lips as I ride the edge of my orgasm.

I'm getting so close, and he hasn't even touched me yet. Our show alone could do me in. He blesses me with more pressure to grind against by pressing deeper into me.

"Dax!" I gasp, my inner walls clenching.

He sucks in his teeth as I grip him. "You don't know how long we've waited for you."

His hand curves around my neck as he holds me still. He squeezes my throat, and my mouth forms an "O" with the sudden loss of air. Standing over me, he watches me as I writhe against his desk. He steps back, his cock leaving my mound, cool air caressing my scorching pussy. I whimper at the loss of his heat and pressure. As I reach new levels of frustration, my hips wiggle to return the stimulation.

A sadistic grin forms on his face, tilting his head as he watches my face constrict. He's basking in my struggle. His hard cock is evidence.

"Fuck y—"

He tightens his grip, snatching my speech from me, then slaps my pussy lips. The sting tingles as his hand retracts, then another comes down on my clit before he clutches my mound.

I hiss from the pain, frustration heightening as he gives me *something* yet not enough of it.

He clearly didn't like me disrespecting him in front of his men. I note this for later—for when I choose to use this to anger him.

"You don't want to do that, darling," he coos.

Fuck. I forgot about his telepathic predictions.

"Not when this can feel so . . . damn . . . good."

As he finishes his sentence, his middle and ring finger find my opening, and they spread my lips, baring myself to his view. His fingers enter me and massage my inner walls, pressing the button inside. Leaning down, he nips at my lower abdomen, trailing bites and kisses down to my clit, then takes the swollen bud into his mouth.

His digits press against my g-spot, building my orgasm with his thrusts as he fucks me with his fingers. His tongue laps at my clit, circling the hardening bud, building my orgasm to maddening heights. His lips suck on it, the sensation too intense and driving me over the edge.

Dax's mouth upturns into a mischievous grin. Despite my delirium, I finally find the words to ask why he's smiling, but the ability to relay them is snatched from me by his rapid lapping to my heady flesh.

Like a roller coaster ride, I explode violently, shouting his name on the way down. I'm panting through every spasm. My skin is hot to the touch. Unclenching my rump, letting my trembling legs slowly part, the orgasm subsides.

I prepare to relax, but I'm met with another uphill climb. Dax continues to draw out my release, draining my body of all coherent thoughts with his tantalizing fingers and tongue. Squeezing my butt cheeks together, I clench my stomach. I want to beg him to stop, but my desperate whine makes for an unconvincing plea.

Dax doesn't stop, and I come undone once more. My voice bounces off his study's walls, the whole kingdom hearing their "future queen's" cries. I lie on the desk, out of breath and unable to form a coherent thought. The only thing I can make out is the pop Dax's mouth makes as he unlatches from my throbbing clit.

He grumbles, licking his fingers and lips clean.

Leaning in close, Dax mutters, "They can smell your submission." He nips at my ear, and heat rushes to my cheeks. "Stand up."

I'm in too much of a euphoric haze to argue. It's like he's created a drug, and I can only continue to feel this way under his allowance. Intoxicated and drunk off my ass, my body hums under his command. The craving creeps in again, and I'll do anything for my next fix.

Dax steps to the side of the desk, ensuring he's blocking the view of my swollen pussy. I stand on shaky legs, my feet carrying me.

I search his face, questioning where he wants me. Even when fully exposed, he finds a way to keep a part of me only to himself. Only *he* can see me this way.

Fisting my hair, he leans in close, clenching his jaw. "They can watch you come for me, but they don't get to see what's mine. This"—he grasps my tender flesh, growling—"is *mine*."

His lips crash into mine, his tongue forcing its way into my mouth, and I'm gasping for air in between lip-lock.

"On your knees for me, darling," he says, easing me to the cold floor. "I want them to watch how good you take me."

His words are a deadly promise for me and an order for his men in the study.

Dax stares down at me, parting my bottom lip with his thumb. My hips wiggle, adjusting my knees to the hard floor.

He strips his clothes, his girth no less impressive than he. Wetting and biting my lips, I watch him stalk forward. He presses his erection against my lips, encouraging them to open wider. The flat of my tongue laps at the salty, delicious precum, and it retreats as I moan.

"Don't tease me, darling." He flexes, causing his length to twitch and bob.

Pressing an emboldened kiss to the tip of his dick, I slide the bulb of his cock past my lips. My mouth stretches wide, taking in his expansive girth.

"Fuck, Alaina."

Taking him deeply, I bob my head along his length, stroking his shaft with my tongue. As I elicit grunts from his lips, Dax meets my movement with frantic pumping of his hips, eager for more. I match his rhythm, increasing my pace, gagging when his head reaches the back of my throat. His size forces tears to well in my eyes.

Peering up at him, I feel my ego soar at my ability to coax such music from the king of werewolves himself.

Dax meets my stare, and a grunt followed by a shudder leads his seed spasming down my throat.

COME FOR ME

"Good girl," he says, wiping a tear from my cheek.

My pussy quenches at his praise, and it is then I know my soul no longer belongs to me. I say a quick prayer to the Moon Goddess. Surely, drinking the devil's sin doesn't come without consequences.

He grasps my arms, pulling me to my feet. Dax moves to the side with his leather chair, pulling me into him and lifting me to the desk once more. He pulls me closer to him by my ass, giving him deeper access to suck on my neck.

Feet shuffle in behind me, and I try to look over my shoulder to see what's happening. Dax buries his face into the space between my breasts, leaving open-mouthed kisses all over. I glimpse blonde hair and a masculine build before Dax clasps the back of my head with a growl, demanding my attention with a devouring kiss.

"Eyes on me."

A throat clears, but Dax ignores the intrusion with loud pants, switching from the assault of my lips to my jawline and sucking on my neck.

I exhale a whimper.

His need to consume me has me forgetting someone was trying to get our attention until the interruption occurs again.

Someone clears their throat. Still sucking at the spot on my neck where my mark would go, Dax feels around his desk until he finds what he's looking for, then chucks it at whoever it is, a solid object clattering against the wall.

The man is insistent on Dax's attention, and I am in no mood to share him. Dax's hand pumps his cock at my entrance, gearing up to enter me.

I gasp, needing him now.

"Your Majesty," the male says.

Dax's eyes glow, sparing a glance over my shoulder, then rubs the head of his cock on my clit.

"What is it, Sam?"

Great, that's twice today he's caught me with my ass out.

"Olivia's here."

Dax pauses our enmeshment at the female's name, the mood shifting instantly.

A jolt of jealousy encroaches me.

Dax glares at Sam. I follow his gaze to a smirking Sam standing in the middle of Dax's study. Sam jerks back when his gray eyes connect with my wolf's glowing set.

I suppress a growl, demanding to know who this female is who's come between us and what about her arrival is so amusing to Sam to have Dax throwing daggers.

Sam's eyes dart from me to Dax, unclear what to do. Dax takes a step away from me, running his hands through his hair. My mouth opens at his need for distance, and my heart races.

Who is Olivia?

Dax snatches a book off his shelf and hurls it at the wall.

I flinch to the side and look around at the other men in the room, and none of them seem fazed by their king's outburst.

That's a red flag, right?

Dax covers his reddened face before putting his hands on his hips, focused on the ground, following an audible sigh.

Moments pass like this, and Dax still hasn't explained who this Olivia is.

"Alaina, go with Sam."

My eyes bug. *Excuse me?*

"He'll show you around until I can catch up with you later."

I consider crossing one leg over the other, as well as my arms, refusing to go, like a child throwing a tantrum. Not wanting to show him that side of me, I opt for a softer approach.

"I want to stay with you," I murmur, reaching out to touch his arm.

He looks at my hand, then turns and walks to the other side of the room to toss me his shirt.

I catch it and blink rapidly. *Why is he being so cold?*

"Alaina. *Go.*"

What's his problem? One minute, he's all about me, with his chauvinistic ways—the next, he's casting me aside at the mention of another woman. He couldn't get away from me fast enough when I went to touch him again.

I tug his shirt over my head.

He's a king. Did you really think you were enough for him?

Despite my rage, I go quietly, sending daggers to the back of his head.

Sam leads me out of Dax's study, through the castle corridors, and into a hallway. The crown moulding near Dax's dwellings subtly directs us to the king's wing. Sam rambles off tour-guide babble. If he's attempting to distract me, he'll have to do better than lavish staircases and high ceilings.

It isn't until we make it up the stairs do I eat my words when I spot a gallery spanning the hall of oil paintings displaying previous rulers and other royal family members.

Studying the faces of royals, I'm drawn to the portrait of a young female with dimensions of chocolate-brown, dark-walnut, and champagne-blonde highlights cascading in curls, resting perfectly at her shoulders. Though the portrait doesn't move, her curls dance around her features, framing her heart-shaped face with sparkling brown orbs. Other portraits pose the same intimidating, somber stare as they ponder off into the distance. If the intention is for this to scream power and confidence, it only screams self-importance and constipation. This glowing portrait is the only one smiling out of the generational monarchs dawning this hall, and her naturality alone holds the most power.

The use of bright colors matches the woman's magnetic energy. She's clearly someone who lights up a room with her welcome. The gilded frame complements its regality. Whoever she is, her work was recently polished and cared for with love and admiration. *She must be loved to merit such care.*

Turning my attention to Sam, I notice a royal crest mounted above ornate double doors behind him. Sam motions to the sitting room behind him meeting the wing's entrance. Floor-to-ceiling bookcases line the walls, couches and chairs circling the middle of the room.

I'm drawn to the massive stained glass window illuminating colorful light throughout. Cushions line the seating beneath the window, providing the perfect reading nook to gaze out at the mountains and forest peeking into the view. Admiring the craftsmanship and watching as the light dances across the floor, I take in the view of the kingdom, my eyes exploring the lands I'm meant to call home. As I'm captivated by the view,

Sam's voice drifts into murmurs. I think he said something about my stuff being here, but I'm not sure.

I move to the window. The view becomes more breathtaking when I discover my mate in the grassy field, standing with his back toward me. Rubbing the pendant on my necklace, I search for safety in my ability to admire Dax secretly. I may be mad at him—and still am, as far as he knows—but at least I can admire his moody ass from afar.

Seconds later, a man looking to be in his mid-to-late-forties with salt-and-pepper hair and a petite blonde with red lips approach him. Their bloodred eyes paired with the lack of rise and fall of their chest tells me they're vampires.

That breathtaking view is poisoned when the woman flashes a loving smile, placing her cold hand on my mate's chest. My wolf surfaces to get a closer look, violet eyes glowing and adding another color to the window.

She whispers something in his ear, and I glimpse her white fangs when she smiles inches from his neck. Their body language indicates they're intimate.

I muster up the most pleasant tone possible, not wanting to appear jealous in front of Dax's beta.

"Sam? Who's she?"

I'm unsure if I'm successful in my delivery, unable to tear my eyes away from the bloodsucker with her dead hands all over my mate.

Sam stops directing staff, who are carrying my belongings around the room, to peek over my shoulder. "Olivia. She's a piece of work."

So, that's Olivia . . .

"They seem pretty . . . *friendly* with each other."

I have no confidence I can bite back the jealousy coating my tongue. Especially after watching her slide her hand down his chest to intertwine her fingers in his.

Olivia's happy to see him, but I can't glimpse his face to see if he's just as thrilled by her presence. She kisses his cheek, and he doesn't move. And that's enough to make my blood boil.

Sam walks away without commentary, sounding off alarms in my brain. Over the years, you learn that not responding is a response.

"Sam," I say, not diverting my eyes, "if I'm to be queen, I should know everyone who lives here."

Nothing. *Goddess, it's like pulling teeth.*

"Sam, you know something. Start talking."

"She's Dax's fiancée," Sam says.

CHAPTER TEN

Dax

Today, we were supposed to announce to all the newly mated wolves we are engaged. While wolves don't follow the normal tradition of engagement, Olivia and I were to be wed through our arrangement by the royal council.

Olivia doesn't know that won't be happening.

I would've told Olivia I had found my mate had I remembered, but it was hard to think of anything but Alaina. Our so-called arrangement became null and void the minute Alaina came into the picture.

Even the council couldn't support a marriage of myself to the heir to the vampire throne over a true mate—no matter what peace it was meant to bring. There's nothing stronger than a bond made by the Moon Goddess Herself, regardless of the species.

Olivia arrived with Ash, the former vampire king, now Olivia's advisor, preparing her to take the throne.

Ash has never been one to say much. I only know his pyrokinesis once made him a formidable foe until he lost his mate. Mates among vampires are rare. Most choose to engage in eternal bonds, making someone into a vampire.

Outside of Ash's former mate's existence, I know nothing of his late mate—or how she died, for that matter. Over time, the loss of her weakened him, losing his edge. It only made sense for the royal council to suggest he step down upon Olivia receiving me as a mate.

Face-to-face with Ash, I can smell why the council has been so persistent in their efforts to form this union. Ash is dying. Ash didn't put up a fight for his throne, as losing his mate was the only battle of importance. Nothing else was worth fighting for. Something I didn't quite understand until I met Alaina.

When a werewolf loses their mate, we weaken and rapidly age. When a vampire loses his mate, they diminish into nothing over time, like a starving soul no longer receiving the nourishment from blood. Regardless of the species, once the heart recognizes the existence of a mate, marked or not, it can't withstand its absence. Unless one chooses to mark or bond with another.

I used to think Ash was dumb not to, but now I understand why. I couldn't imagine being with anyone else but Alaina, and I've just met her.

Ash proves me wrong he's not as ignorant as I think by not hesitating to excuse himself the minute Olivia gives him permission, likely as annoyed with her.

COME FOR ME

Olivia's eyes follow Ash's exit. Satisfied with his distance from us, Olivia jumps into my arms, wrapping her cold legs around me, her arms slithering around my neck.

Reluctantly, I return her embrace.

Detesting her proximity, I consider dropping her, letting her fall on her bony ass but then remember, for many reasons, this is not someone I want to anger. With my mate here, I don't want danger on our doorstep. If we can maintain civility, Olivia will still consider joining forces to cease the attacks, ensuring protection for my mate and our kingdom.

Despite my best efforts, my acting isn't convincing enough.

"What's wrong?" Olivia coos as she rubs my hair.

Nothing. You're just annoying. And you're not her.

"I found my fated mate."

Olivia's lips part, and she climbs off me while I exhale, my wolf able to breathe again without her near. She knows the contract clearly states my mate would nullify our marital agreement.

Black veins vanish as quick as they appear, and Olivia's struggling to suppress her crazy, while I hope she still has skin in this game. If she knew about my powers, she wouldn't bother putting in so much effort to hide her intentions.

Before she opens her mouth, trying to put up a front that she isn't seething with jealousy, I see her intentions clearly. This woman is *delusional*. She's already telling herself that I'm disappointed our arrangement has ended. I need to set the record straight by letting her know Alaina is the only one for me, but if I still plan to create an alliance with her reign,

I need to know to what lengths her emotions will impact her decisions.

Keep your enemies close...

"Well, this is unexpected. But I'm happy for you," Olivia laughs, punching my arm harder than she meant to, showing me, yet again, the lack of control over her emotions.

Olivia would've made a terrible queen.

Despite her inability to regulate her emotions, I don't pick up on any intentions to harm Alaina—yet. Potential threats like her, I would normally mitigate, but a war with the future vampire queen would divide our attention from ending the invasion.

I'll have to keep an eye on her in case those intentions change.

I allow her to stay here at the castle while we mull over what our alliance can look without uniting our species through a mate and eternal bond.

Olivia agrees with her own motivation: winning me over. As irritating as her inability to accept defeat is, it's better to have her here than to have her scheme against my kingdom from afar.

CHAPTER ELEVEN
Alaina

Olivia walks toward the castle with butlers trailing and carrying her bags. She's not leaving. *How could he do this to me? How could he humiliate me like this? How could he let her stay under the same roof?*

His double standard has me boiling. If it were Caleb, Dax would be throwing a fit. Mate or not, I have no interest in being made into his foolish queen who keeps his mistress under the same roof.

He clearly doesn't respect me. And with that, I grab my chiffon periwinkle sundress off the clothing rack. The fabric flows over my curves, settling right above my knees.

I've been wanting to know who I am my entire life, and I can't believe some jerk who I met less than twenty-four hours ago had me thinking twice about abandoning it all. *Dax wants me to belong to him, but he will never belong to me.*

When Dax broke Caleb's hand, he must've known Caleb never intended to let me go. Which meant Caleb might still want me. *There's still time to fix everything.*

I throw on my sandals and head out the door, determined to finish what Caleb and I started.

CHAPTER TWELVE
Dax

"**Y**our Majesty, Alaina's gone," my pack guard says through the mindlink.

A volcano of fury erupts inside me as the news rattles my brain. The thought of my unclaimed mate alone and left to the vices of my enemies has me feral. It's been a long time since I've felt true fear.

I'm kicking myself for not pushing to secure our mate bond. If I had let my wolf claim her, I could easily track her. Leaving her unmarked was a liability I took too lightly. I let her mewing pleads sway my judgment.

The last time Alaina was truly safe was when she was straddling my lap and wrapped in my arms. I thought I was protecting her by having her go with Sam. I didn't know how Olivia would react, and I didn't want Alaina to be caught in the crossfire, so I trusted Sam to keep an eye on her.

I bark through the mindlink, *"Bring me Sam. NOW!"*

He better have a good explanation why my queen is unaccounted for.

Moments later, yet not soon enough, my guards throw Sam at my feet, his knees and palms hitting the grass hard. As he bows his head, his eyes dart around, studying the dirt beneath my feet. The muck I stand on is worth more to me than he is right now.

Snatching Sam by the collar, I lift him to my face, his feet dangling. Sam's eyes widen at my sudden force, but he doesn't struggle in my grasp. He knew what would happen next, and his lack of fear leads me to believe that losing her was unintentional. But I don't like to make assumptions. Not with so much at stake.

I call on my powers to assess the reason she went missing. They confirm my suspicion of Sam's fuck-up as accidental, but it's still unacceptable.

"Where is she?!" I growl.

Birds flee at my boom.

"I don't know! She said she was exploring her new home," Sam says. My patience is dwindling, and still, Sam isn't shaking under my rage. The only one scared here is me. "I told her someone needed to go with her. Then she pulled rank." *My mate is already pulling the queen card.* If I weren't so concerned, this would turn me on. "Then told me that she's my boss, twisted my nipples, and ran out."

My guards snicker at Sam's expense, and even I stifle a laugh. But my fear quickly engulfs that laughter.

COME FOR ME

"She's fucking fast!" Sam tries to lessen the blow. He growls at the guards, who are holding their bellies as they laugh.

Sam is fast, so the fact Alaina could lose him is impressive.

I toss Sam, letting his humiliation hold him instead, and he lands on his ass, not daring to get up.

My wolf roars as I pace, contemplating my next move.

Sam and I are the closest either of us have to a brother. We grew up together, survived countless battles and women at each other's side. He was there for me when my mother died and observed my most ruthless tortures. He knows what I could do to a man, how I could torture wolves and vampires, and how I take pleasure in their ruin.

Although he doesn't fear me, Sam isn't stupid. He knows I can't always make an exception for him to the rules he enforces among the wolves beneath my chain of command. Sam is aware I still need to set an example for the others.

I squat to his level, resting my elbows on my thighs, grinning at my sadistic idea of his punishment. Dipping my head like a vulture preparing to devour its prey. "If you're not strong enough to protect her, I'll make you." I stand, turning my back to Sam. "Hold him."

Footsteps and grunts commence behind me.

My men march toward him and pick him up by his arms. Sam holds his head high, knowing he fucked up, ready to take his punishment like a champ. Fueling my fear for my mate into something more productive, I allow my wolf to come forward, canines protruding, making my way toward my target.

Sam should've alerted the guards to keep watch. He should've informed me the moment she left his sight. She doesn't know the area yet.

The beta's role is to detect potential danger and run the pack when my energy is expelled elsewhere. I must be confident in his skill and ability to lead the kingdom in my absence.

If Sam cares for his life, he'll ensure this never happens again. While protocol around the queen hasn't been trained for just yet, common sense should have directed his actions. Nonetheless, Sam can serve as the first lesson on protecting their future queen from any harm.

I can see the strategy in my enemy's action. Taking her from me would mean my destruction. In war, casualties are commonplace. She'd be a pawn in their schemes and the end of my world in its entirety. We aren't dealing with civilized werewolves; these rogues hold no ground for decorum. She could be near the clutches of death, and I wouldn't know where she was or how to save her with us being unmated. Without the mate bond, sensing her and tracking her is more difficult than it should be.

If my enemies wanted to attack, she'd be the perfect victim. Even unmarked, my wolf is bound to her. The center of my universe has shifted, and without her near, I'm off orbit. I'll be out of control until she's within my grasp. I've seen the savagery of our enemies; unspeakable, unimaginable tortures await her as their prisoner.

Unless it's the mutt, whose infuriating intentions would've cast her away and mark her unclaimed neck. It wouldn't surprise me if he was behind this little stunt. I'll tear every limb from his body and soak the rest of his dying form in silver. He'll die in agony for taking what's mine. If that's the case, she might as well run forever because I won't try to control my wolf when I find her. I'll let him wreak havoc.

I meant it when I said I would mark her if she went near him again, with or without her consent. As much as I wanted to mark her at our first encounter, I understand she might have needed time.

Shit, I needed time myself. I needed time to make sure everything was in place to protect her before my enemies could discover she's my only weakness.

I gave Alaina a choice: to be marked on my terms or hers. All she had to do was follow one simple order, to stay away from the mutt.

But now I have to mark her—regardless of whether she went near him. Not as punishment—as there are more pleasurable ways of doing so—but to keep her safe, knowing there isn't anyone who can protect her better than me.

I was a fool to think my mark would endanger her being associated with me. Alaina and I will make each other stronger once the mate bond is complete. We'll be formidable. My enemies may become hers, but so will my soldiers and our allies. People will lay down their lives for their queen.

Or they'll die as traitors to the crown.

Another possibility stops me in my tracks. *What if she wasn't taken or confused at all? What if she left me?*

My last interactions with Alaina play out in my mind like a bad flashback. I pushed her away. She has shown she could be vulnerable by telling me what she wanted from me without having her mind clouded with arousal, and I turned her down at the mention of another female's name.

This is all wrong. Could she really think I don't want her? Does she not know how much she already means to me? I'd kill for her. I'd die for her. *How could she think I was rejecting her?*

My pack has only seen me smile when I'm scheming or torturing someone. Clearly, I'm not the best at expressing my emotions outside of anger and boredom.

I owe no one justification or explanation; my men are trained to blindly follow. I remain stone faced before my enemies. I'm king, after all. I haven't had to worry about upsetting anyone since my father—because what could they do to me? Who would take me down? But going after Alaina . . . Fuck. I can't even think about that.

I have to explain things to her, to make her understand. This can't be over already—it's hardly begun. I've just found my hope of escape from the council's twisted plans and a future of misery with that vampire. *She can't leave me. I've waited too long to find her, and I refuse to lose her.*

My wolf roars its dread as we descend into madness without her, control slipping from my grasp.

"Find her. NOW!" I growl at my men.

My wolf rages a war, wanting to tear down the dense forest and pulverize every boulder between us and our mate.

My skin stretches taut over my growing form, transforming into fur. Claws and canines descend. My wolf's viciousness is unmatched, but now, with our mate on the line, the brutality in which we'll destroy the world would make the devil himself fear us. My wolf is prepared to deliver destruction to all in her name. The suffering he will inflict on those around him will surpass the agony I'm feeling without her. Today, I'll be bathing in blood, collecting souls, and burning their tattered flesh.

Echoing anger turns into a growl as he snarls, spooking the birds resting in the trees. Claws tear at the ground beneath as I lurch forward. Almost no time has passed, but every second feels like an eternity, my mercy diminishing with each moment.

I curse the Moon Goddess for making my mate so careless about her safety, who's choosing to be unmarked as a war wages against my kingdom. A sweet aroma of black raspberry with hints of vanilla wafts through the breeze.

I howl, signaling to my pack I've caught a whiff of her. The scent of unmarked males follows her delicious fragrance, and my pace quickens. In an instant, we race toward my mate's scent, the forest blurring, panic fueling my inhuman speed.

Fear and fury battle the ice-cold cage around my heart as the possibilities race in my mind.

I'm coming for you, darling. Just hold on.

CHAPTER THIRTEEN

Alaina

Shouts of laughter and merriment draw me from the castle's walls to the courtyard. A cacophony of fated mates flirting and single wolves drowning their sorrows are signs of the after-Hunt party.

He *had* to be here. As future alpha, his duty required his presence, welcoming and congratulating new pack members. Roaring music negated my attempts to shout my alpha's name.

Faces I hardly recognize blur while I frantically search the crowd for Caleb. As night creeps near, string lights lining the courtyard cast shadows on some and illuminate others from their canopy in the trees, the setup intending to give new lovers privacy.

Caleb is my last hope to help me escape a fate worse than I can endure, one where my mate refuses to be monogamous. Urgency leads me to weave through tangled bodies sweating on the dance floor.

COME FOR ME

I have to find him.

After pushing my way to the edge of the courtyard, I climb on a trellis of rambler roses for a better view.

Standing at the refreshment table is Caleb, holding a beer in his bandage-free hand, talking with Tyler. Judging by the red on Caleb's cheeks, he's had a little too much to drink. They laugh together, but Caleb stops when he sees me. His eyes widen like a deer in headlights.

I leap down and approach him, and he scans the courtyard, likely looking for Dax.

I curse Dax for making Caleb so scared to be around me.

"You can stop worrying. He's not here."

He relaxes but doesn't move or speak.

I roll my eyes and grab his arm, pulling him away.

"What're you doing here? If he catches you with me, he'll kill me. He'll kill you."

Caleb isn't wrong. Dax would kill him in a heartbeat. Unfortunately, death is not something he'd grant me. Getting away from him would never be that easy.

"Relax, Caleb. He doesn't want me."

Caleb chuckles. "Yeah, his whole wanting to tear out my throat could've fooled me." He swigs his beer.

I take a deep breath. "I found him with his fiancée's legs wrapped around him."

Caleb almost spits out his drink.

Wiping the dribble on his mouth, he says, "Fuck, Alaina, I'm sorry. He's an idiot."

I see it in his face that Dax was right. Caleb still cares. *Which means I still have a shot at everything I want.*

"We can still be together," I say.

Caleb's eyes bug. "Are you crazy?"

"You could take me as your chosen mate and take over for your father."

He shakes his head. "He'd kill me. No way."

"He has a fiancée who can unite our species. It's probably why he let you live. He was always going to reject me."

Caleb looks away, contemplating.

He's wanted to lead ever since he was a pup. The council would never agree to a vampire as Dax's mate over his fated, but my heart aches at the thought that Dax might prefer her anyway.

I turn Caleb's head toward me, my wolf sickened to touch a male who isn't my mate. Those sparks I feel when I touch Dax are absent.

"Please," I whisper to Caleb, "make me yours." I smash my lips into his.

At first, he doesn't move. Then his touch and kiss are soft and sweet. My wolf whimpers, and I feel like I'm going to hurl. My wolf craves Dax and everything about him. Caleb's smell of beer and bonfire don't compare to Dax's heavenly scent of spiced leather. Caleb hesitates and is gentle, while Dax takes what he wants and doesn't treat me like I'm fragile.

The harsh reality hits me. I'm missing Dax.

I consider running back to Dax, apologizing for leaving, and begging for him to mark me. I consider what life would be like if I stayed with him.

Then I remember his fiancée, my pack, and everything waiting for me back home.

COME FOR ME

I've heard stories about the mate bond increasing after meeting them.

My heart and body ache for my mate, yet I focus on the harsh truth: Dax is probably enthralled with his vampire fiancée, not missing me at all. I recall how he didn't flinch or move away when she wrapped her legs around him. How lovingly she looked at him. He'd probably keep me for strength and keep her on the side. A guy like him couldn't possibly be satisfied with just me.

Could he?

Caleb's voice rids me of my indecisiveness as he breaks our kiss. "Ow, Alaina!" He steps back, pressing his good hand to his lips, and inspects his bloodied fingers.

"What happened?"

"Shouldn't I be asking you that? One minute, you were whimpering, the next, you growled and bit me."

The metallic taste on my teeth confirms it.

Caleb turns up his nose as I'm unbothered by the taste, which makes sense, since I was told my mother's indifference to blood is what made her such a great nurse.

"Sorry, I didn't mean to."

Caleb's guard softens, and he sighs. Stepping closer to me, he puts his arms around my waist, leaning back to get a better view of my face. "What's the matter?"

The smell of alcohol and his blood hit my nose.

What's the matter is that you're not him.

"Nothing," I say.

He laughs. "You're a terrible liar. It's okay if this isn't what you want anymore."

Is he right? Do I not want this?

Tears well in my eyes, and I break down at how complicated everything is. Just as fiercely as I longed for the life I've had, I also long for Dax. The comfort my people had once brought me is incomparable to that of Dax's arms. That part of me knows Dax would become my family, and the pull of that bond grows stronger with every passing moment.

At my decision, the air becomes bittersweet around us.

I look up at Caleb, and he catches a tear and smiles down at me. When he leans in to kiss my forehead, I pull back.

"Oh goddess, Caleb, your lip! It's still bleeding."

Caleb dabs his lip, checking for smeared blood. Werewolves heal fast, even more so when you have alpha blood. Surprisingly, he hasn't healed yet, though I don't think I bit him that hard.

Just when I'm about to crack a joke about his old age preventing him from healing, a twig snaps, followed by growls.

Two large wolves pounce on Caleb, and he swiftly kicks free from their hold and leaps to his feet.

The party halts, and a crowd forms around the three of them. Confusion and shock shatter the festivities as wolves divert their attention from their mates and try to get a closer look.

These are Dax's men.

My hands shake.

Caleb scrambles, fighting off the two wolves. Annoyance and anger splash across their faces as Caleb swings, elbowing ribs as he escapes their hold time and again. The three wolves are caught in a dance of elbows and fists, their thwacking muffled by vibrating music and Dax's men commanding Caleb to cease resisting.

Caleb, despite the repeated jabs toward his chest, stomach, and sides and being heavily intoxicated, holds his own.

I stand, frozen, hoping Caleb will be okay, seeing how his swinging slows as his strength recedes. The fight for his life becomes more frantic, and Dax's skilled men notice how his wolf skips its rhythm.

Punches and jabs pummel Caleb as he falters, blundering back a step, as the warriors advance on him in coordinated attacks.

A fist slams into Caleb's jaw, causing him to stagger. The bone cracks as the other wolf strikes lower and grapples Caleb. As the warrior's body collides with him, Caleb yelps from his clenched jaw, ribs cracking as his head hits the ground.

Gasps whisper among the crowd as I look on in horror. Caleb's breathing becomes labored as they pin him to the ground.

With a growl from Dax's men, the crowd returns to the party, diverting their gaze.

I move to help Caleb, but a familiar scent hits my nose. The hairs on the back of my neck stand. When I turn, I jump at how close Dax was able to get without me realizing.

Dax stands there, silent, with his arms crossed in a white T-shirt cutting into his bulging biceps. Eyes almost black, he stares down at me, not blinking, chest heaving in anger. His scent provides me with no comfort, body language speaking louder than any words could.

His look shakes me to the core.

As his nostrils flare, his mouth presses in a tight line. Those cheekbones are further defined as he clenches and unclenches his chiseled jaw.

When he caught Caleb trying to mark me for the first time, his feelings weren't directed toward me. His alpha presence is stronger than any I've felt before, his royal right as the king evident in the power he radiates.

My wolf whimpers, and the urge to bare my neck in submission at his dangerous aura rolls through me. He had immense control before, but now he's beyond that, in complete dominion.

Refusing to submit, I straighten and lift my chin to meet his gaze.

He started this.

I step to him, an unmistakable challenge in the wolf community—probably the dumbest thing to do.

His eyes glint gold. Another wave of his fury hits me, almost pushing me over. Dax roars at my public display of defiance, his booming growl bringing the celebration to another halt. Glass clatters, and the wolves from all packs turn their attention in my direction in hushed unison.

His wolf is in control now. The wave of anger directed at me is more animalistic than man. His wolf means to bend me to his will, to have me bow and submit to him. Rage threatens to bend me to my knees at his feet. I've disrespected him, challenged him in front of everyone, and he will correct this behavior.

Dax lifts his chin to his men, and Caleb is hoisted up by his arms. Caleb looks exhausted but keeps his head up, which is covered with cuts, blood, and bruises. The guilt hits me.

"Where do you want him, boss?" one of his men says.

He doesn't take his eyes off me when he says "dungeon" in a voice so deep it sounds almost demonic.

My eyes widen, and I look at Caleb. Fear crosses his expression, but if I didn't know Caleb as well as I did, I wouldn't have caught it.

I can't let Dax hurt Caleb for my mistake.

Dax growls as he grabs my arm and drags me through the party. His claws dig into me, leaving trails of blood.

The crowd clears a path, mouths agape as they watch him escort me past the festivities. My feet struggle to keep pace, hustling like a child being chastised and taken out of the room for misbehaving.

Guards stationed at the castle door present a warning and display of power to those on its grounds. They'd keep anyone out—or in—at Dax's command, their presence a new addition from when the Hunt began. The poorly veiled threat is clear.

When we reach the castle doors, we approach them. They address him and bow their heads. Dax doesn't acknowledge them and busts open the door so hard it bangs the wall, almost coming off its hinges.

I look around the castle, not having seen it without its ethereal shimmer. While power and authority still emanates from the structure before me, gone is the welcoming energy. Where I wanted to explore and get lost in its interior, the threat of no escape is foreboding. I wouldn't be found if I strayed off the beaten path, and Dax knows that.

He ushers me through the foyer and to the staircase. My heels click briskly on the floor, echoing throughout the castle, but they lose their rhythm as I try to keep up with his pace. This doesn't stop him. Instead, his grip just tightens, preventing me from falling. Mercy is the furthest thing from his mind.

When we're up the stairs, we turn down a large hallway lined with dimmed lights illuminating portraits of royalty blurring past my peripheral. We're heading to what I can only assume is his bedroom. My mind races, and I struggle in his grasp.

"No, Dax, let me go!"

Dax lets out a low, throaty laugh that sends more chills, and I realize I'm dealing with his wolf. I try to pry his fingers off me. My tanned complexion blanches under his white-knuckled grasp.

Fear ices through my veins as my brain scurries to reveal his intentions. With his wolf in control, I can only imagine what cruel plans he has for me. The tips of his claws indent my skin as his grip tightens. I thought Dax had control issues, but his wolf displays more possessiveness than I expected.

I know what it looks like for Dax to hold back his beast... What happens when he lets him out?

My mind races as fast as my feet. He's relentless as he drags me back to his lair to do who-knows-what to me.

His temper sparks fear to swell my heart.

COME FOR ME

Will he force himself on me? Will he mark me against my will?

My inner wolf judges me, insulted I'd ever think our mate would harm us. The pain shooting from my arm doesn't help my wolf's case. My skin will surely be bruised.

With his back to me, his shoulders move up and down as he breathes heavily. Standing in the hallway, he towers above me, his massive body competing against the size of the solid doorframe. He's enormous, and his size presents more danger than in the expanse of the forest. Confined within the castle walls, he's a caged beast, threatening to destroy the stone imprisoning him.

"You have no right to be angry."

This only seems to make him angrier. *Good.* He had no right to act the way he has.

"You're the one who—"

He snatches me by my shoulder and neck and shoves me against the wall. "You really need to learn when to stop talking."

My masochist of a wolf rolls over and pants at his dominance.

Me? Not so much. I growl at him. I just chose him over my home and everything and everyone I have ever known. And here he is, proving me wrong with some misogynistic comment.

Moments pass as we stare at each other.

My eyes search for the Dax who's swayed my decision to stay, but he's gone. As his eyes flip between gold and caramel,

I don't dare to look away as his muscles quiver beneath his smooth skin.

Dax is fighting two battles for power, one to keep his wolf from taking over, the other in a power struggle with me—but he knows I won't back down. I need to see Caleb to make sure he's still alive.

I hold my chin high. "I want to see Caleb. Now."

His eyes come to rest in his wolf's and have a steady gold, but it's faint. His teeth grind behind his pressed lips at his inner turmoil, and feral instincts loom beneath the surface.

As I try to discern his next move, a light flickers within his features.

The terror from earlier is like a cheap thrill compared to the switch from pissed to a deranged psychopath.

"You want to see him?" Dax says with a sinister grin. "Fine. Let's go."

Dax walks away, leaving me there in the hallway, shock confusing me with his change in demeanor.

What the fuck just happened?

CHAPTER FOURTEEN
Dax

As I lead her down to the cold dungeon, the acrid blend of urine, dried blood, and fear greet my nose. It took years to build a tolerance to the pungent mix, but I've become accustomed to the smell and what it stands for: the destruction of my enemies and protection of my kingdom.

This isn't the case for Alaina, as she gags and shivers.

The dark stone interior contains a stark coolness from the rest of the castle. Instantly, a sinister chill ghosts through the room as I enter. No one who visits would forget the cold filling their veins when I grace their presence. Bloodstains soak the floor in reddish-brown pools, concentrated around silver chains, strategically placed chairs, and tables designed for my truth extractions.

My hand encircles her arm when her steps falter. With a frustrated huff, I pull her farther into the dungeon, her feet stumbling across the bloodstained floor. *She'll need to grow accustomed to this sight as my mate.*

My grip tightens around Alaina's arm as I drag her through the walkway. I can smell her fear.

She's scared of me. *Good.*

Her fumbling steps echo through the stone interior, a stark contrast to my thudding boots.

My captives' terror at my arrival is a sweet addition to my little game. Their combined fear and anticipation creates a sickening taste my feral wolf loves. I'd prolong my approach, building suspense. But the urgency to deal with the mutt once and for all hastens my pace to put her in line.

The pained groans of captives creates sinister music as the silver chains strip their healing abilities from them. Pleas for mercy and release fill the air as I pass men, telling me I haven't tortured them enough. Others adequately conditioned to not make a peep unless I say remain silent out of trepidation my attention will come their way. Even if my sadistic ways successfully have provoked enough panic to dissuade my captives from their malicious intentions and treacherous plans, death is the only way out after conviction.

I have warned this mutt once to stay away, out of consideration for my mate's clear concern over him and my history with his father. A chance others haven't received. He pursued her after seeing her unprotected and unguarded, preyed on this window of opportunity and her vulnerability, just like I knew he would. Finally, I will end that mutt for laying his paws on my mate.

I've never given anyone a second chance. When I see an intent of wrongdoing, I eliminate the threat. End of story. He should've been grateful the first time I let him live. What a pity he would learn with his life, and I'll revel in doing so.

After walking past numerous cells, we come to a halt in front of the one housing the filthy mutt. Standing before him, I breathe in his rancid scent. I sensed him on Alaina earlier, and the smell has been lingering, permeating the air with his spilled blood. My shoulders square, preparing to deliver a hard reality that apparently needs to be an interactive lesson.

Seeing my mate with the mutt's lips over her, who's defied my orders and publicly challenged me, made my wolf deranged.

Hearing Alaina's angelic voice ask to stay with me nearly broke my resolve earlier. I hated sending her away with Sam, but political niceties were necessary to keep her and everyone else safe.

It won't be an issue for long, as we'll be mated soon enough, making it clear to Olivia my choice is Alaina. While having Olivia here is an inconvenience and not ideal, the political necessity is temporary and easily fixed without the consequences of war. Once Alaina accepts me as hers, Olivia won't want to stick around. Olivia may be desperate in her seductive attempts and unhinged when angry, but she's also prideful.

And when Olivia's gone and Alaina safe from her potential wrath, I can devour all things Alaina. Already, she has become a salve for my soul and comfort for my wolf while dealing with politics. In mere minutes, I was able to rid myself of Olivia's embrace, but panic and unease overcame me upon hearing Alaina was gone.

Immediately, vengeance flooded my sight, and my wolf took control. My wolf sorted through every scenario of what could have been happening to her, whether she was taken by my enemies or hurt, making it my fault because I failed to protect her and brought her into my world—when protection was the very reason for not marking her after she pushed me away.

I would burn down the world, I thought. Immediately, my wolf alerted me of some unknown danger to our mate. Something had to be horribly wrong for her absence to last so long. My men should have found her within minutes. The only logical reason for the lack of her presence was that she was taken.

Imagine my surprise when I discovered she wasn't taken at all but was with the mutt himself, after I had forbidden it. The broken wolf, now slumped in a chair before me, hardly resembles the insolent mutt.

My wolf howls in my head, preening with the thought of teaching him and my mate a lesson they will not forget. I plan to make sure he knows not to push me and for her to take my orders seriously regarding her safety. Otherwise, extreme measures are taken, like killing someone when I don't have to.

This is a lesson I enjoy, as it sets the expectation for their submission. The one I only ever have to teach once, the moment I show people that my reputation isn't just a myth and that I am its legend in the flesh.

The silver-coated chains binding the mutt to the steel chair singe their marks into his arms. Its purpose is to torture and weaken my prey for my enjoyment. *Oh, how I can't wait for this mutt's demise at my hands.*

But I have to calm my eager wolf. I want this lesson drawn out. No tools or implements join the mutt in the cell—only the chair keeps him company. The mutt and my guards, who have now seen the mutt defy me twice, know I don't need tools, that I've had the power to take his life at any moment. Letting him go and his subsequent defiance is a reminder of why my men are trained not to leave room for mercy. And why I never do.

My wolf intends to join in the fun, and I plan to let him loose. Flashes of my wolf flinging his limbs across the cell play out in my mind. The mutt doesn't intend to fight me—he knows he can't, especially in his current state. He plans to take everything like the little mutt he is. But his surrender won't grant him immunity. He and his wolf *will* feel my canines rip off those hands he's so carelessly used to touch my mate time and time again.

My mate, not understanding the consequences of her actions, left Sam's side, roamed the kingdom unguarded, and found her way to danger. With vampire and rogue attacks increasing near my territory, it's dangerous for even the most talented she-wolves to be outnumbered in a fight. If she were discovered unmarked, they'd tear her to pieces and deliver her to my feet. Nothing would protect her from the foes who dared to challenge me, but my mark would give her a chance of survival.

Finding Alaina wrapped in the mutt's arms, his lips bloody and reeking of alcohol, was worse than any fate I could fathom. It was one thing to imagine her wandering off and being attacked by my enemies and another to see the mutt I should've killed to begin taking advantage of her.

I saw his intention to follow that command before I let him go and Alaina's plan to follow my orders. You can imagine my surprise when I discovered she was with the one wolf I had told to stay away from.

I didn't even need my powers to piece together what the mutt had attempted. Between the cheap beer clouding his senses and weakening his resolve and the blood on his lips my mate inflicted, he deserved it.

My mate wasn't scared of the pathetic little mutt. I would've felt that in her aura. She was brave, did what she needed to defend herself, and faced the situation like a queen. But she felt remorse when she hurt him, from having to draw the blood of someone she cares about.

That, I understand too well. Luckily for her, with my abilities, my mate won't ever have to worry about guessing someone's true intentions again. I will prescreen anyone near my mate and make sure they have the utmost purest intentions. I don't want her to ever second-guess her safety under my care.

However tough it was for her to hurt him to save herself, the message served its purpose, as the mutt didn't have aim to advance further when I arrived on the scene.

He has little mind for what he has done, and every atom of his pathetic being would pay. While the mutt will die today, death is a kindness—I could make this into a long torture, but because my mate is intact and I'm eager to claim her, his end will be quick.

Seething savagery courses through my veins and inebriates my soul. My wolf drinks in the chaos, and adrenaline accelerates my pulse, while mercy for my little mate's sake has been tested and reached its limit.

My guys open the cell, and the door creaks. Still holding her arm, I push her into the cell first.

She brings her hand to her mouth, shocked. "What have you done to him?" When she moves toward him, I cage my arm around her stomach, holding her close to me.

I lay a soft kiss next to her ear, smiling as I whisper, "Say, thank you, my king, for not killing the mutt."

She shivers at my words, and I smile at the effect I have on her.

She should be scared and is about to find out just how devilish I can be. My words, although patronizing, couldn't be more serious. It takes great restraint not to kill him on sight, and I feel I'm owed some credit. But he needs to be alive as my mate receives a lesson. While I'm proud of how she handled herself, she needs to witness what's next—her actions have consequences. Had she listened and remained where I told her to be, where I knew she'd be safe, this could have been avoided.

Disgusted by my words, she whips her head in my direction, her eyes wide.

If my words alone create such a look, then she's in for a rude awakening.

"You're insane," she spits at me.

A sinister grin sprawls across my face. "Oh, darling, when it comes to my claim on you, you have no idea."

I tell the guards to hold her, one of the few times I'll ever allow someone else to touch her. When I walk over to the mutt, a smile spreads across my face as my wolf relishes how easily he was reduced to his current state.

While appearing calm and still an ever-prideful bastard of an alpha, the stench of fear is eminent; the putrid smell concentrates around the chained mutt. Blood is caked across his body. My smile morphs into a sneer at the pathetic form quaking in the presence of my aura.

My belligerent nature examines his beaten form. The damage is extensive yet not enough to atone for his defiance of my authority as king and right to Alaina as her Goddess-given mate.

The mutt's scheme to take Alaina before I could claim her verges on treason and will be punished as such. It was selfish of him to risk having a weak king for his own self gain. Without her, my strength would diminish. But he doesn't care.

I grab Caleb's face, cracking his jaw as I whip his head to Alaina so she can stare at her consequences. "You did this to him, Alaina."

Truth is, prior to this incident, I didn't *want* to kill him, either. Jack was there for me before and after my father passed. But I've been known to follow through with my intentions, so much so that my word is law among the kingdom. I intend to make good on every declaration. Otherwise, I'll lose the incentive for people to follow my orders.

"No." Alaina shakes her head in disbelief.

"Yes," I mock. "Or do you not recall the mercy I showed him earlier?"

My voice booms throughout the dungeon walls. I've never felt so crazed before. It wasn't until she showed up that he tried to mark what's mine again. He must've forgotten once he saw her. I almost can't blame the boy for his transgression. My mate *is* irresistible.

I right-hook him across the jaw, eliciting another crack. As he recovers from the blow, I walk behind him, circling my prey. I jam my fingers into the open claw marks on his chest, and the wound my men have left oozes blood. Screams echo throughout the dungeon when I dig and twist.

Alaina tries to look away.

I pick him up by his throat and drag him so he's face-to-face with her. "Take your punishment, darling. Watch your precious mutt as I kill him."

She struggles against the guards with tears as I squeeze his throat.

"Stop, please! He didn't know!"

Lies.

I was clear about what I would do if he was near her again. No one touches my mate. I continue crushing the mutt's throat.

"I saw you with her. Your fiancée."

That stops me, and I drag my gaze to her.

"After you ordered me out of the room, you snuck off to be with your little vampire mate." The words spit from her mouth like venom. "I saw everything." Her nostrils flare.

My mate was hurt, and she left. My mate wasn't just hurt. *She's jealous.*

"I told Caleb you didn't want me anymore, that you had her."

How could my mate ever think I didn't want her?

My anger subsides. The thought amuses me, my wolf enjoying that she might care for me.

"Were you jealous, little mate?"

She growls at me, darting away from my gaze. The sight of her blushing has my wolf howling.

"I know I don't have to ask if you are."

My guards bite their lips to hide their amusement at my mate's sass, and I note their transgressions. They will pay for that crack during their training. They're supposed to be void of emotion, ready to kill without thought, and to not question my methods. My interrogations have specific guidelines. Our efficacy is the fear we instill in others, and cracking smiles is not part of it.

"Let him go."

"No," I say.

"It's not his fault. *I* went looking for *him*."

"You. *What?*"

My amusement fades, replaced by blind rage and hurt at her betrayal.

Oh, she did this out of spite.

The mutt's intentions were true, and my mate was just being defiant and trying to get back at me in a jealous rage. *So, the mutt isn't the problem.*

COME FOR ME

But my mate's behavior is. A pup with a tantrum. Something I'm certain I can fuck out of her later. Thoughts of me fucking her into submission run across my mind. How good that bratty mouth would look with a mouthful of my cock, lodging myself into her throat, causing her to gag, daring her to talk back to me again. She'd cry pretty little tears for me.

Focus on the task at hand.

Right. My mate misunderstood what she saw, and instead of confronting me, she ran off to mate with someone else like a child.

We can't have that now, can we?

I can either spend the rest of my life reminding every male that Alaina is mine, or I can remind one disobedient little mate to make sure everyone who encounters her knows it automatically. They'll smell me on her for eternity and avoid her like the plague. Touching her would mean signing their death warrant.

I can't help the wicked grin that creeps onto my face, displaying my canines. As my wolf registers my next move, I salivate, eager to sink myself into her.

"So, he doesn't need the reminder. You do." I release the mutt's throat, and he falls as he gasps.

My guards switch their holds from Alaina to the mutt as I step over the bloodied mutt.

Stalking toward her, I see Alaina standing tall, not afraid of my wrath, and it fills me with pride to have such a brave mate. Anyone else would be cowering and begging for their life. The cell would be filled with fear, sweat, and—if I'm at my most ruthless point—*urine*. But not my mate.

She will make a brave queen.

A shadow covers her face as I meet her small frame. My enemies would find it easy to throw her around and take advantage of her. One whiff of my scent on her, and no one would dare try. Really, I'd be protecting the unmated males from being slaughtered. After all, I have to think of my people as their king.

I grab the back of her neck and yank her toward me. Sinking my teeth into her flesh, I mark her as mine forever, and I know from her taste, this woman will be the death of me.

CHAPTER FIFTEEN

Alaina

"*Mine,*" Dax echoes through our mindlink for the first time, his voice mimicking a conscience and infecting my body.

Dax isn't emotionless like I thought, making it harder for me to hate him. Tears pool in my eyes when his emotions creep into me as if they were my own. Like Dax, his feelings hold grave strength. The joy and relief I give him, the pain I've caused him, the care he has for me . . .

And the fear he has of losing me.

An instinctual urge to claim him as mine sparks within me. His insertion of himself has made him part of my being. Rejecting him now would mean removing a part of myself.

I don't know enough about myself to begin with, but this part of me that encompasses him feels like home. *A home invasion, maybe.* The thought of giving away this new sense of belonging means more than just denying him of me. It was denying me myself.

Dax must be sensing how hard I'm trying to stifle my tears when he gently holds my face, caressing my cheeks with his thumbs. I take in his vulnerable expression as he waits for me to respond to his claim —to accept him as mine—and it has my insides breaking.

I have him, and now, he wants to have me, too.

A small movement causes me to spot Caleb, who's struggling to bring himself to a sitting position on the stone floor.

But how can I have someone who hurts those I care about? How do I freely give myself to someone who forces my hand out of his own insecurity and jealousy?

I'm weeping, the internal conflict becoming too much. Dax's mark, what is supposed to be a declaration of love, is a life sentence. His possessive nature would never let me leave. I'd forever be a prisoner to this pack.

Before, no one in the kingdom knew what I looked like, so I had a good chance at getting away unseen. Now, everyone will smell him on me and recognize the gigantic mark that'll tattoo my skin. No one will help me leave their king, sentencing their pack to be more vulnerable with their ruler unmated.

Home. Taya. Jemma. Mom. Me.

Jemma always said the right guy would wait until I was ready. Dax doesn't wait. He took my choice away from me. He wanted to punish me; it was my turn to punish him.

So, he could wait forever for my answer, but it would never come.

"I hate you." I pull out of his grasp, my hands balling to fists at my sides.

His brow furrows at my declaration, expression screaming anger. If it weren't for this *gift* to experience his every emotion, I would've thought the look on his face was merely anger for rejecting him, but the hurt I'm enduring says otherwise.

He marked me without my permission. It is *so* like a king to assume I'd melt into his arms and accept him.

He's a king, and he wants us—bite him! Don't act like "rich and handsome" aren't your type.

Although I want to go for what my wolf is insisting, this was the Moon Goddess's and Dax's choice.

Not *mine*.

The Moon Goddess took my mother, took my chances to grow up with a family. Now I know why She has sent me Dax, to take away what I have left.

Fortunately for me, I still have one choice. With the mate bond growing stronger, I have to exercise my right to choose *now* at its weakest.

I silently apologize to my wolf for what I'm about to do.

"I, Alaina Grove, reject—"

Dax squeezes life out of my throat, a stark difference between when he's grabbed me before. Those times, I could breathe, but I'm clawing at him now as I gasp for air, trying to regain that same privilege.

His eyes are gold, jaw clenched, teeth bared, veins popping out of his head and neck.

Caleb's eyes go wide, and though he tries to get to me, his injuries have taken too large a toll.

"Finish that sentence. I dare you." Dax squeezes harder, and spots dot my vision.

His voice is spine-chilling yet soft when he leans into my ears and mutters, "Don't break my heart, darling. You wouldn't survive that punishment. Neither would anyone you love."

My eyes go wide, and I think of Jemma. *Would he kill the closest person I've got to family?* The look on his face answers my own question.

He'll not only do it. He'll *enjoy* it.

I'm struggling to remain conscious when he whispers, "I'll never accept your rejection. *Never* say that shit to me again. I'll make you regret it." He lets go of my neck, turning to the guards, and I gasp desperately. "Take Caleb to the infirmary."

They each grab Caleb's arms, and one guard throws him over his shoulder. Caleb grunts as they cart him out of the cell and up the stairs.

When I intend to follow, Dax seizes my arm, wrenching me back to him.

I stare at him with so much betrayal, hatred, confusion, and loss, while he stares at me with longing and what I decipher as concern.

He's worried. *Good. He should be.*

He probably thinks I'm the kind of girl who would take him back after he's screwed me over. He thinks I'd roll over, giving him what he wants.

Well, he's about to learn even kings don't get everything they want.

COME FOR ME

My lip curls in disgust when I glower at his hand curled around my arm. The rest of my body stays frozen, while my eyes shift from his hand to his pleading deep caramel eyes.

My eyes likely glow violet when he finally relents, drops my arm, and sighs. Rubbing the back of his neck with a look of defeat, he lets me follow Caleb.

* * *

In the infirmary, the royal doctor finishes stitching up Caleb's final wound. He looks better already, with his wolf finally having a chance to heal him. Dax is allowing Caleb to go home once the doctor discharges him.

"What's your father going to say about you returning to the pack without a mate?" I ask.

Caleb pauses, registering the reality. "I'm sure he'll arrange something for me. Or if I'm lucky, he'll make a few calls to get me into other pack borders to search."

He's never loved the idea of an arrangement. The only reason he's considered me is that his parents had already regarded me to be their daughter.

Anyone else would be a hard sell for Luna Kathy. One time, his parents mentioned to me they've felt the aura of a leader in me. I snort at how wrong they are. The only thing I've led myself to is my own imprisonment and to getting their son almost killed three times in one day.

I offer Caleb an apologetic smile on behalf of my mate among everything else after he finishes inspecting his bandages.

He bumps his shoulder into mine as if to tell me not to worry about it. "As much as it sucked ass, I would've done the same thing King Dax did if someone tried to mark my mate before me."

"You would *never* do what he did."

"You're right. I wouldn't have spared him. He didn't do that for my benefit."

Hope they checked to see if he had a concussion.

I roll my eyes and sigh.

Moments pass as I ponder his thoughts, staring in silence at my kicking feet.

Caleb's lousy attempt to side with Dax does little to comfort me.

"Think about it. The king, whose ability to protect his pack and himself, relies on finding his fated mate, and after eight years of ruling alone and seven looking for her, he catches her trying to be marked by another. *Twice.*"

His logic hits me square in the face. Dax found me in the middle of being marked by Caleb. According to pack law, he was in the right to challenge Caleb's choice. Dax is my Goddess-given mate. By design and nature, we're two parts of a whole. For years, he's been merely fighting to protect that part of him.

But I was also fighting to protect myself.

I clung to the need to be with my family and pack so desperately, in hopes of finding out more of who I am. Regardless of the consequences, I was willing to do anything, even hurt my mate and defy the Moon Goddess.

Crap. Is Dax the reasonable one here?

No. Dax is an ass about it.

COME FOR ME

"Give him a chance, babe." Caleb bumps my shoulder with his once more before he gets off the padded table. He then puts on his shirt, careful to not reopen his wounds.

"Careful—if Dax catches you calling me babe . . ."

"It would've been worth it." Caleb winks. Despite Caleb's words, I know he won't dare call me babe again. "Take care of yourself. Let me know if you need anything."

Caleb leaves, and I get off the table and leave the infirmary. His words echo through my mind as I trail through the castle.

Long corridors pass by my feet, and I lead myself to unknown directions, making myself just as lost as I feel.

I consider how I'd react to finding my mate in such positions he continues to find me in.

When Dax took me against the boulder, leaving his scent on me and lay ownership to our bond, he waited and gave me time to adjust to his title and the future.

Dax has shown me his home, has cleared the air and among the Crescent and Bloodhound pack, when Alpha Jack thought I was unrightfully claimed. Dax made sure to claim me then, showing everyone I was his.

Then, when he abandoned me, pushing me aside for his duties to the throne, I saw his fiancée and became jealous. But how did I react? By running into Caleb's arms to be marked.

How mature of me.

Moving through the castle, I take in my surroundings. My pack's grounds don't hold a candle to the grandiose nature of the castle I'll now call home. My wanderings disorient me as I contemplate my life, my wolf's incessant desire for our mate dulled by my need for understanding.

I turn a corridor, my eyes glued to the paintings and ornate trims adorning the walls, when I bump into a hard form and stagger with a familiar scent.

Sam stands before me, his shoulder leaning against the wall, arms crossed over his broad chest with his tongue in his cheek.

It takes me a second to realize why he's looking at me like I'm enemy number one. Then I remember a certain purple nurple.

If he means to intimidate me, he's got the wrong girl.

I narrow my eyes back at him, matching his body language by crossing my arms and leaning against the wall adjacent to the door Sam must've emerged from.

I tilt my head and smile at him.

Sam sizes me up, then chuckles when he sees Dax's mark on me. He thinks I've submitted myself.

Charm seeps from the dimples on his cheeks. Sam strikes me as someone who would be hell-bent on getting your attention at the bar all night, and while blonde-pretty-boy isn't your usual type, his persistence and the innuendos he slathers in his charismatic statements make your entire night. Immediately, you've handed over your power the moment you realize his attention is what's made this night so great. You start thinking his personality makes up for his preppy-boy quality and take him home, only for him to rub your labia raw while trying to find the clitoris and never calls you again.

I'd bet money that's the kind of beta he is, *Mr. Playboy.*

COME FOR ME

As if right on cue, like I have solved the puzzle, a woman appears behind door number one. She looks from me to Sam, taking note of the tension judging by her nervous smile.

The awkward silence is deafening.

The girl goes to leave, clearly not wanting to stand between us anymore. She thanks Sam for tonight and hopes to see him again. In Mr. Playboy fashion, Sam just nods with a quick lift of his chin, then returns to our stare-down.

I give him the *Well, well, well . . . look who was right* stare. I think, and I *know* my face reads "smug" all over. I scan him with my mark for punishment.

I chew on the inside of my cheek, sending a smile intent on casting judgment while also thinking about Taya and how I wish she were here. Mr. Playboy is *exactly* her type. Taya *loves* making players into puppies, and this dog could use obedience training.

"Dax says you're to join for dinner. He guessed his *queen* was likely famished. Now I see why."

His eyes flicker with mischievousness.

This snarky motherfucker wants me to punch him.

He steps to the side, bending forward dramatically, motioning me to the boisterous noise at the end of the hallway.

I huff but make my way toward the two massive cedar doors propped open at the end of the hallway, with Sam snickering as he follows.

Laughter bursts from the dining hall as I near the doors. I sigh in relief when I inconspicuously slither into the crowded room.

Sam clears his throat, cutting off my reprieve, informing everyone of my entrance.

People at the large table turn in my direction, chairs screeching as they rise out of respect for my new rank. The roaring flames crackles in the hearth, sending shadows dancing over the faces before me.

I'm met with silence as they take me in, assessing the she-wolf "nobody" I bet they were laughing about moments before. At the end of the table are two empty velvet high-back chairs, the largest clearly meant for their king at the head of the table, while the other is placed to its right.

Olivia sits in the chair to the right side of where I assume I will be sitting—the high-back chair next to the throne meant for the queen.

She's probably trying to claim her status as the king's mistress. Her aura seethes with arrogance and royalty . . . *I can't stand her.*

The male vampire I saw in the field earlier is seated next to Olivia, who stares at my chest before meeting my eyes.

I follow Sam's lead.

"Alaina, this is Olivia and her trusted advisor, Ash, the King of Vampires," Sam says.

"At least until I take over," Olivia snickers.

Ash's red eyes are dull compared to the sparkle in Olivia's, and I get the sense he doesn't really care much for his title.

Olivia extends her hand to greet me. "Hi, I'm Olivia, Dax's"—Olivia pauses—"friend."

COME FOR ME

Catching the fake-nice-girl act I thought we left back in high school, I squint, giving her an insincere smile before grabbing her cold, dead hand.

"I wish I was as brave as you," Olivia says.

My face scrunches. "What do you mean?"

"I can never go out in public before making sure my nails are done."

I force a laugh, then peer over my shoulder at Sam, pleading for him to get me out of this. It's all I can do to not ruin everyone's meal by starting a brawl.

Sam ushers me to my seat. As soon as my butt hits my chair, everyone else follows.

The wolves resume serving themselves and eating, and the vampires sip blood from their glasses.

Sam, sitting directly across from Olivia on Dax's side of the table, shovels steak onto his plate before cutting into it roughly.

Leaning across the table to him, I whisper, "Where's Dax?"

"Probably burying himself in work. He always eats in his office," Sam says with his mouth full.

If I have to be here for this awkward dinner, so does he.

I pluck the napkin from my lap, fling it onto my empty plate, and march down the hall toward his study. I can smell him as I get closer to the doorway.

Dax is in his office, with papers sprawled out on his desk and floor. His chin rests in his hand, a finger to his lip as he lounges back in his seat. One foot is crossed over his other leg, balancing reports, as he reads a paper.

My shoulder rests on the doorframe as I take in his formal attire, much different from the clothes I've seen before. His hard muscles stretch under the unyielding fabric. Everything about him emanates how hard he works to care for and protect his kingdom.

Silence of his study stills around us as he flips papers.

Is this where he spends all his time? If I hadn't come to fetch him, would he have stayed like this all night?

I glance to the couch lining the wall, the worn cushions likely a makeshift bed for restless nights and long hours alone.

"Alaina," he says, eyes still glued to his reports, voice resembling smoke.

My wolf's spine shudders, stretching beneath the stroke of his power from his gravelly voice.

I take that as my cue to enter his office. "If I have to endure this dinner with your fiancée, then so do you."

He looks at me as if processing my statement. Sighing, he tosses the papers on the desk. "Fine." He stands and buttons his suit jacket.

We walk back to the dining room.

Everyone stands when Dax enters, waiting until he and I have both taken our seats to follow suit. The royal formalities have me rolling my eyes.

Dax digs into his steak and potatoes as he engages with Sam in a discussion about attacks happening in the north. He sticks with business and politics, something I imagine are his only topics of conversation as of late.

I turn my head to Ash, who I catch staring at my breasts intently. Again.

He darts his focus toward his glass, and I shift uncomfortably in my seat, knowing I was being eye-fucked by the old man.

I turn my attention back to Sam and Olivia, who are having a tense discussion about whose species is better. Sam is clearly *not* a fan of Olivia. *Something he and I have in common.*

Dax notices my discomfort and stares at me with concern, but I feel like he's looking right through me.

I'm about to mouth that I'm fine when Sam slams his fist on the table, causing me to jolt.

Sam's eyes are glowing, body shaking, his wolf ready to make an appearance.

Olivia *accidentally* spills her blood-filled glass onto Sam's plate. He scoots his chair out, shoulders and chest heaving, teeth bared and growling.

Dax's dominant aura emanates into the room, glaring at him. "Sam . . ."

At Dax's warning, Sam's eyes return to their normal blue.

He gives Olivia one last glare before tipping his chair over and storming out, muttering, "Fucking whore."

Heat encompasses my chest at the word—because who else's whore would she be than her fiancé's?

I study Olivia's face to gauge her reaction.

She rests her hand on Dax's arm. "Thank you, love. I'm sure Sam didn't mean it." Olivia sips from her glass, seemingly unbothered.

A growl emits from my throat before I can register it's me who's growling.

Dax and Olivia look toward me. Dax leans back in his seat and smiles knowingly.

He's enjoying seeing me like this. Jealous and possessive—like *him*.

I don't regret the display, only the satisfaction it's bringing him.

Olivia looks at her hand and clears her throat before moving it back onto her lap, then smiles. She strokes the stem of her glass. The act is suggestive in itself. "Forgive me. I forget sometimes how territorial you werewolves are."

When she giggles, I swear her dead red eyes turn black with her fangs showing. If she did, it was as fast as a blink.

With my wolf surfacing, my eyes switch between a calm sea to a violet hurricane. I struggle to keep control of my wolf until I sense Dax's arousal at my territorial display.

I shift my gaze to Dax to see him still smirking at me.

That smug bastard.

His caramel eyes mix with gold as his wolf emerges.

As much as I want to rip her to shreds, I am too stubborn to lose the ongoing war with Dax.

I inhale my pride and exhale my decision.

"Excuse me." I leave the table and head upstairs.

Determined to find an unoccupied bedroom, I scour through the long hallway, when glass shatters.

A woman runs past me, almost knocking into me.

"Sam, stop!" the woman shouts.

Another crash follows a grunt from Sam.

There are so many rooms on this floor I haven't explored enough to know what's behind them or who resides where. *Is it only high-ranking individuals?*

That sounded like Dax. Paranoid and guarded.

I follow Sam's cologne a few doors down from Dax's. The essence of cedarwood seeps into the hallway, and I am confident this is Sam's bedroom from earlier.

I cautiously creep forward, and a flower vase flies into view before it clatters against the cracked door. Gently pulling the ornate handle, I peer inside.

Sam is holding a Victorian-style cherrywood chair over his head, glowing gold eyes locked on the she-wolf. Curls of chocolate, champagne, and dark-walnut swirl about her features.

Something about how she stands her ground with unwavering courage against the raging, destructive beta sparks familiarity.

Where have I seen her before?

Recognition smacks me in the face that she's the woman in the portrait. *Does she live on this floor as well?*

The woman cocks her head at Sam, giving him a silent *don't you even think about it* look paired with a pointed finger. She reminds me of a mother warning her child before he gets in trouble.

"Sam. Put. It. Down."

Sam fakes like he is going to chuck it, then smiles at her as if to say *Watch me*. Sam throws the chair at a wall.

She says something in another language I interpret as French.

At the most beautiful statement I ever heard and don't understand, Sam's eyes return to their normal blue.

No longer engaging in his tantrum as King Kong, Sam approaches the woman, then stops once his heaving chest is inches from hers. They have a clear stare-down.

Are they about to fight? Hope she kicks his ass.

To my surprise, Sam grins, picks the woman up by her thighs, and spins her. She laughs, hugging his neck.

Who was this woman? A former lover? He softened so quickly.

I inch farther into the room, causing the floor to creak. The sudden noise causes them to turn in my direction.

Sam drops the woman from his arms.

Was I not supposed to see Mr. Playboy let his guard down?

"Alaina, come meet River." Sam nods.

"Alaina?!" River's eyes widen, and she looks at Sam, who continues nodding. The confirmation has River beaming, her straight teeth nearly blinding me as she rushes toward me and hugs me. "It's so nice to meet you! I've been dying to meet the woman who tamed the beast!"

River holds my hands, and I can see the resemblance to Dax.

She is warm and sweet, reminding me of Taya. Taya never seemed to notice how her warmth instantly lit up the room.

"I could say the same about you and Sam!" River's expression contorts into confusion. Then she bursts out laughing.

What did I say?

COME FOR ME

"I am *not* Sam's mate, dear goddess." She chuckles. "I couldn't see Sam commit to anything except maybe a mental institution."

I like her already.

"Sam is practically my older brother. We grew up together," she explains.

River thinks she's helping put the pieces together, but I've heard the sibling justification before.

I continue to try to decipher the meaning behind the sibling statement, studying them carefully. Waiting for any indication that screams they've fucked before.

If River chose to remain friends after a night or two with him, I'll have to withdraw my earlier thought and question her judgment.

"She's Dax's little sister," Sam clarifies.

Now I believe her.

Dax would never let Sam live if he fucked his sister. Scratch that—Dax would kill Sam the minute he sensed any intention of sniffing his sister the wrong way.

Why haven't I met her before? How come I didn't know he has a sister? What did Dax tell her about me? Did Dax tell her about me, or did Sam?

River apologizes for not coming to see me first. She was taking a nap until she heard Sam throwing a tantrum. River tells me she has been traveling across the world, learning cuss words in every language, trying all the cuisine . . . in more ways than one. River cut her trip short when she received word that Dax found his mate; she always wanted a sister.

River is extroverted, bubbly, and free of obligation. Our conversation leads us to the room housing most of my belongings. The traditional, vintage interior contrasts against the natural wood features, and I gasp at the view before me. Gold and emerald decorate the walls.

But it's not the royal decor or the window's breathtaking view of the surrounding mountains that surprise me. My collection of watercolor paints, brushes, and palettes are displayed across the art table, assembled into my very own studio in the castle. My well-loved easel was positioned by the window, basked in the perfect lighting the room had to offer.

My heart melts as I think it was designed to make me feel at home. *Did Dax do this for me?*

The familiar smell of leather and spice wafts into my nose again, and I turn and see Dax in the doorway. As River continues talking, I instinctively move to examine the blank canvases propped behind the easel, keeping my back to Dax and Sam.

"There you are. I've been looking for you," a she-wolf coos, and I whip my head toward the sultry tone quicker than I would have preferred.

Her hand drapes over Sam's shoulder, and my wolf settles, returning to River's stories. The she-wolf pulls Sam away as they scurry off for "stress relief."

He mutters to Dax with a sly grin and winks on the way out.

River rolls her eyes at Sam's playboy tendencies. She chuckles. "Some things never change. Do you have some time for me to show you around? I can tell you some stories about Dax."

I turn away, processing her comment, still acknowledging Dax, who continues watching us. Hanging on every word, I try to learn more of River and Dax's life growing up in the castle. It's not like *he's* offering up any details. Might as well use her chattiness to my advantage.

The more I know about my enemy, the better.

I nod.

River's eyes light up as she leans closer to me, linking her arm in mine, eager to spill all the tea on her older brother. She ushers me out into the hall, gaining space between us and his super hearing. River giggles, looking back at Dax after she whispers to me about the voice-cracking stage of his life.

Dax mutters something, and we bust out laughing like gossiping teenagers.

I think I found my ally.

River leads us past many of the corridors I've already explored, pointing out her favorite things. We peruse the kitchen, dining room, library, pack offices, and she points out the various gardens, some of which I note to return to for painting, along with the many waterfalls and landscapes.

She boasts about the stories of her childhood home creating the perfect setup for the ultimate pretend play with her friends, as well as the mischief the grounds allowed her to get into as a teenager, causing Dax's nose to wrinkle.

Dax speaks to me through the mindlink while River talks, likely to distract himself from River's coming-of-age stories.

Although Dax doesn't reminisce stories of his own, Dax can recall every legend and battle, explain the function and protocol of each safety feature, and point out details in architecture most would miss.

His words register in my brain like they are my own inner thoughts, a tour guide narrating from inside me. Normally, I would ignore the tour guide and just enjoy the view, but with Dax, I am hanging on his every word.

If he were a demon, he could command me and coax me to do anything with his gruff purr echoing in my mind. Dax communicates through the mindlink with such clarity and passion. His memory recall and attention to detail speaks of his intelligence, making him even sexier.

River's squeal pulls me out of my trance, and she insists we take a trip to some of her favorite places in the world and use my creative license to decorate her bedroom with the views.

I suppress a smile. *What else did Dax tell her about me?*

"Neither of you will be leaving the castle grounds anytime soon, especially without guards. There's been an increase in attacks nearby," Dax says, reminding me I'm not just his mate but that I'm his prisoner.

I don't know when or *if* I can ever go home. No one knows when the attacks will stop.

That must be what was bothering Dax when I found him in his study. I've heard whispers about the attacks, but our pack never saw any.

Dax leads us back into the castle and into the king's suite in silence and requests River allow him and me some privacy.

River raises her eyebrows and smacks her teeth, smirking. "Try not to break the bed. It's an antique. Very expensive."

And with that, she's out the door.

Dax closes it behind her.

"A little warning before meeting your sister would've been nice."

"I didn't know she was coming."

"Were you even going to tell me you had a sister?"

How is it possible someone so guarded is related to someone so open?

He raises an eyebrow. "I was a little busy having to remind you not to go near the mutt."

I cringe at his clipped tone. *Touché.*

Dax pulls back the bedspread. "Bedtime. We have combat training at six."

"Combat training?"

"Yes. Is that a problem?"

I throw my hands up to surrender, shaking my head as I make my way to the bed he's drawn.

"I guess I'm just used to you arguing with me," he jokes.

I laugh.

I wouldn't miss a chance to kick his ass.

Dax pulls the cotton sheets over my body, tucking me in. While he fusses with the pillows, my curiosity gets the best of me.

"About the rogue-vampire attacks—"

"Nothing you need to concern yourself with."

I sit up. "If the attacks are happening to what is *supposed* to be my new pack, I think I should know."

Dax leans on the bed, caging me with his arms on either side of my legs, and searches my face. His lips pucker as he squints at me, and I wish I knew what he was thinking.

I think how soft his lips are and fight the urge to lean in and suck that bottom lip of his, to nip at it. Dax fingercombs my hair above my ears and grins. But this grin isn't the evil one I've seen surface before he kills. This soft smile holds adoration.

My wolf howls at his proximity and tries to make sense of how I can get him to look at me this way later.

"I like hearing you say 'your pack,'" he says, stroking me. I remain perfectly still, afraid to ruin this moment. "They haven't entered our borders, but they attacked the Midnight pack a few hours ago."

I bite my lip, averting my gaze.

The Midnight pack is just a few miles north of here, which means they're getting uncomfortably close.

Dax must sense my unease as he pulls my focus back to him. "I won't let anyone harm you."

I believe him. He may be able to anticipate my next moves, but I've never had to predict his, since he follows through every time. Except for when he said he would kill Caleb, which I'm not complaining about. Part of me thinks, however, that he only speaks his actions into an unchanging prophecy because he knows no one can stop him even if they wanted to. He'd see it coming.

He kisses my forehead. "Get some rest." Then he turns for the door.

I grab his hand, sparks returning from the touch, shocking myself and him. "Wait!" I cringe at how eager I sound. "Isn't this your room? Where will you sleep?"

He pulls my hand up to his lips and kisses the back of it. "I have some things I need to take care of." He smiles. "Then I'll join you."

"In here? With me?"

"Where else?" Dax chuckles as if I asked the dumbest question in the world.

"I thought you'd offer to sleep on the couch like a gentleman."

"Nothing about me is *gentle*." Dax leans in, grabbing my chin. "I plan to sleep in my bed—with my mate." He places a peck on my lips and walks out.

With his promise, my mind races with all the things I now need to do to make myself look good before bed.

Fuck my life. Do I own anything silk?

I open the armoire to find Dax's clothes, then scour the rest of the bedroom and come up empty with the exception of noting what hoodies to borrow later and a shirt of his to wear as backup.

In the midst of scanning the room, my legs brush up against each other.

I just shaved recently. How are they already prickly?

I scurry into the bathroom.

"Please tell me I have a razor," I pray to myself, rummaging through the drawers under the double sink and vanity. "Yes! Now to just find something to wear."

Dax had Sam bring in my things, so where are my clothes?

I spin in place, looking around the bathroom, then stop when my focus lands on double doors connected to the bathroom.

"Please be a closet."

Moving toward them, I pull open the doors to the mother of all walk-in closets, causing my jaw to drop. Stepping through, I'm hit with a scent of an expensive perfume. The motion-sensored lights illuminate the space. Clothes with tags hang from the many built-in shelves, with multiple drawers stacked and attached below. Shoes of all kinds, some new and some mine, line the back wall. Peeping red-bottom heels are showcased to me.

Walking deeper into the glorious closet, I'm drawn to the glass countertop island in the center. Upon closer inspection, jewelry and tiaras sparkle in its casing under the lights.

"Holy shit."

Focus.

Remembering what I came here for, unsure how long until Dax gets back, I shake my head. Drawers under the jewelry case offer silk, lace, and other luxurious lingerie and pajama sets, all in my size.

I need something casually, naturally, unintentionally sexy, but everything screams, *Look at me, fuck me.*

I settle for a silver silk nightgown, closing the drawer carefully. Rushing out of the closet, I run to turn the shower water on. Afterward, I chuck off my clothes and jump in before I give it a chance to warm up.

After shaving and bathing every nook and cranny, the silk set against my skin is heavenly. I admire myself in the mirror.

My tousled hair adds the perfect amount of hot mess to the elegant piece.

The sound of Dax's voice through the hall makes my heart race. I turn the lights off and race across the floor, jump into the bed, and turn on my side. The door opens and closes, followed by my mate's footfalls and seductive smell.

Dax makes it to the bed, and the mattress dips as he lies down. When he reaches around my waist, I'm suddenly being dragged backward until I'm firmly held against him as the little spoon. My ass collides with something hard.

Dax palms his hand over my legs, hips, and ass. "Did you wear this for me?" He nibbles my ear, sending goose bumps all over my skin. After he trails open-mouthed kisses on my neck, it isn't long before he's deepening his devouring pecks and caress to grope me and suck on me.

I bite my lip, fighting the urge to moan. "No."

He flips me over to my back, hovering over me, growling. "You know my powers . . . and I know you're lying." He kisses the swell of my breasts.

I think about how they might look while I'm on my back . . . *Are they flopping to the side?*

For a split second, I consider covering myself up.

Before I get the chance, Dax takes my hand and places it on one side of my head, followed by a click. I'm too busy inspecting the bed restraint around my wrist that I don't react quick enough before he does the same to my other.

I go to protest, but he covers my mouth. "Don't try to hide what's mine from me again. You understand?"

I can't resist the brat inside me. I close my legs in obvious rebellion. My lips curl into a smile against his hand.

Dax, however, isn't as amused.

"Oh, baby girl . . . Did you just disobey me? When are you going to learn your fucking lesson?"

His tone is meant to intimidate me, but I add a shrug to my snarky smile.

"Quit being a fucking brat." He crawls backward, pulls me down to the bottom of the bed with him by my ankles, and fastens me in with restraints connected to the foot of the bed until I'm spread eagle for him.

Staring down at me, he admires his work. "Mm . . . I love having you spread open for me like this."

My smile fades, and I struggle against the restraints. I frown when I realize it's no use.

"Aw, what's the matter, sweetheart? You lost your smile."

Bastard.

Dax chuckles. Pulling his shirt over his head, he tosses it to the floor, and mounts me. "So helpless." He pushes the gown over the top of my breasts, exposing my hard nipples begging for his attention.

And the underwear I didn't put on.

He hums in approval, running his hands over the sides of my bare stomach. "Do you normally not wear panties to bed, or did you forget them just for me?"

"I normally don't wear panties to bed."

I lie again, but his ego doesn't need my help.

He raises an eyebrow at me, unconvinced, and smacks my pussy. "Lie to me again, and I won't let you come for me tonight."

My body purrs when he tells me what to do.

He thrums my clit with his thumb, and I sigh at his touch.

"I'm going to do whatever I fucking want to you. You understand? This body is *mine* to worship."

I nod, wanting him to continue his torture, willing to do whatever he wants.

"Say, 'Yes, my king.'"

"Yes, my king."

"Good girl."

Dax sucks my neck where my mark is, and my neck rolls to the side, closing my eyes. He trails kisses to my breasts, closes his mouth over my nipple, and sucks until he releases my bud with a *pop*.

I open my eyes to watch as he moves to the other side, dragging his tongue in circles around the nipple, gazing up at me.

I clench my cheeks together, desperate for friction. Dax ignores my need, returning to trailing open-mouthed kisses on my chest. The erotic sounds of his breathing and slurping have my pussy throbbing.

"Please, my king."

"Use your words and tell me *exactly* how you want me to play with you."

I want to tell him to fuck off, but I let my wolf decide for us to roll over and beg. "Please, my king . . . Please, eat me out."

"Mm, yeah? You want me to lick your pussy, baby?" he says between peppering hickeys on my skin.

"Yes, my king," I pant.

He hums, easing his kisses down... down... down and...

His mouth clamps down on my clit, alternating between flicking his tongue against the sensitive bud and sucking my flesh into his mouth. Spreading my folds with his fingers, he dives back in, making my toes curl and my ass clench.

My knees try to turn inward, but the restraints restrict me from the movement I need to chase and tame the orgasm before it erupts faster than I can keep up.

"Oh, fuck," I moan.

Stopping his feast, he sticks my finger slowly like the tease he is into my pussy. "Yeah, moan for me, just like that. Your body responds so well to me." He returns to his torturous licking until I'm on the cusp of this orgasm, close to exploding all over his face.

I gasp and sigh, my mouth forming an "O" and brows furrowing together.

"Mm... Does that feel good, baby?" He flicks his tongue against me.

Fuck, he knows it does.

"Yes, my king."

"I love this fucking pussy."

"I'm close."

"I know, baby," he says with such fake empathy, ceasing his suction on me. "But I want you to come on my cock."

I whimper at the loss.

Dax stands, removing the rest of his clothes, revealing his erect cock.

It's so sexy that he's just as turned on from lapping up my juices.

He crawls up my body, dangling his hard flesh in front of my face. "Don't worry, baby, I'll take care of you. Spit on it."

I do as I'm told.

"That's my good girl, getting my cock ready for you," he praises as he rubs my saliva all over his dick.

When he undoes my ankle restraints, he throws my free leg over his shoulder, kneeling in front of my needy faucet.

My pussy welcomes his dick home with ease. My mouth parts, and I cry out.

"I love the sound you make when I slide inside you."

While thrusting and rolling his hips into me faster, he strums my clit. His eyes roll to the back of his head, and the visual of him receiving pleasure from my body adds to the lethal combination. It doesn't take long before I'm teetering close to the edge again.

"Fuck, you feel so good. You gonna come for me?"

"Yes, my king," I whimper. *If he'll let me.* "Please."

"Go ahead."

I erupt under his command, with him grunting his release right after.

He undoes the other restraints and fixes my nightgown, then collapses on his side. After pulling me into a spooning position again, we fall asleep to the smell of his leather, my vanilla, and sex.

CHAPTER SIXTEEN
Alaina

Stretching across the soft sheets, I pause when my hand brushes something hard. My heavy eyes drift to Dax's naked form, and my palm itches to trail a path down his muscles. He seems so peaceful. I give in to the urge to caress and soothe his taut, tattooed chest.

Reaching over to caress the center of his broad chest, I see his eyes open abruptly, glowing aggressively gold.

Dax is on me faster than I can register. Snatching my hand, he rolls on top of me in one swift motion, growling like a predator defending its territory. His free hand wraps around my neck, tightening pressure points, sending stars to my vision, stealing the breath from my lungs.

Registering it's me, Dax stops growling, and his caramel irises return at the calming of his wolf, wide with concern. I'm doused in guilt, mine and his, for managing to startle the number one apex predator out of his sleep, causing him to feel so unsafe in his own home.

"Shit, I'm sorry," Dax rasps, removing his hand from my throat.

"No, I'm sorry. I didn't mean to wake you."

Dax sighs and buries his head into my face, lowering the rest of his body onto mine, causing something hard to press against my center. "I know you didn't."

My wolf squirms beneath him, unintentionally wiggling against his erection in delicious ways, pleasure jolting like lightning from the contact.

Unfortunately for me, commotion outside the hallway pulls Dax's attention toward the bedroom doors.

Dax stands, turning away from the bed.

Sitting up, I ask, "Where are you going?"

Dax runs his hand over the back of his neck, his tan muscles rippling with the lift of his arm.

He opens the door, and Sam is waiting on the other side, leaning in the doorway.

Sam regards Dax with a nod, looks my way, then back at Dax. "She ready?"

"Only one way to find out."

They study me.

After looking back and forth between them, trying to figure out what they're up to, I finally stop on Dax. "What?"

"You're going to start training with Sam."

"Him?"

"That's right." Sam straightens, walking into our bedroom. "If you're going to protect a kingdom someday, your little titty grab from earlier isn't going to cut it."

Another one of Dax's men appears in the doorway.

"It might if they have your pepperoni nipples." I get up from the bed.

Dax laughs, patting Sam's back before walking to greet the man at the door.

Based on Dax's instructions about how to warm up the pack for training, I assume he's a warrior.

I make my way to the closet, change into active wear, then return to the bedroom and plop on the bed.

Sam stands in front of me, glaring.

My snarky demeanor doesn't falter. It's so easy to get under his skin.

"You know," he says low, "it's custom for the beta to train with the royals . . . Should I go find Olivia?"

I spring up from the bed to lunge at him, but before I can gouge his eyes out, a strong arm snakes around my waist, pulling me back.

Sam snickers at Dax's intervening, knowing full well if it weren't for his king, Sam would be dog food.

"You sure she can handle herself in a fight?" Sam instigates. "She's quick to react on emotion."

Muffled swear words are all I can say to his haughty comment, with Dax's hand covering my mouth.

"She's my girl. *Of course* she can handle herself."

My wolf howls at our mate's praise. *Mate believes in us.*

Sam clicks his teeth. "I don't know . . ."

I'm kicking and squirming to desperately get out of Dax's clutches to show this beta why he's second-in-command and not first. With all the jerking, my head accidentally makes contact with Dax's jaw, followed by a click of his mouth closing hard.

Dax groans.

Sam made us hurt mate. My wolf's decision on who to blame leads to her further aiding my attempt to escape our strong mate's grasp, gnawing at Dax's hand, tasting metal.

Goading him, Dax says, "Want me to let her go so we can find out?"

Yes, please.

Sam shakes his head fast.

"You sure? You said she was fast. I'd love to see just how fast . . ." Dax hums.

The wicked deviance in his gravelly voice is unmistakable.

"Oh, shit," Sam exclaims before darting out of our bedroom and down the hall, giving him a head start.

When Sam's footsteps hit the staircase, Dax kisses the top of my head.

"Go get him, babe." Dax releases his hold on me.

Sprinting after Sam, I'm determined not to let our mate down.

Sam shouts when I march toward him, our mate's laughter booming behind me.

I barrel out the front door, careful not to knock into the wait staff crossing the foyer into the kitchen, who's cleaning up this morning's meal for the pack. I jump down the front steps of the castle, my feet hitting the grassy field. When I sprint after him, it only takes me seconds to be right on his tail.

Pushing off my feet, I try to jump on his back but miss, my arms wrapping around his waist, accidentally pulling his pants down while tackling him. I go with it anyway, capturing his pants, leaving his butt-naked self and his dignity in the dirt where they belong.

Bolting in front of him, pedaling backward, I wave my trophy, taunting him with it.

"Hey!" Sam shouts after me, trying to decide between covering his package and where the good Goddess split him.

I give him my favorite finger before turning and darting toward the training field, where the pack will be waiting.

At the bottom of the hill, I come to a stop, in awe of the countless wolves who've shown up. I've never seen so many people gathered to train. Especially a pack as diverse as this.

The field before us is divided into training areas, arenas, and tracks designed for strength-building, agility, and fighting skills—all of which are necessary to protect all within the castle. Wolves young and old scatter about the field, younger pups stretching out on the grass as they fight sleep's call, some failing as they wait for training to begin.

Sam's panting and the shouting of my name halts my astonishment. I turn around to face the top of the hill, and Sam appears, covering his package. I shouldn't be surprised when, instead of being embarrassed, he nods with a quick upward tilt of his chin at the female wolves huddling in the corner, who are snickering and whispering. Some even whistle.

I roll my eyes at their bashfulness. *What do they see in him?*

As I wave Sam's shorts around, they grab his attention from the pretty she-wolves. "You called?"

COME FOR ME

Sam stops and glares at me. "Give me my shorts back!"

"Come and take them."

I'm being childish, but he questioned my fighting skills and mentioned a certain ex of my mate, so I no longer care how I might appear to others. *He'll eat his words.*

Sam stares at my arm. I raise my eyebrows and nod to the shorts, encouraging him to come and get 'em. Sam slowly makes his way over to me, narrowing his eyes. An arm's length away, he snatches the shorts out of my hand and slips them on.

I really don't want to fight him while he's naked.

Once they're on, I swing at his face. Sam flings his head back, dodging my punch. Backing away from me, Sam *oohs* at my miss and bounces around on his toes with his arms up by his face.

"You drew your arm back before punching, telling me you were coming. That's why you missed. Don't wind up."

I continue doing what Caleb taught me, circling my enemy, making sure not to cross my feet to maintain my balance. Standing to the side, not dropping my fists, I jerk my right leg, aiming the inside of my foot to the side of his face.

Sam steps out of the way and trips me.

I fall flat on my face.

Probably worried I'm about to cry, Sam mutters a curse, extending a hand.

Taking advantage of the opportunity, I snatch his hand, pulling him with me. He lands on his face, eliciting an *oof*.

Catching him off guard, I climb on top of him, pinning his arms behind his back, pushing his head into the dirt. "Say her name to me again."

My ears perk up at the most melodious laughter.

"That's my girl."

At Dax's praise, my heart skips a beat, my wolf wagging its tail.

He holds his hand, and I take it, letting him guide me off his beta. "You underestimated her."

Sam pops up, hawking at the ground. "She still has a lot to learn."

I roll my eyes. *Whatever.*

"Seems somebody's a sore loser," Dax mindlinks me.

"It would appear so."

Dax and I regard each other, smiling.

I'm too busy enjoying being on the same team as a lighthearted, playful Dax that I don't pay attention to Sam.

Irritated, Sam asks, "What're you saying about me?"

Regaining my senses, I divert my eyes but notice the rare appearance of Dax's inner child is gone when I peer at him again. The assertive king has returned. What was once a playful aura is replaced by dominance and need. Gold swirls appear within his caramel soul keepers.

I bite my lip under his gaze.

Dax clears his throat, shifting and saying flatly, "I trust you'll teach her whatever she needs to learn."

Confusion and disappointment swirls in my head at Dax's abrupt end to our moment.

I hate him and don't need to make sense of it.

"Let's take a break," Sam suggests.

Dax turns to face his pack, his presence stifling the air in the field. Wolves, in their human and altered forms, spring to attention, eyes shifting to him, awaiting their king's command.

I fall behind Dax, and we join the crowd. He sorts people into groups by age and skill with warriors as their designated trainers.

Sam reports to my side. "Dax has everyone in this pack train."

"Everyone? Even the pups?"

"Especially the pups. Dax believes the younger they start, the better. He says they're the most vulnerable if we fail to protect them."

That last sentence hits me hard. Pups mean future generations, making them easy targets. They're also used as bait in wars with enemies. A shiver runs down my spine at the thought of innocent pups in the hands of the evil lurking outside our borders.

Afterward, despite Dax's best efforts, the pups never tired out. They protested when it was time to move on to the teenagers. I was surprised to observe Dax's teachings were primarily focused on defense techniques, given he was such a renowned predator. I would've thought he would them to become little assassins.

A male with shoulder-length brown hair who can't be any older than sixteen appears.

"Let's see what you've got, Tom," Dax says to the boy.

Tom looks nervous, with his fists up, but relaxes when Dax circles him. Dax bounces around like a boxer, which makes Tom smile. Dax eggs Tom on, reminding him what he's worked on and to take it when he sees an opening. When the youth lunges for a swing, Dax ducks out of the way, while the boy's smile fades, and he apologizes. Which puzzles me because what he's apologizing for is *not* punching the king in the face.

"Don't apologize for making an effort," Dax says as he throws a blow.

Tom's quick, though, and darts out of the path. Unfortunately, Tom moves so quickly another female his age doesn't have time to get out of his way and falls on her ass.

"S-Sorry," Tom says to the girl who scrunches up her nose at him. He reaches out to help her up, but she rejects it and storms off. Tom looks around, clearly anxious about what people might think of him, the awkward guy who just knocked down the pretty female.

"It's fine, Tom."

Tom's eyes water, but he blinks the tears away. He stands in front of Dax in a fighting stance with his feet staggered but forgets to protect his face.

"Hands up, Tom, hands up!"

"Sorry."

Dax growls and swings punches left and right, but Tom leans his head back out of the way of Dax's fists. Dax keeps on him until he backs him into a tree.

"Stop apologizing for existing." Dax lodges his claw into the tree bark beside Tom's head, then leans into his face, snarling. "And start making people sorry for standing in your way."

Tom nods and stands straighter.

Dax smiles and pats his shoulder.

Tom's confidence bodes well for him through their roughhousing.

Dax spews words of encouragement at the outcome when he listens, laughing and smiling with the kid.

Tom still has a lot to learn, but he has the chance to be great if he stops second-guessing himself. Dax must see the same potential in him as the reason he spends the most time working with him. Tom's training regime is more mental than physical. His lack of confidence, the constant apologizing . . . To stay safe, he must be used to making himself smaller so he's not a target. Tom wants what most teenagers his age want: to be accepted, to be loved, and to fit in. He looks to exist without conflict, but it's clear the world hasn't always let him. But people are less likely to hurt you if they don't know you're there.

Dax's training methods toward Tom encourage him to take up space without remorse or fear. Which is starkly different from how he trains the other teenagers and kids. With them, he instructs to get in and get out fast.

Maybe Dax isn't as my-way-or-the-highway as I thought. He's willing to adjust his training methods and set aside special time to make sure everyone has an equal opportunity to learn in a personalized way. It makes me swoon . . . just a little.

Yeah, only a little.

"Keep coming, keep coming! That's it!" Dax coaches as Tom chases after him, punching Dax in the ribs, not holding back.

Tom lands solid punches. Others stop fighting to watch them, impressed at what Dax was able to pull out of Tom. And I hope, one day, Tom realizes he was never meant to fit in because, when he's his most authentic self, he stands out.

Dax pats Tom's cheek in praise, then moves on to training with a younger pup.

Rumors about the young king's fighting skills and power never did him justice. Dax is always steps ahead of his opponent, never missing, and can't be touched. Watching him, my wolf squares her shoulders, holding our head high and nodding with approval at our mate's impressive capabilities.

Sam catches me staring. "Impressed? He was always a good fighter, even when we were pups, but once he got his powers, he was unmatched."

Dax waits with his hands behind his back while the kid gets himself off the ground. He offers Tom tips and critiques, and the kid hangs onto every word. Dax pats the boy on the back and moves on to the little pups, who all have bow staffs as they work on defensive techniques.

Dax walks over to the smallest of the group and playfully growls at him, pretending to be the attacker. The little pup laughs and emits a tiny growl. Dax feigns fright, and the kid laughs and progresses toward him.

It's the first time I've seen him smile and laugh that isn't laced with murderous intent. Seeing him with the pup has me wondering what he was like at that age. Dax is always so serious, so it's hard to imagine him carefree and playful.

"What was Dax like as a child?"

A long silence leads to a shift in the air.

Sam rubs the back of his neck and sighs. "Dax . . . didn't really have a childhood."

"What do you mean?"

"As soon as he could talk and walk, Dax's life was training and meetings. When he wasn't doing that with his father, he and his mother tended to the community. His father was . . . strict. And his mother never questioned her king. None of us in the pack really played with Dax growing up. I don't know if he ever got to just be a kid."

A twinge of sadness settles in my heart.

Surely protected in the safest place in the kingdom, inside castle walls, he could freely roam and enjoy life. The image of a disheartened Dax forced into a joyless childhood pulls at my heartstrings.

The cold, serious-armor Dax wears makes even more sense now. He's business all the time because that's all he's ever known.

The little pup jabs him with the bow staff. Dax clutches at his heart, pretending to die. When the pup gets closer to him, Dax roars and pulls him to his chest. The pup screeches and chuckles.

"Someone forgot rule number one—first opportunity to run to safety, you take it!" Dax tickles him, eliciting little giggles from the pup.

I can't help but melt at this paternal side, wishing I could see more of this man who protects his pack and smiles when he's not thinking about murdering someone.

Dax meets my stare, his dark, intense stare igniting heat in between my legs, building a need for friction. As this need increases, his eyes scan my body and stop when they reach my center. When his flashing gaze meets mine again, a knowing smirk spreads across his face.

He struts over to me, his shoulders dipping as he walks, the cuts in his muscles gathering sweat on his glistening tanned skin.

Goddess, he's all male.

Stopping at my side, he leans into my ear. "I can smell you. You wanna play, little one? Let's play."

He's baiting me. Again. He knows I won't turn down the challenge. Especially when it involves the chance to kick his ass.

When he steps behind me, I let my claws elongate in my right hand and turn to strike him across the face.

Leaning away just in time, he laughs at my attempt.

I go for another combo, aiming for his throat and gut. He blocks each move and punches me in my ribs instead.

In disbelief, I glare at him, shocked at his audacity. Meanwhile, my wolf wags her tail in approval.

"I'm not going to take it easy on you, darling. Neither will our enemies."

I don't know why he's saying "our" as if we're on the same team. He's the only enemy I see around here, as I'm reminded of the people from whom he took me away. The home I probably won't see again.

Someone clears their throat, breaking the tension.

I stare down a bigger pain in my side than the punch Dax gave me.

Olivia.

"Pardon the interruption. I just think that if we're up against vampires, Alaina here should train with one," she coos to Dax.

Olivia knows the right strings to pull with Dax through preparation, training, and protection.

Dax gestures for Olivia to take his spot in front of me and steps aside.

I raise an eyebrow at Dax, looking for any indication he doesn't want me to have the chance at beating his ex-fiancée to a pulp. He gives me none. Instead, he looks as though he approves.

My wolf purrs at the opportunity.

Don't threaten me with a good time.

CHAPTER SEVENTEEN
Dax

Olivia doesn't give a warning or hesitate to lunge at Alaina. It takes everything in me not to intervene knowing Olivia's next move. I remind myself these lessons are better had now in training than a real fight.

Olivia slices at Alaina's arm, instantly drawing blood. Alaina clutches her arm. Olivia's eyes calm as she stares at the blood, no indication she's losing control indicating her years as a vampire. Olivia walks to Alaina, grabs her hand covering the bleeding wound, licks the blood off her fingers, and smiles.

Some might find that hot. Man or woman, I don't like to share my mate.

Alaina backhands her, causing her head to whip to the side at the force. Alaina doesn't wait for her to recover. Instead, she hits her with a right hook before sweeping her legs so she lands flat on her face.

Alaina looks at me.

COME FOR ME

My little wolf is handling herself well against Olivia. Pride surges through me as Alaina knocks Olivia to the ground.

"That's my girl."

Alaina smiles at my praise, then turns and raises her eyebrow at Olivia, whose eyes are no longer that beady red I detest, but now, they match her heart, cold and full of darkness.

Olivia doesn't intend to accept defeat when it comes to me. I saw her plan to seduce me even after I ended the engagement, which is part of the reason I wanted Alaina to fight her today. Olivia needs to see Alaina will rule beside me. *And kick her ass if she tries anything.* Alaina's constant efforts to pull away from me haven't helped in deterring Olivia from recognizing she doesn't have a chance.

Mate is stubborn but sexy as hell.

Olivia's plan plays out like a movie in front of me.

Olivia uses the hatred Alaina has for her against her to make her jealous. She does this by getting close, threatening to mark me.

Olivia remains ignorant of my abilities—something my pack was *politely* ordered not to breathe a word of lest they want to die. I want Olivia to show me who she truly is.

I allow her to play out her plan. Olivia doesn't have the balls to mark me without my permission. She may be conniving, but she's also desperate for my attention and approval. The moment she met me, she intended on having me, not letting anyone get in her way, Sam included.

Sam hates vampires as much as I do; his mother was killed by a vampire when he was young. On top of Olivia being a manipulative wench, it didn't take much for Sam to become protective over me and hate her.

Olivia caught on to Sam's intention to make her time here worse by telling her when she's missed a bloodstain on her face and that she smells like she's a rotting, dead corpse. It's juvenile but effective. She has a short temper.

Alaina lunges at Olivia, but she ducks away and slithers behind me, with her fangs uncomfortably close to my neck. Remnants of blood and flesh lingering on Olivia's breath makes me want to gag.

I don't move. Olivia's intention may not be pure, but the lesson is there. I need to see how my mate manages her emotions in the heat of a fight.

When Alaina's jealous, her nose scrunches, and she gets this look that'd make a lesser man cower. It's fucking sexy as hell. I may just have found the motivation for my stubborn mate to accept me.

A vision of Alaina's plan to rip Olivia's throat plays out before my eyes.

Alaina lunges forward in incredible speed, a blur of fur as she shifts and twists me to the side away from the threat. Her wolf roars as she tears Olivia's throat out, then spits out the vile flesh and muscles.

My little wolf radiates with possessive claim over me, even if she's unwilling to admit so to herself.

My wolf nods. She can hold her own in a fight, which eases my mind. Alaina and Olivia sparring holds ulterior motives; it allows me to determine just how I need to protect her if it comes down to her presence at my side in a battle.

COME FOR ME

Truthfully, I won't care if Olivia dies. I even contemplate letting Alaina wreak havoc by killing Olivia. I know I'd enjoy the possessive act for her king, but the kingdom doesn't need a war with the vampires.

I smirk and move toward Alaina. Sparks ignite when I grab her, and she relaxes at my touch. She makes that sound of possessiveness for her king that hardened my cock at dinner last night. I love that Alaina has a desire to kill anyone to protect her mate because I would do the same for her and more.

Interesting. It seems murder is my love language. I wonder what Alaina's is.

I pull Alaina into me by her stomach. "Easy, darling." I walk us away from Olivia.

Alaina's sweet plans involve ripping her to shreds. In this vision, she's got that sexy, murderous look in her eyes. *My little killer.*

"You exposed your vulnerability. You weren't worried about me getting to your mate at all." Disinterested, Olivia inspects her nails.

Ah, shit.

Alaina struggles in my grasp to get to Olivia again, kicking as I lift her and turn the other way. I spin her to face me.

My little queen's aura radiates grave hatred for Olivia, and it's so fucking sexy watching her ferocity. I love that she doesn't back down.

I sigh, fully aware of the backlash from what I'm about to say next.

"Alaina, she's right."

She puts her hands on her hips, cocking her head and parting her lips.

I place my hands on her shoulders and shuffle backward in case she decides to kick me in the balls.

"When your enemies know your vulnerability, they'll use it against you. You lunged at her without thinking, letting your instincts get the best of you. Putting me—and yourself—at risk."

She rolls her eyes.

"If someone grabs you in the middle of a fight, it's over. I've lost. They've got me."

Her chest heaving, she looks at me, wanting me to continue as she holds onto her anger.

"There is nothing I won't do to keep you safe, and my enemies will know this. If they get to you, they're getting whatever they want from me. You're my weakness, Alaina. They will gladly use you to get to me and vice versa."

She scrunches her face, contemplating my words.

I see her plan to push me away, and I don't understand why. She furrows her brow and gives me her famous death glare.

Shit. What did I do now?

Alaina's hair whips my face as she turns from me. As she stomps back to the castle, anger rolls off her.

My wolf grows more and more anxious the farther she gets. So, I follow her. Part of me thinks she wants space, but my wolf won't let her be without me protecting her. Although I'm not sure a vampire or a rogue could compare to my little wolf's temper. Whatever is going on in her head, she's fuming.

Almost to the top of the staircase, she throws daggers my way upon me entering into the foyer. Practically breathing fire, she rolls her eyes, stomps up the steps—and for a moment, I thought I saw smoke come out of her nostrils.

Where's my little volcano off to?

My wolf prays she's headed toward our bedroom and the possibility of angry sex. Alaina doesn't tell me not to follow her or to go fuck myself, so I take it as a good sign.

My wolf begs to hunt the prey who's swinging its hips in front of me as she saunters down the hallway to our bedroom.

My wolf flips inside, excited for his mate to take her anger out on him. I lean in to kiss her, and she moves her head away from me.

Okay, so maybe angry sex isn't on her mind.

"As your mate," she begins in a biting tone, "I don't want your former fiancée here."

Ignoring her tone, my wolf and I growl in approval at her, recognizing that she is, in fact, ours.

Mate is jealous. The beast inside grins wickedly.

I want to reassure her there's no need to be, that Olivia has *nothing* on her, but she's so sexy when she's steamed it's hard for me to focus, let alone take her seriously.

But I try my best to hide my smile by covering my mouth. She places her hands on her hips, and I know I'm caught. "Why are you smiling?"

Her sass is just . . . *Damn.* I adjust myself.

"I love how you're not afraid of me."

"Un-fucking-believable." She throws up her hands and paces.

"What?"

I know what.

She glares at me, the look our pups will one day magically comply under. She'll make a terrific mother, strong—one who won't take any shit from anybody, not even me. Something I've always wanted in my mate.

I'm able to breathe, regaining my composure. "Okay, then, what do you want, Alaina? 'Cause I want you. You can't keep refusing to claim me as yours and then make demands of me by pulling the mate card. It's one or the other."

Alaina crosses her arms, scoffing in disbelief, buying herself time to come up with a good response.

Anything to avoid admitting she wants me almost as much as I want her. She can't hide from me, though, nor can she ever truly push me away. I'm not afraid of my little volcano, as long as it's me causing her to erupt. The only thing I do fear is losing her.

"I want respect. Keeping your ex here sends the wrong message." She turns away from me, shoving her pants to the floor with a huff.

Her shirt is pulled over her head, and her tension causes her to shake, keeping her muscles tight beneath the bra and panties on her dewy skin.

Ah, deflection—nice try, darling.

This isn't about her anger or appearances in front of the pack. This is pride and jealousy.

But I'll bite.

If Alaina wants everyone else to know she's mine in every way, I'll give it to her.

COME FOR ME

I walk toward her, place my hands on her hips, and pull her into me. "What message would you like to send? I'll have you scream it." I guide her toward the bed until her calves hit and lay her down, staring into her eyes. Every reaction, from her nipples hardening to her hitched breath, can't hide from me.

"Tell me you want her gone, and I'll make that happen. All you have to do is stake your claim." I bare my neck to her, baiting her. "Take what's always belonged to you, darling. Be *my queen*." I growl the honorific.

Her heart skips a beat, lip quivering, and her canines descend unintentionally as she fights her wolf's instinctual urge.

I'm too eager for the real-life version that I don't let the whole vision of her intent to mark me play out, letting my guard and my powers down to be present.

We know what this would mean. I can be calm in any battle, but she leans in, and it takes everything for my heart to not beat out of my chest. I've never wanted anyone more than I've wanted her. *I fucking worship my mate.*

Alaina leans in to mark me. I don't move, more than ready for her to seal the bond officially. Then moisture hits my cheek.

Did she just spit on me?

Note to self, don't let my guard down to anyone, not even her. My father would've kicked my ass if he could see me now.

I wipe my face and groan.

Irritation boils inside of me. Alaina scoots up the bed and away from me on her elbows. She hugs her knees to her chest and avoids looking in my direction.

I don't expect Alaina to be anyone but herself. But in public, she can't act this way. Any public display of disobedience toward me could perceive me—us—as weak. Any indication that we're not united makes us a target for enemies. If people don't fear me, they'll rise against me, against her. And I don't want to have to kill an entire kingdom, but I will if it means she's still standing.

My mate is playing a dangerous game. I've tortured countless enemies, and she is, by far, the most stubborn. She keeps pretending she doesn't want me. *That's fine. I'm a patient man. And I always break them in the end.*

"Just because I don't want you around her doesn't mean I want you for myself."

I raise an eyebrow, and I can't help the smirk tugging at me.

Wanna bet? My mate continues to lie to herself and me.

I grab her freshly shaven ankles, more evidence she *does* want me. She could have easily covered her legs with pants, but she didn't. She chose to shave in preparation for when her king decides it's time to play. I think about my mate's curves in the shower, soaped up and wet, consciously making a decision to be groomed for me.

In one swift motion, I drag her down to the edge of the bed, pinning her arms with one hand above her. My wolf wants to take her roughly, and I have to fight the urge.

"Those torture methods I used against my enemies? I'm going to use them to turn you, my defiant little mate, into my wanton whore."

Her cheeks flush, and my darling is trying like hell to get out of my grasp. I enjoy the feel of her rubbing herself against my package as she writhes beneath me.

She notices my growing member and stops struggling. My little wolf's eyes glow violet at my erection's pressure against her thighs, and her breasts rise and sink. Her nipples harden through the thin fabric of her sports bra.

After spreading her luscious legs, I position myself between them. "Your body tells a different story." I trace down her face, cleavage, and stomach until I reach the edge of her lace panties.

The intricate details of the lace, the sheerness, and the color tells me she chose these with me in mind. My finger grazes her pulsing clit, and her heart beats even faster. Sparks between us create an electric shock on her bud.

"Your wolf responds so beautifully to her king." I growl and bite my lip.

Dipping my head, I trail my lips across her stomach, wanting nothing more than to taste every inch of her. Wanting to prolong her torture with the promises of never-ending pleasure, I end up torturing myself.

I kiss her clit over her panties, and she shivers. My wolf is in sensory overload at her arousal. The thumping of her body tells me what it needs when she refuses to.

"Oh, baby, you're pulsing," I tease.

She lies back and closes her eyes, drinking in my words. My voice, calm and hypnotizing as I carry on, narrates her slow torture. The thin fabric of her panties reminds me of how silly it is she even wears them.

As if this thin barrier could keep me from taking what I want.

My wolf reacts to the idea of anything and anyone keeping me from her. Within an instant, I rip the thin fabric off her voluptuous body with my canines. Straightening up again to see her bare mound, I spit the remnants of lace to the floor beside me, not taking my eyes off her body—*my* body.

My poor darling's pussy continues to pulse, begging for her king's attention and swift mercy. I lick my canines at the taste of her wetness on her panties.

A growl leaves my wolf at the sharpness of my canines, pleasure mixing with pain as they threaten to sink my teeth into the pretty little wolf moaning beneath my gaze. She needs me just as much as her pussy pleads for mercy and release.

I grip her thighs. "Nothing about this will be merciful, darling."

Not afraid of my beast's dark nature, she lifts her hips, gravitating to my warm breath as I inhale her scent. I'd bathe in her secretion, have her juices marking me as hers, even if she refused a more permanent claim. My lips twitch as she fights against my hold, my fingers digging into flesh as she mews, fighting to close the immeasurable distance between my tongue and her bud.

She inhales, likely to berate or demand orders from a king she refuses to yield to. But I steal all thoughts from her, my tongue dipping between her flesh and flattening against her throbbing center. Slowly, painfully so, I lap up to her clit, flicking the hardening bud as my eyes flash to her closed ones.

"Eyes on me, darling."

Her violet pair sears into my soul.

"Yes, fucking beautiful."

A devilish moan escapes her. Whatever insult she intended for me fades as my lips pucker around her clit.

Smirking, I note its efficiency in silencing her complaints as I apply pressure and suck. I tease her pleasure higher, pulsing the sensation around her bud, my fingers massaging her thighs as I pull her to me. Her breathing quickens, and I chuckle. I'd cause her destruction buried between her legs like this. Black raspberry and vanilla bursts across my taste buds as I drink in her juices, the salt of her sweat enhancing the flavor of the sweetest cream I could imagine.

Her taste and moans threaten to turn me feral, begging for a release I need just as much as my own. I note the hymns coming from the bed above me.

She's close.

My wolf hungrily laps and dips into her entrance, my attention diverting from her clit and giving her moments to calm the orgasm building inside her. Her breaths are erratic, chest heaving as she fists the sheets and fights for control of her own wolf, body quivering beneath my touch.

Her palms caress her breasts, squeezing as her pleasure heightens, an attempt to tumble over the edge of release. With one swift move, I snatch her wrist in an instant, ripping it from her heaving chest, then squeeze her throat with the other.

Only her king will be giving her pleasure.

"Stay," I command as I lick and massage her folds.

My hand remains on her throat, her wolf fighting the surface of her strong will, subsiding when her muscles relax against my touch. Heat floods her pussy, waves of scent teasing my senses and drawing my focus back between her thighs. Holding her hands above her head, I travel down her chest.

My wolf growls at the thin fabric of the bra veiling her from me, and in an instant, the material is shredded, ripped from her body in my wolf's impatience. I tweak and pinch each nipple between my teeth, licking and sucking the hardened points as my free hand moves to feel her slickness forming. My fingers slowly circle her clit as my attention travels down her writhing form.

Fingers are replaced with my tongue once again, slowly drawing circles closer to her throbbing anatomy. She's so responsive to her king, each lick and pass of her clit has her arching against me.

My tongue teases her opening, dipping in the center to lap at the source of her essence. Her gasp sings through the room, the pleading sound more beautiful than anything. *Music to my ears.*

My wolf growls in hunger, fighting our control, my tongue swiping from her tight entrance to her clit. I pinch her painfully hard nipples, whimpers and mews escaping her lips with gasps for air as time passes.

Again, I taste her. Long, slow, agonizing tastes torture my wolf, who fights to rut our mate with fever and frenzy. Her scent soaks my tongue and permeates the room as her climax nears, the world outside the room no longer relevant.

So fucking sweet.

Her bud tightens as she nears impossibly close to her orgasm, her intent to come flashing before my eyes. I watch the release, indulging my wolf with the magnificent sight before denying us both. Her lips part, a hole for me to fuck later.

She tenses as I taste her one last time, teetering her on the edge. As she breathes out my name, my tongue stills, my body lifting from her as I cease my pursuit.

A whine escapes her lips. "Dax."

"What did you call me?"

"Dax." She smiles. Such a dirty fucking mouth.

I can fix that.

"Take off my pants."

She does as she's told, scooting to the edge of the bed, staring at me with doe eyes.

My cock springs free in her face. She looks at me innocently, but her intent reveals she's challenging me.

I grab her chin with force. "Open."

When she doesn't, I squeeze her cheeks and pinch her nose closed until she has no choice but to open her mouth.

"That's it. I like when your mouth is open for me like that."

I force her to take me to the back of her throat until tears roll, and she's gagging, pushing on my legs to regain control.

When her eyes flutter closed, I deliver a sharp tap to her cheek. Her eyes shoot open, the colors of the Caribbean Sea greeting me as she gags on my girth.

Her wolf dances along the surface of her control, and the concentration on my dick falters as she gasps for breath. Deep violet gleams in adoration as she services her king. I take advantage of her widening throat, thrusting deeper into her as she gurgles around her king's cock.

"Eyes on me, little wolf. I want to see you take all of your king between those pouty lips."

My wolf fights for control, my hips bucking faster over her soft orifice, hands gripping her hair hard by the roots, holding her in place, my pace unrelenting.

Her eyes widen as she takes more of my length, knees quivering as her scent thickens between her thighs. She'll never admit it, but her need grows when I use her like this, and I revel in her response to me.

Air escapes her lungs, and I force more of my length down her throat. I take what's mine, fucking her devious little mouth as I please. My wolf growls as he takes more from our mate, consuming every inch of her inner walls.

Her thighs attempt to squeeze together, seeking her own pleasure in her servicing of my cock, but my feet spread them wider, preventing the release she seeks.

"I'll get to your other holes later, darling. You don't need air. Only me and the pleasure I bring you."

My wolf inhales the sweet scent of her need, pooling deep within her, threatening her release as I take more of her mouth. Salty tears slide down her flushed cheeks.

"My little wolf is wet for me."

Choking and gurgling combined with drool and precum escapes from her lips as I dislodge my length from her throat. She gasps for air, while a moan and whimper leave her as my tip slaps against her lips. Sweet music her body emits from my touch fills the room as I fist her hair, and I bury my hard dick deep and fast into her soul once more.

Tears pour from her doe eyes, and I sneer at the pleasurable pain only I can evoke. Choked gagging only draws my length deeper in her throat, my balls pressing hard against her chin. My fingers massage her scalp as she cries around my dick and gasps for air.

"Who do you belong to?" I ease her off my length.

"You, my king," she says in between breaths.

"Good girl." I run her lips down my length again, fucking her mouth. I push her off me, the little force I exert sending her quickly flying into the soft mattress. Her back hits the bed, a little rag doll tossed aside after playtime is over.

My little plaything needs to fall in line . . . She'll see how I need to play.

"Spread your legs."

Her sensitive pink flesh glistens with her need.

She stills as if she's shy, uncertainty written on her face.

"So fucking beautiful. Touch yourself."

Alaina thinks about what I'm asking.

I'm growing impatient when she finally eases her right hand down to her sex, rubbing her bud in slow, tantalizing circles. It's not long before she starts moaning, her back arching. Alaina cups her swollen breasts, kneading them to the tip.

"That's it, darling. Rub that pretty pussy for me." I stroke my cock.

Alaina's fingers pick up speed, and her moans become more frequent.

She's about to come.

I step closer to her, my shadow, once again, blanketing her body.

"Do you want to come, darling?"

"Yes, my king."

Fuck, her submission is beautiful.

"Beg me."

"Please, my king. Please, may I come? I'm so close."

Never did begging influence me until now. She's come close, though. I'm used to my torture subjects' pleas.

Grabbing her hand to stop her release, I smirk as she looks at me in disbelief, as if I've betrayed her.

"Not yet."

I let go, and she whimpers as I position myself at her entrance.

Tension builds between our two panting bodies. Sparks crackle between us, the mate bond fighting to pull us together and the gravity of her pulling me in.

My hips threaten to buck and drive my hard length deep into her center and settle home within her. I belong there, sheathed in her warmth and wet core. Instead, I palm my cock with my left hand, gripping my length as I calm my wolf.

My fingers spread her opening, friction sparking her clit as they prepare her for my hard cock. I tease, slowly pushing inch by inch into her slickness, the length retreating to be joined by another one of my digits. Curling them inside, I find the spot along her inner walls that promises immense pleasure.

Her breathing catches as I massage and coax her orgasm higher. My speed is torturous, slow, and unbearably teasing her, judging by the moans and pleads forming along her lips. Her hips buck and meet the thrusts of my fingers, moaning and whimpering for me, needing more. And, *fuck*, do I want to give her what she needs.

My fingers slip from her entrance, rubbing her wetness along my length before returning to circle her clit.

She frowns, and I shove my fingers in, stretching and filling her as my cock would soon. They tease her g-spot, threatening to send her over the edge in a frenzy fueled by tension and need.

The need to claim her is overwhelming and all consuming.

"Is this what you want?" I say with condescension.

If only she weren't so stubborn, she and her wolf could both get the release they need.

She nods.

"What was that?"

"Y-Yes, my king."

"Then, say it. Tell me you want me to fuck you."

Desire hides behind her prideful lies.

"I want you to fuck me."

I groan as I stroke myself faster, wanting so bad to give her what we both want, but I know that pride is still there.

"Tell me you want me."

"I want you."

Her body is ready for me, pulsing with a need only I can give her. My wolf growls and scratches the surface, fighting against restraint.

It takes everything in me to ignore her body's calls, but my little queen had brought this upon herself.

I grab her throat, loom over her as I smile and, barely above a whisper, say, "I knew it."

And I do the hardest thing I've had to do: walk out, leaving her unfulfilled. Her torture becoming my own.

CHAPTER EIGHTEEN

Dax

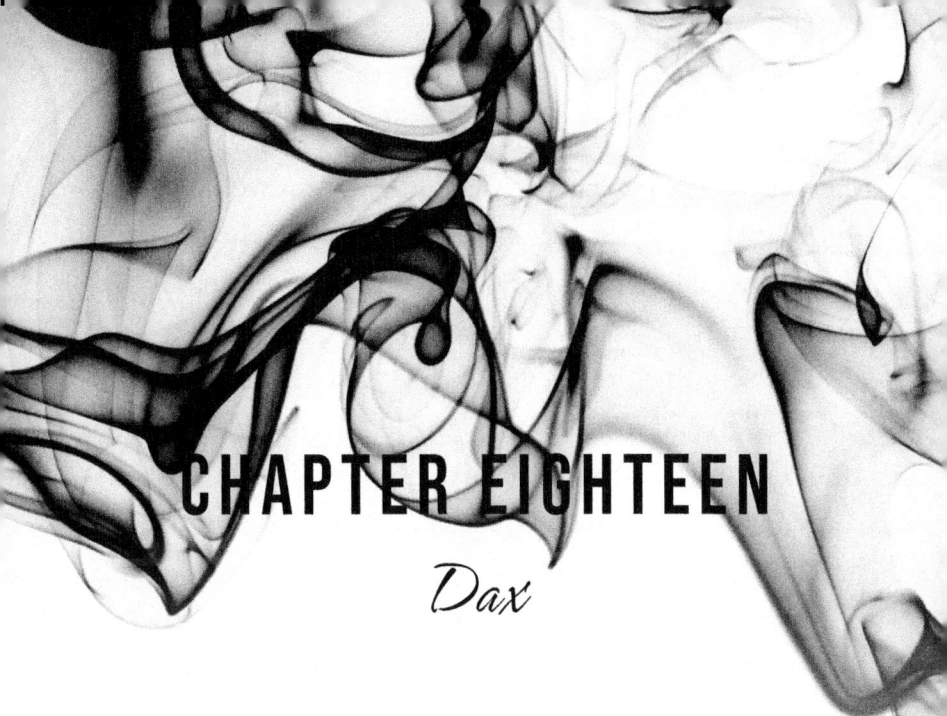

Adjusting my crotch, I can confidently say this is the first time I've had a hard-on in the dungeon.

Sam catches me, and I shrug.

I came down here to displace all my pent-up sexual frustration from my queen onto my new prisoners by engaging in interrogation.

Storming across the cold darkness as I walk through the long hallway, my stomping boots are unmistakable to my prisoners. Fear lingers as I scrape the silver-coated cell's bars. The silver now tickles after years of my own torture as a pup. I laugh at the sensation while others would shriek in agony.

My father, *may he rest in hell*, used silver on me as a form of punishment. He thought it would make me stronger, and for this, he was right.

My father taught me how to torture prisoners when I was twelve, which led to torturing my first person to death at thirteen. He said the rogue killed and raped a pack member.

It was the same thing for a while. They'd bring me in, the thirteen-year-old executioner, and my victims would laugh—until I began. Word spread about me being the demented child who enjoyed torturing people. My reputation still precedes me.

The screams, the cries, and the collateral damage is all a means to an end to ensure the kingdom is protected. Anyone would gladly take the throne from me if they thought they could, and they wouldn't care about the means to make it happen. And neither will I.

If torturing and killing others means protecting what's mine—my pack, my kingdom, and my queen, it's easy. If someone thinks you're merciful, they'll ask for forgiveness, not permission. And I can't have that. I must be feared.

If asked a month ago what was better, to be feared or loved, I would've chosen fear. Historically, tyrants lasted longer than loved figures, and being loved doesn't keep you safe from betrayal. Now that I've met Alaina, I can't say confidently that—if she were to love me—anything would be better. My reputation protects us now.

After hitting double digits, I stopped counting how many lives I've taken and stopped caring. "Feelings are a weakness," as my father would say. Not even when I was alone did I cry after killing my first person until my mother died when I was twenty.

Anger was the only acceptable outburst my father allowed me. He saw it as a form of strength and intimidation, but I prefer to be calm and menacing.

COME FOR ME

Our home was never quiet when my father was alive, as he would always yell or throw things, any commotion to show his *force*. Father was always like that, loud and chaotic, but I got used to his predictability. What was truly terrifying was when he got quiet. You never knew what he would do next.

When there was nothing left to break and silence fell, the silver whip came out, and it was time to hide. In addition to physical, he loved psychological torture, his specialty.

Like using my mother to get me to comply with his insanity. Even she couldn't protect me from her mate. She loved me the best she could when it was safe to show love, as my father also felt love opened us up to enemies.

It's the same with Alaina. She's done everything up to almost being marked by another to shield her true feelings from me. But the connection, the sparks, and the raw heat between us is undeniable.

When I found her at the Hunt, I ordered Jack to release the pack records to me. And it gave me more insight into why she fights me so much.

There wasn't much in her file, but I read every word, determined to learn everything about my darling.

Her mother ran from her mate when she sought refuge with the Bloodhound pack. Her father wasn't listed, but her mother had said he was powerful and didn't want to risk him finding her. Having power meant enemies—enemies her unborn daughter would adopt. So, she left her mate before he could mark her to ensure her best chance at remaining hidden. She was two months pregnant at the time.

In the transcript, Jack follows up with necessary questions to gauge the risk of helping her hide, to which her mother had responded her mate wouldn't hurt anyone. She also mentioned using an ale obtained from a witch to disguise her scent.

Jack's men had confiscated upon her entry into their borders. After he determined Alaina's mother wasn't a risk, she was allowed membership into Bloodhound on a probationary period.

The first thing she did was see the pack doctor. He ran blood tests to ensure everything was normal. When the doctor drew blood, Jack stepped back, hating the smell of it, and asked Alaina's mother why it didn't bother her. The doctor noted the ale's odor resembled that of a satiated vampire, which made her nonthreatening during her days' long journey. Exposure to the smell made her feel safe when her cortisol levels spiked.

This explains Alaina's higher tolerance of blood, as she barely reacted to the bloodied mutt.

Reports show she was well-liked during her probation. Jack noted the smell of blood not bothering her, making her the perfect nurse to assist the pack doctor. When she wasn't working, she spent most of her time sitting in a tree. She fit right into the pack, lifting her probation a month after her arrival. While seemingly happy with her new home, she was often spotted spending several hours in a tree.

Immediately following Alaina's birth, her mother passed away, having not been strong enough to survive the birth after being away from her mate for seven months.

COME FOR ME

Then it goes into Alaina's records, and I've memorized every word. Each new report has taught me patience and how to find appreciation in my little mate's defiance. While well-liked among her pack, she got into several fights. My pride and fascination grew when I read they were often people she had no business fighting, as they were often bigger than her. No doubt someone who thought she'd shy away and take whatever shit they threw at her. I had to laugh at that very wrong assumption because I've learned my little mate doesn't back down to anybody or any challenge.

But no one knew then they were dealing with a queen.

While she's small, reports of her speed being outmatched allowed her to avoid punishment for fighting with other pack members. "Punishment" was lost on her because no one could ever catch her to hold her accountable, giving her no reason to ever listen to anyone but her own impulses. *She may be the fastest runner, but she will never escape me.*

My little mate needed to be tamed; she needed me. I let her believe that by not sinking her teeth into my shoulder that she's "denying me." But I already possess every part of her. Her body instinctively responds to my touch and presence, her wolf calls for me, and her pretty little mouth pleads for my attention—even when she's telling me to fuck off. She knows I'll follow through with punishment when she disrespects me, so why does she keep defying my orders? Because she wants my attention regardless. And while she doesn't yet realize it, she's lucky to have found me.

While she can pretend to deny me, there isn't any part of her left for me to claim. Every inch of her belongs to me. Even the parts I haven't fucked yet, like her pretty little ass.

Though she won't admit it, I'm forever seeded inside her, mind, body, and soul. Greedily encompassing her body, possessing her, filling her until I'm all she knows and can't survive without me. She thinks her not confirming I've marked her means she isn't claiming me. I think that's what scares her and why she refuses to mark me.

Another thing my mate is wrong about: the love I have for her has been there from the moment we connected, and it's the same for her. The mark doesn't bring on new feelings; it only intensifies and solidifies what's already there.

Now, whether she's lying to herself by investing in this denial or if she was truly never taught that about the mate bond and marking, I don't know. I don't want her to feel bad if she wasn't informed. She did lose her mother, after all, something that would've probably been brought up during the birds and the bees talk. But if she does know that's how it all works and if investing in the denial makes her feel safe, I'll let her. Anything for her safety.

Which brings me to my next theory as to why she won't mark me yet. I say *yet* because she will when I'm done waiting. Thoughts have crossed my mind about fucking her for days until she's delirious and doesn't know she's doing it. I'd have her heavily addicted and seemingly drunk on my cock.

Once sober, it'd be too late. She would've already marked me. After she'd tell me she hates me, I'd grab her throat, eliciting the sweetest scent from her pussy, and gladly oblige to her body's call by fucking her again. Her disputes would turn into those soft moans resembling a damn siren call. Her pretty little mouth would call my inner beast forward, turning me into this rough, savage mess as I figure out which call to answer, which hole to fuck.

Fuck, I'm getting sidetracked.

I adjust my hard package.

Part of me wonders if Alaina is worried she'll suffer the same fate as her mother. She'll gain enemies. That, she wouldn't be wrong about. But she'd be wrong to assume I won't keep her safe. Women like to think their men soften after meeting them, but not me. My pack was important to protect before the need to secure my reputation as a ruthless, sadistic king. But now, my pack matters little—I matter little—if she's not part of it.

I keep walking past the cells and stop when I no longer smell fear. To confirm, I sniff the air again, no fear, sweat, or urine. I don't hear teeth chattering, either.

A vampire leans against the stone wall. His aura is minimal in power, indicating he's a newly made vampire. With red eyes, he stares at me, calm and emotionless.

Hellooo. What's this?

I nod toward the cell for the guard to let me in, and he opens it.

Sam grabs him from behind and pushes him toward the interrogation room.

He doesn't protest or struggle, and if he didn't have anything to hide, he'd be begging to be let go.

This guy knows something.

His calm nature exudes confidence, as he thinks he can hold up under torture. But his presentation and blatant arrogance tells me more than he wants me to know.

My reputation is too well known for him to not know who he's had the misfortune of falling into the hands of. This means he simply doesn't care, which leads to two possibilities: his master is also ruthless and torture is something he's not a stranger to. *Somewhat likely.* Or he's exceedingly loyal to his puppet master, whoever he is. His lack of perspiration shows me the puppet master is just that, the show. He doesn't run the operation and doesn't call the shots, just carries them out.

This guy's a pawn, a major piece in completing the ring leader's mission, yet disposable. Judging by his smug look, he's succeeded in carrying out his master's wishes. And now he'll die for it, just like the show runner and puppet master intended.

Unfortunately, this means whoever is behind these attacks are a step ahead of us. This guy doesn't know who is actually in charge. I know I won't get that from him. It'll get us one step closer, as whoever sent him out today to head these attacks answers directly to the person in command.

This guy is going to help me.

I've learned overtime that the ones who aren't fazed by the dungeon and the sounds of torture are the ones who have intel I want. They're not scared because they've accepted their death, as they'll die before they give anything up. They're usually the toughest to crack, but they make the sweetest sounds when they finally do sing. And they always do. His symphonies will spill his secrets.

We walk toward the torture room. My guys strap him to a chair.

I pull up another chair in front of him and drape my arm over the back of it. One foot planted in front of the chair, the other stretched out. I cock my head as I assess my new victim.

Based on the wounds on his side and forehead, he hasn't fed in a while, causing him not to heal as fast.

He's not a randomly made vampire like the others and has earned his new immortality. His attire tells me he's closely associated with wealth.

Although disheveled, his hair had gel in it, which tells me appearances matter wherever he's from.

We sit in silence as I scan him from head to toe.

The bloodsucker flashes his fangs at me, hissing, "I'm not telling you anything."

Having heard them all before, I flick my wrist with a dismissive wave. I mindlink Jerry, ordering him to come to my side. He doesn't hesitate.

Jerry, although a decent fighter, has turned his back on the pack. During the last battle, I caught him ignoring a brother's plea when he was taking on too many. Sam informed me the two had a dispute over a she-wolf, and Jerry was upset. A wolf whose loyalty can change is like catnip to my enemies. And I can't have that. Jerry is nothing more than a threat to my pack's safety now. And I have no use for a warrior I can't trust.

"Slit your throat, Jerry."

His eyes widen. "Wh-What, sir?"

I exhale. His stuttering presence irritates me as he feigns innocence. "Our guest is thirsty and hasn't fed in days. Slit. Your. Throat." At the last part, I use my alpha command.

Jerry reluctantly takes out from knife his holster. The blade glints in his shaky hands. He swallows when it reaches his throat and squints as he starts slicing his skin with the knife. Jerry bleeds out, gurgling blood.

Black veins travel up the bloodsucker's neck as his eyes go dark. Blood sending him into a feeding frenzy, he thrashes violently.

"Have I got your attention now?" I stand and stroll toward Jerry's spasming body. I grab him by his collar and lift him to bring him just out of reach of the vampire's fangs. "If you want a drink, all you have to do is talk."

Instead of going for Jerry's bloody carcass, the vampire tries to bite me.

I drop Jerry's body when Alaina pokes at the mindlink, something she's never done.

"Alaina, what's wrong? I'm in the middle of—"

She pants and moans.

"Alaina . . ." I growl, knowing exactly what she's doing to me.

"I just thought you should hear what I'm capable of"—her breath hitches—*"without you."*

She's trying to prove a point that she doesn't need me, but her determination is only proving the opposite. My mate's smart but bratty as hell and she knows if provoked, I always deliver on my punishments. To prove her wrong by defiling her body in unspeakable ways on *her* terms, she wants to bait me and wants me but only if it means being vulnerable and admitting that she does. Nonetheless, I'll buy into this cat-and-mouse game.

"*Don't provoke me, little one. We both know what happens when you do.*"

"*Oh, fuck, this feels so good.*"

Sensing she's on the edge, I close my eyes, trying to regain my composure. While I know what game she's playing, she's currently winning. My little mate is apparently well-versed in the art of torture, her silly facade evident but effective.

I'm struggling to keep calm. I belong to my little wolf just as much as she pretends not to belong to me. All this feigning is fucking hard on my self-control. My wolf fights to take and claim her for the world to see. She makes me fucking crazy. *I'm fucking crazy.*

Needing to distract myself with cries that aren't hers, I direct my attention back to my victim. I'm amused at his expression when I motion to my men to hold his mouth open and he sees the tent in my pants.

"*Why continue to deny yourself? We both know you're touching yourself to me. Are you going to come for your king, darling? You're so fucking pretty when you come.*"

Her soft moans continue, telling me *I'm* now baiting *her*.

Knowing I've won, I stand over the vampire with pliers, and his eyes widen as he begs for his life.

Annoyed at his loss of confidence earlier and that his pleas are drowning out my darling's, I shush him.

Her breathing quickens, and I know her pussy's contracting. She's mere seconds away from coming, and I want her to come with my name on her lips.

"*Tell me who owns that little pussy you're making feel so good.*"

"*Caleb!*"

My heart stops.

I yank out one of the vampire's fangs, his screams in sync with hers.

The fuck she just say?

My mate had the audacity to speak the mutt's name. The one I've saved against my better judgment *several* times.

Now she's using it to throw in my face? My mate's defiance has no limits.

Like Alaina's moans, my shock dissipates into waves of rage threatening to take over. My wolf claws at the surface to sink our teeth into my disobedient mate's mark, sucking all words from her until her vocabulary is limited to my name. I can't correct her now, but I'm already fantasizing about all the ways I'm going to make her eat those words later.

I chuckle and grasp at what's left of my sanity, trying hard not to kill this motherfucker before gathering information.

I click my teeth. "Oh, darling... What a big... fucking... mistake. I'll see you soon."

I close the mindlink. This game has gone far enough.

No more hiding, my queen. It's time you bowed to your king.

CHAPTER NINETEEN
Alaina

Turning the showerhead on, I revel in the satisfaction from my win beaming inside me. Convincing myself what I did weren't the actions of a dumb bitch but the work of a skilled . . . queen?

No, don't start thinking that.

Mastermind—*we'll go with that*. He shouldn't have underestimated me.

Stepping into the shower, I wince as the scalding hot water kisses my skin, amping me up more.

If I proved my point to Dax I don't need him, I only proved to myself that I do. After having him, no amount of masturbating could compare to the ecstasy he summons from my core. But I'll never admit that to him. His ego would explode.

Massaging my scalp with the shampoo Dax fetched from my old home upon my arrival causes me to sigh. Behind me, I grab Dax's bodywash and flick the lid open. Shamelessly, I lift the bottle to my nose, gently squeezing to unleash the spiced fragrance, and my insides quiver. I lather it over my skin, comforted that I smell like him. But guilt creeps in because I may have hurt Dax, causing my wolf to whimper and my heart to ache.

My thoughts wander to him hovering over me on our bed. Water streams down my curves, and my hand follows, my thighs widening as I touch myself, circling my clit. Our scents swirl among the steam and combine in the sweetest combination as my need rises.

"Dax," my moan sings with the soothing sounds of the shower.

Get ahold of yourself, Alaina.

Coming to my senses, I frantically try to wash off his stench, practically rubbing my skin off in the process. But it's no use. So, I take my bodywash to cover up his spiced soap.

When my stuff arrived, I asked one of the maids what happened to my lavender soaps. Apparently, Dax ordered them to be thrown away and replaced with the black raspberry vanilla instead, saying that it "suits me better."

Did I go too far?

I screamed a former lover's name. Someone who had me, to whom I looked to give myself over multiple times. Scratch that, someone who I *have* given myself over to multiple times. But that was before I met Dax. Everyone has a past. Let's not pretend the king of werewolves hasn't fucked before.

The thought of him with another, however long ago, enrages me instantly. My argument starts fading. Olivia and Dax aren't together, but I'd be naive to think they've never been before. If he had screamed Olivia's name, what would I have done?

Leave. Run. Hate him. Kill her.

That's when the anxiety comes in full force. The steam suffocates me, the heat quickly becoming unbearable. I turn the knob to the left and gasp as the cool water hits my body. Dropping my head back, I'm able to breathe again.

I calm my anxiety with the only evidence I have to support that he's not leaving me, *at least not yet.*

I'll see you soon, he said.

You'd think my intrusive thoughts would stop there. Big fucking nope.

What will he do when he comes for me? When will he come for me?

A slamming door breaks me from my thoughts. And like the water coming out of the shower head, my blood runs cold. A sudden eeriness lingers as I wait for footsteps that don't come. Everything seems to shift and still besides my thudding heart against and the hissing shower. The water seems to roar louder than before to compete with the silence.

Goose bumps erupt along my body as I shiver under the cold instead of turn off the water, scared to make a move or a sound. There's no curtain, so the figure that I've convinced myself is behind me would have a nice view of my ass right about now.

My cheek meets the stone wall, and my hand is pinned behind me. I gasp at the sudden contact. Sparks from his touch are a welcome contrast to the freezing water.

He's come for me.

His aura is dangerous, threatening, promising ruin. And I know he'll forgive me but not before he makes certain I'm sorry.

His grip is sure to leave a bruise, claws protruding and breaking the skin around my wrist. The faint smell of blood mixes with the bodywash's.

Dax is still in his clothes, which are drenched and sticking to his chiseled muscles. The ridges and hills of his abs show through the translucent article. Veins in his neck and forehead pop out to witness my demise. Water droplets dangle from strands of hair and the tip of his nose.

His eyes are flickering from gold to their normal eye color as his control wavers.

And I know whether his eyes choose to show calm or storm depends on my answer to his question.

"You think you can take care of yourself better than I can?" He vibrates into my skin, voice is husky and low, like he'd just woken up.

An invitation for pure sin, and our tension is gravitational.

I should apologize and bare my neck for this feral creature behind me.

But giving in isn't me, and it isn't us. It's not the game we play. The game that has his member hard and pressed against my back.

So, instead, I dig myself deeper into the hole. "I respond to you the way I would to any domineering alpha male."

My voice quivers, and he's not convinced. I'm not convinced of the words coming out of my mouth, either. It's all lies, and he knows it.

His grip tightens further, and blood beading from my wrist runs toward the drain. He then whirls me around, slamming me against the other shower wall.

I grunt as my head hits the stone. My eyes bug, and my wolf wants to claw her way out of my body and exaggerate her willing submission. But it's too late for pleas and forgiveness. He wants my blood, my tears, and my torture. I've seen him look this way at Caleb. Only this time, this look of anguish is directed at me.

He allows his walls to come down, and I feel his hurt and betrayal. My justifications for my actions don't matter anymore.

He growls when he registers that I understand what I've done. And I start to wonder, *When was the last time someone hurt the king? And did they live to tell the tale?* Seeing how infuriated Dax is, I would imagine no one. And I can't confidently say I'll be the first exception.

When his walls go back up, his hell-bounding aura hits me in the face again. His eyes stop glowing, dimming out, as he's regained control.

"Let's put that to the test. Shall we?"

I contemplate running, but his powers will alert him of that intent, and I curse his gift. The sudden shift of energy vibrates through the room, and I don't dare to move. The room is deathly silent once more.

The eerie silence is broken when he breathes into my neck and inhales my scent, followed by a chilling, deep, reverberating laugh.

Sweeping his lips up my neck, his breath warming and caressing its way up to my jawline, he whispers, "Run."

I blink in confusion. *He can't really be asking me to run.*

"W-What?"

"From me, *Alaina*."

He says my name with such disgust. Alaina. Not darling. Not queen.

No amount of distance has ever felt farther when he straightens.

"You provoke me, disrespect me, and disobey me every chance you get. In public, I might add. I'm done with this cat-and-mouse game. In fact, I'm ending it now. This"—he motions his finger in the space between us—"ends now. Run."

His words are harsh, and the delivery is a solid impact. My heart feels as if it were just stabbed, my chest tightening and heart rate increasing at this rejection.

Blankly, I stare at him, searching his eyes for answers.

He's letting me go. He's giving up on me, on us.

Fighting back the tears, refusing to cry in front of him, I step out of the shower and bend down to throw on a pair of jeans and a T-shirt but stop when Dax growls, "Leave them."

He wants me to be humiliated, to leave naked with nothing.

I swallow my pride and leave quietly, shocked this is what things have come to.

Never did I intend to hurt Dax. I just wanted to prove a point. But I crossed a line even my own mate couldn't accept. I never meant for any of this to happen. Sometimes, it's not the intention but the impact that matters.

COME FOR ME

As I stare out at the empty woods in front of me, I see the consequences of my actions. Not a single guard or pack member is out here in the woods to see their pathetic luna leave with her tail between her legs. At one point, I craved the privacy that comes being the king's mate. Now that I have it, I'd give anything to be surrounded once more. It would mean my mate cares for and would protect me, that I mattered to the king.

But I ruined that.

Dax doesn't care about what happens to me anymore. I mean nothing to him now. Surely, that's why I am unprotected—why waste perfectly good men and resources to keep me safe if he no longer cares?

He wouldn't, and he didn't.

I walk into the lonely woods, the moon lighting the way. The castle appears farther and farther away, disappearing behind me as I move deeper into the forest. I stop to look at the balcony attached to what was once my bedroom, where Dax will soon have Olivia take my place as his queen. Someone who always chose him, made him feel enough and desired no matter what.

My wolf doesn't growl or whimper at the thought of someone else loving him the way I should have. The way he wanted me to.

Tears pool in my eyes, and I lick my lips and taste the bittersweet drops.

I don't get to cry. I caused this. And there's nothing I can do to change it. I need to move on.

After taking one last look at the castle, the place I was destined to call home, I turn and continue my path. I don't think I ever accepted it as home to begin with. I never gave any of it a chance.

Even when you're a werewolf, the woods can be creepy. I've walked through the woods naked and welcomed the moonlight on my skin many times before, normally after a long run with my wolf. Someone would usually help if I got into trouble.

This time, no one is coming to help me. I'm an outcast, no better than a rogue. Even worse, I am a rejected mate of the king.

The soil feels cold on my bare feet. Every now and then, a branch snaps under me. I'm thankful for the summer nights making being naked bearable so I don't freeze. Trees sway and softly hiss in the breeze. Somewhere in the distance, an owl hoots, while bugs chitter around me. Fog adds a nice horror-movie touch, along with the whoosh of flapping wings and birds sounding like alarms.

I'm cautious and do my best to not alert anyone. Not everyone knows I'm an outcast. Some may still believe I'm someone that holds leverage over the king. Not to mention, I'm naked and alone.

My heart races while my mind conjures up scenarios that do little to calm my nerves. It doesn't help that I get this sense I'm being watched.

CHAPTER TWENTY
Dax

I mindlink the pack to warn them to stay out of the woods. Close behind her, I watch her wet hair stick to her back, sending droplets down her perfectly round ass, getting lost in her crevice. Her hips sway as her toes press into the soil, tits bouncing as she carries them in her arms.

Alaina thinks she's alone and that I've sent her away. And for now, I'll let her believe that.

I meant what I said, but what she thinks I meant by it is far from the truth. She puts so much effort into trying to convince me she doesn't want this life, this pack, *me*.

It hurts.

She wanted to stay when she realized the choice wasn't hers but mine. When she tried to grab her things to leave, I stopped her. I want her bare, just as she's stripped me of my walls. Making me no longer an immortal beast but a beast who bleeds and finds life within such a wild beauty.

She's quickly becoming a headache, disrespecting and disobeying me like this, but pain can be pleasurable.

Feeling pain is quick proof you're alive. Self-inflicted pain stops the numbness, offers a sense of control, and distracts you from the true pain of the world. The bleeding that follows becomes just as addicting. But my darling queen has provided much more than a reminder that I'm alive—she has shown me how it feels to live, and I only bleed for her now.

I wanted her to run from me. She would have if she knew of the plans I have for her. If only she'd left me, I would do anything to make her happy, but I could *never* truly let her leave me. That's the one thing I can never give her. All I could offer her is the illusion. I thought she wanted to run, for the chance to leave. Why else would she continue to push me? But I saw her tears as she gazed up at the castle; she wanted to stay just as much as I want her here.

She doesn't realize I would never let her go, though. Part of me had to laugh when she cried. It's humorous she even thinks I would, let alone I would just let anyone have her. From the moment I met her, she was doomed to spend the rest of eternity with me, never to be without me. *If she only knew how fucking addicted I am.* How her mark is forever the flame to my moth within. Despite her defiant nature, no one else will have her. No one fucking touches her. And I swear to kill anyone who tries.

In the shadows and darkness surrounding us, she bathes in the moonlight of her actions, regretting it all now, calling out that mutt's name.

COME FOR ME

But regret is not enough this time, darling. I want us to share this pain.

Despite my powers showing me her intentions weren't to hurt me by saying his name, it won't save her. *Not this time.*

Even with my powers, I had a moment where I allowed her playful brattiness to get to me, and I doubted myself, my abilities, and my worth to her. I showed her that I was hurting but only momentarily. I wanted her to understand there are lines not to be crossed. While some may think this punishment is too harsh or makes us even, it doesn't. Not even close. Everything I do is to keep her safe. Whereas what she did was to keep herself safe *from me.*

Damn her walls and her efforts to push me away.

I've dealt with forces of nature and creatures her little pack still believes are nothing more than stories told by the campfire. She can fight with me for the rest of our lives, but she can't fight *against* me anymore. A king and queen at odds displays weakness and invites destruction. *It ends now.*

My very vulnerable queen looks behind her after I purposely step on a branch. She doesn't know it, but at times, she stares right at me, wondering what lurks in the dark woods.

Since meeting Alaina, my abilities have only strengthened. My hearing has reached new heights. Her pulse drums loudly in my ear, and it's only increased since I've stalked her through these woods. My sense of smell is impeccable. I can practically taste her blood as cuts form on her bare feet. What's become better is my strength, especially my speed. She makes me better. I can only imagine how much stronger we will be when she marks me and accepts me as hers.

At the snap of another twig in my hand, she whips toward my direction. I toss the same twig to the other side, and it lands in bushes, startling her as rustling leaves echo through the forest. She looks in the direction of the twig and stops walking.

Her eyes widen when she sees my golden eyes glowing in the dark. I let out a growl, a warning to my delicious prey not to run from her predator. Her flight kicks in anyway, and she takes off.

CHAPTER TWENTY-ONE

Alaina

I don't have time to shift before my feet decide to flee, and suddenly, I'm barefoot, running through these unfamiliar woods. Attempting to shield my face with my arms as I run through brush, I duck under branches, swinging myself around trees. My limbs are stinging and my lungs are on fire, but I don't care.

I'm not dying out here, especially not like this.

I saw glowing golden eyes, but I couldn't register who they could belong to, my head reeling from fear and adrenaline. I don't even know what's chasing me, but I can hear it, and it's gaining on me. Footsteps pound against the ground, and they're getting closer, just waiting for me to slip.

The creature seems to know my every move. No matter how many times I duck at the last minute, change, or fake the direction I'm going, it's still there on my tail.

I'm going to die.

My only chance is to know what I'm dealing with and fight.

I look up at the stars and pray to the Moon Goddess that this isn't Her plan for me. To die, naked, alone, and afraid.

I don't think of my next move, allowing my instincts to take over. Without thinking, I veer off the path and cry out as I throw myself into the bushes beside me. Before I know it, I'm tumbling down a slope. Falling, I pick up speed as I'm rolling over twigs, rocks, and leaves. I reach the bottom of the small hill, landing in more piles of leaves, branches, and debris.

I spring to my feet when a loud thud hits the ground. Backing away until a large stone is at my back, I recognize the beast in front of me. The smell of my blood and all beings of nature clouded me from seeing it before. But as I stare at him now, he's unmistakable.

Dax.

Like the dark predator he is, a beast in its natural habitat, he stands, licking his lips, leering at his prey. Specks of dirt cover his face, his once-white shirt, and his arms. The look he has is the same he gets when he hunts for food, like he just caught prey he's ready to devour. A look he's given me many times before.

Before he told me to leave.

His eyes flash from bright gold to normal as his broad, muscular shoulders heave with every loud inhale and exhale.

Why did he come for me?

Even now, as he's hunting me, he looks devilishly sexy. And after everything, the thrill and fear of being stalked, chased, and cornered, arousal forms between my legs.

Dax can smell it and shows no shame as he breathes me in. His chest rises and eyes close as he sniffs my embarrassment. He exhales, his eyes, now bright gold, open and land on me. He growls and takes a step closer.

Doubt stops the fantasy as my hurtful thoughts invade me. *This is just his possessive nature, the effects of the mate bond. He's just giving into his desires, a momentary lapse in judgment. Later, he'll throw me out. He doesn't really want me. The Dax that told me to leave is the real him.*

Confusion whirls around me as I try to make sense of the events. The broken parts in me want to have misinterpreted the events that occurred, but I have to protect my heart from what he said. He truly did want me to go. Until I know for certain, he's not getting anywhere near me.

"Dax, please, don't." I put my arm out.

He doesn't listen and continues his pursuit.

"Dax, stop!" My wolf surfaces, causing my eyes to flash as I stand my ground.

Confusion etches his face, and he stops, seemingly wondering why I would stop him, as if he's never said anything hurtful to me. His fake innocence enrages me.

"You told me to leave," I yell through breaths.

"I told you to run."

His voice is gruff, just as out of breath as I am. He's gotten faster. I have a feeling he was toying with me before, that he could have caught up to me if he wanted to. But he let his sick hunt pursue.

"Same thing."

"Is it?" He stalks forward, lifting his eyebrow as he cocks his head. "You think I'd ever let you go? You belong to *me*, Alaina." He licks his lips at me, a predator salivating for its prey.

My wolf purrs at such a possessive act.

Fuck, why am I like this?

I blink rapidly, my lips trembling.

He was never really done with me. Relief washes over the fear and heartache. My heart starts picking up its own broken pieces.

Dax reaches for me, and I swat his hand away. He let me believe he was done with me, that I was being cast away in the most humiliating way. *He doesn't get to just come back like nothing happened.*

"I didn't say you could have me." I lean my head back against the familiar boulder.

Once again, yet under entirely different circumstances, he has pinned me against the same stone where I met him during the Hunt, looming over me.

He stares at me. "I didn't ask."

Swiftly, I'm up in his arms, my legs wrapped around his waist. He slides his nose from my ear down my jawline to where my mark is. Nipping and trailing light kisses along the way, until he sinks his teeth into my mark. The slow, sunken bite is a stark contrast to tender caresses.

COME FOR ME

I gasp and claw up his back, while the other hand grabs his nape. The most pleasurable burn supersedes the pulsing pressure and tingling sensation as his teeth sink into my neck and mark my soul. He growls before lifting his canines out of me.

"You're mine." He sucks and licks at the spot and then walks with me in his arms to a nearby tree. When he crashes his lips onto mine hard, I can already tell they'll bruise come morning.

Our tongues dance as they slide and caress each other.

Everything after is a blur. He enters me, not waiting for my body to adjust, and hammers into me, an animalistic claim. Suddenly, the tree bark scratches my back as I'm thrusted upward. My werewolf abilities heal the scratches as quickly as the bark inflicts another stinging bite, a perfect cocktail of pain and pleasure driving me up further toward release.

"You're fucking mine. Say it," he growls.

"I'm yours!" I gasp in ecstasy. "I'm yours, Dax, I'm yours."

I'm meeting him thrust for thrust, getting closer to the edge. *Just a little more...*

He stops and searches my face. I'm panting, my thighs and ass slowly unclenching as the orgasm dissipates. His eyes flash gold and narrow. He leans into me and grits out, "I don't believe you."

His alpha king voice is evident, meant to invoke fear and intimidation, and in some ways, it does. In other ways... it sparks something deep in my core.

My back is pulled away from the bark, and the tingles from the healing properties sizzle on my back like sparklers, causing me to hiss at the soft electric shocking my skin. Cool blades of grass kiss my skin in the breeze, and the sparks subside.

He towers over me with his large frame and leaves trails of kisses down my body. Throwing my legs over his shoulders, he bites down on my clit, and I gasp. The sting of his bite payback for the name I dared to echo.

His lips devour me, tongue flicking my aching, pulsing nub. Feelings and sounds from us breathing, moaning, and him sucking on my flesh echoing in the woods only amps me up further. He drags his hand up my stomach and splays it over my breast, moving in circles. The vibration of his moan sends me further toward the edge.

Oh, keep it right there.

When he stops, I cry out in frustration. Face glistening with my juices and licking his lips, he sits up. He wipes my juices from his mouth and wipes my arousal lazily over my face. I let him.

"So beautiful," he says. He grabs my chin between his fingers, pursing my lips together, and lays a kiss on mine softly, tasting the mess he's made of me. Our lips make that suction noise as his lips leave mine, and he pats my cheek. "Good fucking girl."

With only one of my legs over his shoulder, his manhood centimeters from my entrance, he strokes himself as he stares down at me. He lays his hand on my mound, strumming my clit in circles with his thumb.

"Dax," I say breathlessly, "please."

I'm grinding my hips in search of friction, needing more. Instead of giving it to me, he smirks and chuckles, finding amusement in my pleas for release.

He leans down to my ear, his abs rippling. "I thought you said you didn't need me?"

I can hear him smiling.

"I-I don't."

He removes his thumb and smacks my center. "Play with yourself, then." Pumping his length, he issues a warning growl, his patience thinning.

Emboldened by his hungry stare, my hand moves to make eager circles across my aching sweet spot. I moan under his gaze, my breath quickening. My other hand strokes the side of my neck to my breast. Alternating between squeezing my nipple between my thumb and the base of my pointer finger, I squish and roll my flesh.

"Yeah, keep doing that. Fuck. Does that feel good, baby?" He sucks in through his teeth. "You're so fucking sexy when you're making that pussy feel good."

It's hard not to feel sexy with the way this male looks at me, and my inner sexual goddess turns me on even more.

"You like when I touch myself?"

"Fuck yes," he grits out, veins protruding from his forehead and neck. "Feel how wet you are for me, darling."

At his command, I dip my fingers in, and he's right. I'm coating the ground beneath me. I watch him watch me stick another finger inside myself, moving in and out slowly. Only coming out to swirl the juices around my pulsing clit. I bring my fingers up to my mouth, and Dax growls in a heated warning.

"Do it, and I'm fucking you."

I raise my eyebrows. "Promise?"

A wicked grin spreads across my face. Enveloping my mouth around my fingers one by one, I slowly suck and moan as I drag each across my tongue, then pop them from my lips.

You can practically hear the last bit of his patience break before he buries himself inside me, unable to control himself and adjust. His thrusts are unrelenting, our skin slapping and moans rattling the trees.

My mind reels. I don't know if this is the art of war or the art of seduction anymore. They both seem one and the same, and I don't know who's winning or who's losing. Every thrust of his hardened length speaks to our game of tug of war, both wanting the same thing but aching for the other to succumb to one another. It's not enough to meet in the middle and call it a tie and admit that the bond is a mutual need. Instead, someone needs to lose so that both of us can win and end this miserable game. And his pull is stronger, his side convincing *and* tempting.

My body is erupting with him inside of me faster than I can catch up. I open my mouth to scream, but he slaps his hand over my lips to muffle my cries. Arching my back, eyes rolling up into myself, I try my best to close my legs to weaken the powerful release threatening to explode. His thrusts slow to a rhythmic pump, pouring himself inside of me.

"Shit, Alaina," he strains.

Dax spasms, and my legs shake as we come down. Sweat runs down the center of his chest. I smile, never thinking I'd be the reason the king of werewolves would break a sweat.

He tucks a strand of hair behind my ear, rubbing his thumb on my cheek. "Fuck, never stop looking at me like that."

I hold his pleading gaze, and there's a feeling I haven't felt from him I can barely read. *Fear? Sadness?*

"Never leave me."

Both. Because while this was all a clear misunderstanding, I still left without a fight.

Dax cradles me against his broad chest. Exhaustion sets in as I'm encased in his warmth. "Sleep. I've got you. And when you wake, I'm going to punish you."

His tone is playful, with a hint of dangerous mischief.

I smile into his chest and flick a dismissive wave. "Yeah, yeah, yeah."

Whatever it is, I'm sure I'll brat my way out of it.

* * *

My eyes flutter open, and the silk caramel sheets indicate that I'm back in the castle. Sunlight seeps through the floor-to-ceiling curtains that dress the large windows overlooking the kingdom.

I sit up and stretch.

In the corner of the room, the light fails to hit. Slumped in the chair with his legs spread and arms hung over the armrests, swirling caramel-colored liquid in a short glass, Dax is sitting in a velvet crimson Queen Anne armchair. His white shirt is unbuttoned, showing his tanned chest, while black slacks struggle to keep his package contained. He must've come from a meeting.

Dax stares at me through his lashes. His cheekbones flex and eyes narrow.

I could devour him.

Tossing the bedspread off my body, I'm confused when I look down to see myself in a cherry-red chemise, with lace splaying over my breasts. I wasn't wearing this earlier, nor is it a part of my wardrobe.

Did he dress me while I was sleeping?

Already knowing the answer, I focus on the male in front of me. I crawl to the foot of the bed with every intention of climbing into Dax's lap and lick up his chiseled jaw.

"You don't leave our bed until I tell you to," Dax states, his tone dark.

This stops me in my tracks.

Huffing, I roll my eyes. "Yeah, oh-kay." Dismissing his demanding nature, I swing my legs over the front of the bed.

It isn't until my feet kiss the floor that I'm stopped, a wave of shocks licking up my neck like a jellyfish. A vibration buzzes against my clit, in my velvet center. . . and something pumps in my ass. I fist the sheets and cry out.

Holy fucking shit—what was that?

Once the sensations subside, I blink at him, confused.

Dax sips his drink, holding a small remote. He looks unbothered, but under the surface, his anger is a monsoon. Dax's hostility is a spectrum, one where I can pinpoint which stage he's in.

Where he stands now is what I've dubbed "the calm before the storm" stage. During this phase, his wolf circles me, his prey. He knows he has the upper hand, and therefore, I don't get to see the explosive anger. Instead, I get the indifference, the "I couldn't care less about you" and the "boredom."

He's not easily amused with my bratty behavior during this stage, and he will get what he wants because, in his eyes, I've already lost, making his win inevitable. For Dax, this is the time he is finished torturing his victims and moves in for the kill.

Dax grins.

What has he done to me?

Frantically, I grab at my neck, hoping what I experienced isn't the punishment I think it is. Any hope I have is crushed when I feel a thick metal ring snug against my neck. I claw desperately for even the slightest bit of a gap, but there isn't one. I feel around the metal for a flaw, a crack, a clasp—*something*. With all my strength, I try to pull it off, bend it, but there's no use. His smirk tells me this thing's not coming off until he wants it to.

Something pumps out of me in a place where no man has been before. I trail my hands down and stop at a rubber bulb at my bud. Sliding my hand back, I notice that connected to the rubber device on my clit is another he's inserted into my vagina.

I suck in a breath and trail more to find another device lodged into a forbidden space.

"Do you like it? I had it made just for you. Seems I need to create new ways to torture you."

"What the f—"

He sends another electric current to my neck, cries erupting from my throat. The pain perfectly balances out with the pleasure from the humming against my pussy and the pumping into my ass.

I'm so full. It's too much.

I bite my lip to keep myself from yelling more expletives.

"Good girl."

Dax sets his drink down on the cherrywood end table next to him and licks the scotch off his lips. He clasps his hands together, folding each finger into the crevice of the other, and rests them on his belly.

"You screamed his name," Dax chastises.

His wolf's aura moves from calm to storm, which is only ever directed one way, unhinged and merciless.

Poking the bear anyway, I feign innocence. "Who? Caleb?"

Dax sends another current to my neck, and my pussy is drooling between my thighs. I'm overwhelmed. My body has a mind of its own now. It rolls and rocks, screaming unintelligent things.

Pinching my legs together isn't enough this time.

I'm both relieved and disappointed when the pleasure stops.

The fear and thrill of being under the control of this merciless king is strangely arousing, and he can smell just how much.

I need a therapist. I note to myself to search for one later.

"There's nothing wrong with you," he says, interrupting my thoughts. "Your safe word is 'mutt.'"

Safe word?! I swallow hard.

"Nod if you understand."

I do so.

"Good girl." He sighs. "If roles were reversed, and I had said Olivia's name..."

I growl.

I'd be livid and hurt.

It's negatively affected him, but with his emotions guarded, I'm not able to discern how he's feeling.

I took things too far, but I thought we made up last night. Judging by the look in his eyes and the danger in his tone, he plans to make me pay just a little longer.

But I don't intend to let him.

I get up from the bed to pounce and take the remote from him.

"I think it's time you bowed to your king," he says without paying my attack any mind while he presses the button.

Crashing to the floor, I cry out as shock waves pulse around my throat.

He leans forward, elbows posted on his thighs. "Didn't I say to stay in our bed?"

I'll combust if he presses it again.

"I'm sorry," I squeak.

He leans forward, placing his hand behind his ear. "What was that?"

Normally, I'd cuss him out, but this new device is taming me.

"I'm sorry."

"For getting out of bed or for saying the name of your ex-lover while pleasuring yourself?"

I hang my head. *We've hurt mate.*

"If you want to act like a bitch, then I'll treat you like one. Crawl to me." His finger hovers over the button on the remote.

The mere suggestion of him wanting me to crawl like a female dog is humiliating and degrading. Dax was forcing my hand, leaving me with only one choice: *his.*

Tell that to your wet pussy, my inner self teases. But, dammit, is she right.

My body and pride are at war. If I'm honest with myself, I want his dominance and control. But can he respect a queen crawling on the floor? Would I?

"I'm not asking for your submission anymore. I'll just take it," Dax mindlinks.

I guess I don't move fast enough because a lick of electricity crawls up my neck again.

Dax doesn't want me to think about whether to follow his words but to obey.

"I believe I told you to crawl to me, darling," he drawls.

Lowering myself, I place my hands on the floor, then slowly crawl toward him, sticking my ass up in the air, dropping my shoulders.

"Damn, you're so fucking sexy." He licks his lips.

With the way he's looking at me, it's hard to feel anything but desire.

I'm on my knees. Dax pulls me by my hair into him, crouching to meet me face-to-face. Inhaling my scent, he exhales, and his eyes flash gold.

I'm greeted with a single possessive kiss, a reward for choosing his need for my submission over my pride, which is, apparently, worth one praise kink.

Worth it.

"I find it hard to believe you didn't have this device long before you met me to use on all your bitches," I retort, half joking, half curious yet fully disgusted at the thought.

I don't know why I ask questions that don't benefit me.

Dax smiles against my skin as his lips brush over my mark, sending tingles down my spine. He sinks his canines into the spot, causing me to moan. His teeth slide out of my flesh with ease, leaving bite marks.

Dax laps up the blood, moaning as he tastes me, and hisses, "Didn't have to. They listened."

Damn him.

I scoff and look away, pissed at the comparison.

Dax tips my chin toward him. "Does that make you angry, my queen? That someone else has felt me inside them?" He cups my breast.

"Speak."

He commands like I'm his dog.

"No," I lie.

Waiting in silence, he raises an eyebrow.

He's not buying it.

I sigh. "Yes, my king."

"Good girl. I thought so." Leaning back, Dax unbuttons his pants, letting his hard cock spring to attention. "I want you to choke on it for me like a good fucking girl."

I wrap my hands around his throbbing cock, wetting my lips. Dax moves my hair out of my face, gathering loose strands in his fist, easing me down. He guides and controls my head with the push and pull of my hair knotted around his hand, and I gag immediately. As he thrusts deeper, he hits the back of my throat.

My instincts kick in, and I move to pull away, my hands pushing against his thighs as he shoves his hard length past the gag.

"Breathe through your nose."

I do as he says, and immediately, the panic subsides, and I moan.

"That's a good girl. Fuck, yeah, just like that." He sucks in air through his teeth. "Shit! You give good head."

My pussy soaks itself as he moves my mouth over his cock, heat pooling as my slickness spreads with my movements. I grow needy as he continues using me for his pleasure. My hair pulls and stings with the thrusts he takes. My hips writhe against the pain of his pull on my roots and the slam of his dick deep into my throat. But here, on my knees, I swear nothing feels as good as him.

I stand corrected when currents lick my neck and the vibrator hums, the device plunging into my ass.

My eyes widen as I let out a muffled scream with him still in my throat. When my lips meet the base of his cock, he strains and groans.

COME FOR ME

Dax throws his head back, neck bared to the room, hissing with pleasure. My eyes water, but through them glints the glorious sight of the pure alpha male, hard muscles clenching and veins prominent in the arms holding me to his mercy. Tattoos dancing up his arm and across his chest lead my eyes to the throat my wolf longs to lick and sink her teeth into.

My mouth waters, slickening his cock further, sending him deeper as the added sensation flutters his eyes to mine. He pounds deep into my throat again and again, the room filling with slurping and gagging and his wolf's grunts and groans.

I'm frozen with the fear of such a powerful release inside of me. All I can do is watch this man lose control of himself while still in charge of me.

Meanwhile, my orgasm has built to a pace I can no longer keep up with, outrunning me.

I am at the mercy of the least merciless man to exist.

"Oh, fuck, I'm gonna—"

The pleasure device ends with a click of the button. My pending orgasm halts. He pulls me off him by my hair, I hiss from his tight grip.

"Say thank you," he instructs.

"Thank you."

"'Thank you for letting me suck your cock.'"

"Thank you for letting me suck your cock."

"Who do you belong to?"

"You."

"Good girl." He nods, gesturing behind me. "On the bed."

My legs are shaking, but I make it to the bed and stick my ass out on the edge of it on all fours. I'm needy and soaked. Eager and ready to take all of him.

"I'm not fucking you yet." He takes the collar off, a heavy hand slapping my ass to turn me over, switching on the devices buried inside me.

"Oh," I moan, and my arms shake with my entire core.

I rock my hips, climbing up . . . up . . . up . . .

Then it stops, and I collapse to my elbows.

He spanks me again, making soothing circles over my cheek with his palm.

"Please, Dax, I'm sorry."

"Aw . . ." He kisses my back. "No, you're not. But you're about to be."

Fuck.

"Sit up."

I push up off my elbows and brace myself.

* * *

He clicks the device off again, ignoring my pleas and bestowing another denial on me. I know now why people told stories growing up about Dax, the king of torture. After an hour of his pleasure tool without being allowed to come, my legs are trembling uncontrollably. My mind is in a haze.

"Aw, baby, you're shaking. You really wanted to come, didn't you?"

I nod, whimpering.

Tears slide down my sore cheeks, my mouth parted in a silent plea as I fight against the orgasm he's teased to new maddening heights each time he's denied me.

Somewhere throughout the night, I've shifted from resistance and fighting him to embracing the pleasure our bond has brought us. I now fight for—not against—his power over me. I need the release only he can entice within me. Pleasure has blinded me to anything except my king and has inflamed my soul with desire. I craved my own liberation, but most of all, *I crave him.*

He builds another orgasm in my core. He does as he pleases with my body, claiming it and my mind as his, just as deeply as our mate bond has claimed my soul.

I need Dax.

I collapse on the bed.

"How does it feel to be so close to something you want, just to have it taken away from you?"

"Please, Dax."

I'm desperate. The contracting of my pussy is becoming too much.

"I've waited *seven years* for you to come for me. You've only waited an hour."

Our bond courses through my veins, consuming my every thought. Every breath, sigh, and moan is by and for him. I've lost count of him bringing me to the cusp of release, taking me to the edge of how much pleasure my body can endure before denying my orgasm. I would sell my soul for one more lingering moment of his touch, a little more friction, more torture, more cruel caressing fingers, and more tongue. He takes what he wants from me and only gives when it pleases him.

"And as much as you need to come, I need you more than that. So much more, Alaina."

His words, echoing all around me, hypnotize and shock me.

I've become a wanton—a pleading, begging, needy mess at his command. My pride long gone, my walls demolished, and the world outside him nonexistent. Our bond is the gravity tethering me to his bed and holding me captive to his whims.

"Up," he instructs.

Trembling, I lift myself from the bed back on all fours. When he turns the device back on, it hums and causes my body to tense up. I scream. The burning need is too much.

"Agh," I cry.

"You wanna come?"

"Yes, my king."

Like Dax, this device is my undoing. When the plug pumps into my anus, it sends shock waves to my neck and fizzles out with the vibration on my vulva. It's as if it's all connected, rocking me to the finish line.

"Beg."

"What?"

It's hard to focus with all these delicious sensations.

"Beg me."

"Please. Please let me come, my king. I'll be good, I swear."

"Stop denying our bond, and I'll stop denying you." His tone is soft, barely above a whisper.

I wave the white flag and nod.

Dax kisses my mark. My orgasm has been building for so long the climb only takes a second, and like a roller coaster, I'm at the top, looking over the edge at the steep drop.

"Come for me, Alaina."

With that, I scream all the way down, my arms giving out, and I collapse onto the mattress.

"You did such a good job taking that for me."

I close my eyes. My legs are spasming. Dax removes the device and sets it on the nightstand. Another noise goes off, but I don't recognize it.

"But I'm not quite done with you yet."

"I'm dead. I can't move," I pant.

Dax chuckles, kissing my temple as I lie on my side. "Don't worry, I've got you."

After scooping me up, he places me on all fours again. My head is hanging, exhausted. "I want you to see just how good you look as you take me. What men *wish* they could have."

Dax lifts my head, and my eyes land on the mirror across from the bed, an addition to the room.

Before I can get distracted with mundane, irrelevant thoughts, Dax grips my chin, forcing my eyes to lock with his as he gropes my breasts. A moan escapes me as his skilled hands palm the soft skin, squeezing groans past my swollen lips.

Dax's hands travel lower, gripping my hips, positioning his cock at my entrance. He snakes his hand around my neck, biting me as he buries himself inside me, slowly pulling me to his base.

Retracting his canines, his lips pepper kisses along my shoulder. He lifts off me, dragging his hands down my back to grip my hips.

"Fuck, you feel so good."

His hand slips between my thighs and rubs my clit as he thrusts into me, chasing yet another orgasm. Dax moans, knowing exactly what he's doing to me as my pussy clamps around him, his fingers rubbing my bud as his right hand reaches behind his back.

Our eyes lock in the mirror as I grip my breasts, their weight bouncing as he thrusts into me. His devilish grin meets me, sensing what's coming. My eyes widen as he presses the button on the remote, thrusting his cock up inside me.

I wince, expecting pain to course through my body, yet it sends my pleasure reeling up further.

"I want you to watch yourself as you come around my cock."

After an hour of my punishment, my eyes have stopped darting to him in hatred, hurt, or defiance and have softened to lust, need, and desire.

My will battles with my wolf's determination to submit herself to our king, our mate. His control and power over my release crumbles my will to resist and delay the inevitable. My gaze can't divert from him anymore. No matter how hard I try, my wolf is locked in, presenting herself bare before him to be all he desires.

For once, we are on the same page. Our screams and moans echoes through the castle as I come for him, just as he comes for me.

COME FOR ME

***

In the morning, I'm sore, and my body aches in the best way. A smile forms at the sensory reminders. His arm is draped over my waist possessively, and his hardened member is pressed into my backside. I see his many scars coating his arms that are covered by his dark hair. I follow the arms up to the male they belong to and see him sleeping peacefully.

For a moment, he's just Dax. So normal. I selfishly take advantage of his vulnerability, to check him out without him knowing. His chiseled jaw, his unfairly long eyelashes—*screw men and their long eyelashes that they never appreciate*—and his pink lips.

"Darling," he rumbles. He must've felt me move. I look away before he catches me staring at him. "I could feel your eyes on me, little one. Don't hide from me now."

I blush and curse at Dax's supernatural senses.

He moves me and shifts until he's settled in between my legs, resting his elbows on either side of me as he hovers over my face. Dax rolls his hard member into my core, and I moan at the feeling of hunger and a need for mercy, still sore from our previous encounters.

Even after I crawled for him, he still looks at me like I ensure his world doesn't succumb to the hilt of a blade instead of a weak bitch who does whatever he says. Our cat-and-mouse dynamic dwindles, and it's taking more effort for me to deny him than it is for me to give into him. He can see that and growls in approval at me for not fighting him for once.

"I should fuck you more often. You're less defiant this way," he teases as he buries his nose in my neck.

"Hey!"

He laughs, and I make a lousy attempt to push him off of me, then wrap my arms around him, giving up. *Not that I tried hard to begin with.*

"We need to get up."

"No," he lets out a muffled groan with his face planted against my neck. Making sure neither of us can get up and face the day, he goes dead weight on me.

"Dax," I laugh, trying to push him off this time. "Come on, I can't keep the king from his kingdom."

He pins my wrists above my head with one hand, then trails the other to my needy clit and looks at me. "I could make you stay in this bed. Making you come over and over again, screaming my name. You'll be so satisfied and exhausted you'll succumb to sleep, and just when you're starting to recover, I'll have you moaning once more. Never letting you fully come down, I'll have you in my bed for days, Alaina, making sure I'm to blame for your addiction. I'll never let you leave."

I swallow and don't dare touch on the obvious childhood issues that could stem from finding his declaration appealing, his idea that I'd be his prisoner, protected from everyone except him. Not letting me leave until I'm as obsessed with him as he is of me, addicted to him . . . Goddess, it sounds all sorts of psychotic, *but I wouldn't mind it.*

He can smell my arousal, and when he kisses me, we taste each other's hunger. My hips grind against him, searching for friction only he can give me.

Our teenage make-out session comes to a halt when there's a knock on the door.

COME FOR ME

He growls. "Go away. We're busy."

I hit him playfully, and he smiles. Pulling the covers over our heads, he trails kisses down my chest, then my stomach, then my—right there.

Until another knock is at the door.

Fun-loving, duty-free Dax is gone, and Mr. Killer In Charge returns, growling at whoever is disturbing his meal. I can't help but giggle at his frustration as he throws the covers off him and storms to the door.

He swings it open, grabs the man's lapel, and slams him to the wall. "What?"

"I'm sorry, sir, but there are rogues and vampires attacking in the East villages. People are dying."

Dax lets him go, nodding toward the door.

The guy bolts.

Dax rubs the back of his neck. "I must go with them. You'll stay here with Sam, where I know you'll be safe."

Before I can protest, he leaves the room.

I flop back onto the pillow, groaning at the cold Dax, at the unsexy version that keeps me his prisoner. Just when I was starting to feel good about our future.

I can't stay here again. Venturing through the castle grounds isn't enough to distract me from my lack of free will. I need to actually get out of the castle's walls and explore the kingdom that is supposed to be mine one day. And I know just how to make that happen.

I throw the covers off me and cover myself with a robe, then speed walk down the castle halls, the floor cold under my bare feet.

People bow and acknowledge me as "Your Majesty."

"When did you tell people to call me Your Majesty?"

"The second I met you."

This is going to take a while to get used to.

Mr. Playboy himself leans against a column with his soon-to-be-bedded target. By her blushing cheeks, she seems to be returning the favor, liking whatever he's saying. Her strap hangs off her shoulder, skin exposed, as he leans in to kiss her.

I clear my throat.

At the sight of me, the woman's eyes widen, backing away from him, showing her neck in submission, averting from my gaze. She curtsies before apologizing for her indecency and runs away.

Seemingly not happy that I've interrupted his fun, Sam sighs, then straightens, adjusting himself. "What can I do for you, Your Majesty?"

I ignore his tone and realize I've never seen the woman before or any of the other women he brings in here. I haven't explored the kingdom much at all outside the castle besides training outside, so I could use time away and have some fun.

Thinking about what the Mr. Playboy can do for me, I smile.

Ew, not like that.

"I want to go out tonight, and you're gonna take me," I say matter-of-factly.

He laughs, shaking his head. "I'm not taking you anywhere, princess."

"Why not?"

Because I can be quite the handful, I know exactly why he doesn't want to deal with my shenanigans.

"I don't wanna be your fucking babysitter all the time. No, thanks."

Sam likes to act like he hates me, but even on a bad day, I'm the little sister he never wanted.

"I don't need a babysitter. But Dax won't let me go unless you go with me."

"No. Every time I watch you, you turn into that fucking cartoon character, Road Runner, and then Dax gets fucking pissed when I don't know where you went."

I bite my lip to hide my laugh. *Guilty.*

"Not gonna happen," he says as he points in my face and bumps his shoulder into mine as he passes me.

He isn't afraid of upsetting the king's mate like everyone else.

Dammit.

I chose Sam because I thought he'd be my best chance at getting out of this place. It doesn't hurt that Sam would jump at the opportunity to be around drunk women. But I didn't think about what taking me would mean for him. It'd be work, not fun; he'd be responsible for my safety. Baring the mark of the king already puts a target on my back—add alcohol to the mix, and I'd be vulnerable to attacks. Sam wouldn't enjoy himself guarding me all night.

Okay, so beers and drunk she-wolves won't do it for him. Time for another tactic.

"Are you denying your queen this request?"

His footsteps come to a stop, and I turn to face him while cocking my head.

When Sam turns to face me, he doesn't seem rattled by my question. Instead, he's calm, his face emotionless. Dax must've taught him well.

"Last I checked, you're not my queen *yet*." Sam's arms are crossed as he leans forward.

I catch the hidden meaning behind his emphasis.

Sam believes what everyone else does: Dax always gets what he wants, finds a way. And he wants me, and Sam thinks he'll have me. He believes me succumbing to being their queen is the equivalent of my submission to their ways.

"Do I not bear his mark? Does Dax not have everyone showing their necks to me in submission? Are you telling me that if I ordered you, as your queen, that you wouldn't be expected to listen?"

This time, I have him backed against the wall.

He's silent.

"What would Dax have to say about your"—I look him up and down, meeting his gaze head on with my eyes narrowed—"defiance?"

I use Dax's favorite word to describe me.

Sam looks shock at my indirect threat but grins while looking down at me.

"Dax would be pleased to hear you're already calling yourself queen and bossing people around."

Fuck. I didn't mean it that way.

Alright, let's try again.

"I'm going with you or without you. And I don't think Dax would like it if he found out you let me go alone."

He chuckles once more. His laughs are irritating me.

"I'm sure Dax would gladly jump at the chance to take you out and get you drunk, princess. All you gotta do is ask."

I throw my hands up and groan at that.

Sam is absolutely infuriating. I can see why he and Dax get along so well. He is often a grumpy jokester, a weird combination. Even the peppiest woman will piss him off. Then she and I can annoy him together.

"Look, I've been marked against my will and cooped up in this castle ever since. I just want to go for an hour or two and then we can leave. I'll have a couple of drinks, dance for a song or two. I won't cause any trouble. I just need to get away for a bit."

He huffs, seemingly contemplating my decision as he chews on the inside of his cheek.

Okay, so intimidation doesn't work on him, but honesty and vulnerability does. *Interesting.* Not what I was expecting with Mr. Playboy. *Who knew he had a soft side?*

"Fine," he says. I jump with glee. "One hour."

CHAPTER TWENTY-TWO

Alaina

It wasn't just one hour, and it certainly wasn't a couple of drinks. A few beers, shots from some strangers, and I was about done.

With my lack of balance and observation, Sam is my babysitter tonight. He's saved me from walking into walls, using the wrong restroom, and falling flat on my face. I can't count how many times he's apologized on my behalf for drunkenly running into people. I'm a giddy, bumbling mess as the alcohol flows through my body.

Dax's guards are also on babysitting duty. They're taking turns, switching between bathroom duty since breaking the seal. Now I need to pee every ten minutes.

Sam and his guards have been useful, but they're *working*, which hardly makes them fun to hang out with.

The crowd jumps and sings along with the music. Women on the dance floor move in a circle together, smiling, until a man approaches one of them, trying to creep in.

Cringing, the girl shakes her head at his pursuit of her. He shrugs and walks away. Onto the next candidate.

The group bursts out laughing, and my mind wanders to Taya. If she were here, we'd be on the dance floor, laughing at the guys that approach us and stumbling through the crowd together. If we weren't dancing, we'd be sitting at the bar to people watch.

I miss her.

Okay, think about something else before you start crying.

Sucking the rest of my beverage down, I hit that sad, hollow slurp. I spin in my stool back toward the bar, placing my empty drink on the counter, ordering another.

The bartender doesn't waste time to pour me a beer and winks.

Sam leans his forearm on the bar. "You wanna lose that eye, man?"

The glass barely touches my lips when Sam lifts it and hovers it over my head. I try to reach for it but finally give up.

"Fine, I'll just get another one," I huff.

Sam calls the bartender, giving the beer back. He slashes across his throat, gesturing to the man that I need to be cut off.

Ugh, he is such a buzzkill.

"Ooh, I'm Mr. Pwayboy. No fun allowed," I slur.

Sam rolls his eyes.

Like it's the most wonderful realization, I get a sudden burst of energy at my recall of there being *two* bars in this club. I take off, hurdling toward the crowd of people, trying like hell to get to the other bar.

Sam's used to chasing me by now. It's childish, but it's too funny not to.

Dax and Sam should thank me for giving his beta such a good workout.

He can't catch me, but he's learning to call in reinforcements to corner me, so our game of tag becomes hide-and-seek.

I'm hidden in the sea of people before Sam can pinpoint where I am. Far enough away, I peer behind me, glimpsing Sam's scowl through the crowd.

I completely forget about why I ran into the crowd, with "Hypnotize" by Biggie Smalls blasting. I'm losing myself in the music, swaying my hips side to side, until hands are gripping my waist, and a guy's pelvis grinds into my backside. The smell of cheap beer and cigarettes assaults my nose.

I try to move away from the stranger, but he pulls me back to his chest. Turning toward him, I growl, pushing him away.

I thought he would recognize me or my mark as the king's and leave me alone, but he steps closer to me, grabbing a fistful of my hair. When I pound my fist into his chest, my blows are as dull as my senses are. I yell at him to let go of me, fighting to create distance, but he doesn't relent.

A familiar scent hits my nostrils, and a grin spreads across my face.

Oh, this guy's dead.

Misinterpreting my grin as cooperation, he tries to force my lips to his.

Following the ground-shaking growl of my mate, Sam pulls me from the guy's grasp and his soon-to-be new kill.

With his back to me, Dax's shoulders heave as he stares at the guy who laid his hands on me.

The guy is stupid enough to challenge him by stepping to him like he stepped toward me.

Dax punches him in the face, sending him flying, sliding across the floor into the crowd of people. He lifts him by his collar. "Since these don't work anyway..." Dax rips the man's ears clean off, pulling the stringy canal with him.

The man grips the bleeding holes, balled up in a fetal position.

Dax cackles.

I can only imagine what a demented sight it must be and how much more terrifying that scene is without sound. Holding this man's bloody lobe, Dax laughs at his victim's vulnerability.

Like an evil serial killer.

He drops the guy and decapitates him with his claw. Dax marches toward the guards who lost me and breaks their necks, allowing Sam to be free of recourse.

"The first kill, I'll agree with, but that"—I point to the guards—"well, that just wasn't necessary," I slur, sounding more bored than upset.

"They outlived their use to me when they failed to protect you."

His eyes glow bright gold.

Goddess, he's so fucking hot.

"It's my fault I ran." I point back to myself to remind him. "I'm fucking fast."

He chuckles at my fake modesty. "Then, it's your fault my men are dead." As he leans in, the sting of spices tickles my nose as wafts of hardened leather wrap around me, his danger threatening my resolve. His scent is stronger than ever. Narrowing his eyes, he whispers, "Guess you'll have to live with that. As their queen, you'll get used to it."

I thrash and groan. Dax laughs at my attempt to get out of Sam's grasp. He tilts his head up to Sam, and Sam lets me go. When I stumble, Dax puts an arm out to catch me until I can regain my footing.

"Let's go home. Now."

I huff.

I'm not in the mood for him to tell me what to do. So, I raise an eyebrow. "Make me."

He flashes a grin, the kind that, if I didn't know he wouldn't hurt me, would've had me on my knees apologizing. His smile puts the devil to shame.

He throws me over his shoulder, causing everyone to look my way, and *I. Am. Mortified.* The embarrassment enrages me further, and before I can curse at him, he smacks my ass.

"Watch that pretty little mouth of yours."

Damn him and his abilities. But I drunkenly smile, knowing I got to cuss at him in his vision.

CHAPTER TWENTY-THREE

Dax

I couldn't focus on work while my mate was wasted in a club somewhere with a sexy little outfit on. I was only minutes away when Sam told me Alaina had run from him.

Thanks to my powers, the image of what the asshole was planning to do to my mate is burned into my mind. I clench my jaw every time I think about it.

I have an endless list of enemies who will die trying to get their revenge on me—this guy wasn't any different. The moment he saw my mark, he knew who she was to me. In most circumstances, this would've kept her safe. Other times, it'll make her a target.

She's the best thing to happen, not just to me but also my enemies. Before her, I didn't have a weakness for my foes to go after. It's only a matter of time until word spreads.

She won't be going out again without me, not unless we've completed the mating bond. It'll be easier to keep her safe that way.

Alaina and Sam haven't stopped arguing since we left. She calls him a playboy, a man whore, things of the like, and Sam mocks her by calling her "princess."

Now they're bickering about some cartoon called *Road Runner*, I think... Something about Sam being the scheming coyote and Alaina as the bird that outsmarts the coyote with her speed and feigning of innocence. Anytime Alaina tries to speak, Sam yells over her with "Meep, meep."

I want to punch him, but I'm learning this is their relationship; they fight like siblings.

"I knew it. I *knew* you'd run from me." Sam squints as he points at Alaina, who's thrown over my shoulder. "I'm not babysitting her ass next time, Dax. I'm serious. Get someone else. She does this *Road Runner* type shit every time!"

"I don't know what he's talking about," Alaina lies.

He's right. She does run from him every time. It's become a key part of the back-and-forth in their sibling-like relationship, which is why I've stopped punishing him. Only in times like these do I find myself intervening. Otherwise, I ignore when Sam barks into the mindlink to "control my woman."

Instead, I watch Alaina from my office window, who's outrunning Sam's wolf in her human form. I love watching her run; her speed is impressive.

Running seems to make her feel better, too. Some days, she doesn't say much. When I ask her what's wrong, she just shrugs. It's been a while since she's gone on a run, but Alaina is too stubborn to go jogging like a regular person—she always has to be bolting from *something* or *someone*.

That's when I ask him to take her around the castle grounds, knowing full well she can't resist making Sam's life harder. When she returns, she's more relaxed, grinning, and the smart mouth I love resurfaces. While she's not smiling at me, I tell myself I played some part in her happiness, and for now, that's enough for me. It is a welcome break from her hating me.

"On second thought, I'll watch her," Sam says, "but only if you give me the remote to the shock collar."

Alaina gasps.

Sam had to fetch me the shock collar from the dungeon. Sam wasn't too thrilled to leave his newest conquest to fetch anything for my own endeavor yet perked up when I informed him it was for Alaina. He was less than thrilled when he found out I'd repurposed the torture device to a sexual nature, adding components of pleasure. Sam knew then exactly what it was for, his room not too far from mine, something he also isn't loving.

"You told him?!"

Sam laughs at my embarrassed mate.

Alaina lifts off me with both hands, sitting up and scolding Sam. Her claws dig into me, the pain welcoming. *Fuck, hurt me, baby.* My wolf loves when she buries herself into me to put another male in her place, a lethal combination.

Get him, babe.

"Don't think I won't kick your ass, Sam."

A sense of pride hits me because she's all mine. I always envisioned my mate as someone who won't take shit from anyone, drunk or sober. So did Sam. Although I don't think either of us expected the two of them to form such a bond. When Sam finds his mate, she and Alaina will likely annoy us.

Alaina tells him to shut up as he laughs uncontrollably.

"You shut up," Sam retorts.

With Alaina still on my shoulder, I whip around, growling at Sam.

Sam quickly apologizes, and I slowly resume our walk back to the castle.

"Ha," Alaina says.

Goddess, they're like children.

I don't know what Sam did behind my back, but I spank Alaina before the dirty word could escape from her mouth. Queens shouldn't say such things in public. And she curses like a sailor.

Another vision plays out of her, defying me anyway. I mindlink her, telling her exactly what I'll do to that dirty mouth of hers if she says it.

"Fuck you."

A devilish grin spreads across my face.

* * *

"Are you going to be a good girl for me?"

At one in the morning, I'm peering down at Alaina, who's gasping for breath after gagging on my dick. I'm gripping a fistful of her hair, dragging the head of my cock across her plump bottom lip.

Glaring up at me, she's beside herself, contemplating whether she should listen to her body or her pride. Wondering why she gets off on being treated like my little plaything, caught between loving the attention I give her and the desire to punch me.

Specks of black from her makeup run down her face from her glowing violet eyes, her locks frizzy and clothes wrinkled. The aroma of hoppy wheat and black raspberries match her wild state.

I'm fucking addicted.

She chooses her pride. Before she can get those two little curse words out, my dick is back in her mouth.

"Let's try this again." I pull out of her so she can breathe, her chest bobbing as she gasps.

The hatred in her eyes doesn't mask her lust for me.

I see her intent to wait me out, thinking I'll come soon, knowing what her mouth does to me.

I forget she's used to the average wolf, like that mutt of hers. But I'm the king, which means I don't need the breather. My recovery time is nonexistent—both in killing and fucking. I'm insatiable and relentless. She'll learn only when I'm satisfied will I stop.

I lean in, my voice barely above a whisper. "Your mouth isn't the only hole I can entertain myself with, and I've got all night. When it comes to your safety, I won't tire, and I won't relent."

"I don't care if you cuss. Fucking cuss at me, darling. But you're *royalty* now. You have to be mindful of appearances."

"Why?"

"Because I'd rather spend more time fucking you than killing anyone who intends to judge you."

With that, her disposition becomes sweet submission.

"You'll have guards with you at all times from now on. If you leave castle grounds, you are not to run or hide from them. Do you understand me?"

She nods.

"Good girl."

CHAPTER TWENTY-FOUR

Alaina

I am in a toxic relationship with beer.

If it weren't for the sun shining through the window, I would've easily slept past noon.

Waving around the empty spot, I open my eyes, expecting to feel Dax.

Instead, he's sitting on the foot of the bed with his head in his hands. Immediately, I'm wondering what's wrong and if he's been here the whole time.

The stench of urine and blood assaults my senses, answering my question. He must've been in the dungeon torturing someone, and he's returned empty-handed.

A tinge of guilt hits, knowing I haven't helped ease any of the worries he holds. Between dealing with my defiance and the attacks of the kingdom, this poor guy can't catch a break.

Crawling toward the end of the bed, deciding to give this man a bone just this once, I run my hands across his chest from behind. He tenses under my touch, and my wolf whimpers.

Mate doesn't want us touching him.

I pull my hands away. "What's wrong?"

"Nothing."

Bullshit.

"Then, why'd you get all tense when I touched you?"

"I was trying not to move." He hangs his head, rubbing his hands together, strong forearms resting on his thighs. "Figured if I did, you'd stop."

Oh.

He doesn't turn as he waits for my response, but his honesty renders me speechless.

Dax sighs, rubbing the back of his neck before rising from the bed.

Mate thinks we don't want to touch him. Mate's hurt. Mate needs us. Do something!

Instinctively, I grab his hand. "Wait!"

Dax's eyes meet mine, his lips parting.

Now speak. Tell him.

"I . . . I do . . . want—to touch you."

Surprised by my admittance, Dax gawks at me as his heart races. Closing his mouth into a tight line, he recovers, tilting his head.

He doesn't believe me.

For a guy with the power to see intentions, he must see I'm telling the truth. But considering everything I've done, he has every reason to question.

Mirroring his actions, I tilt my head, giving a small smile, gently tugging him back down to the bed. I resume my graze,

COME FOR ME

adding a kiss to his head and neck, right where my mark would go.

Finally melting into my arms, he leans back into me as my hands roam his body.

Gratitude fills the air. I'm grateful that, despite everything we've been through, both of us are able to share such an intimate moment without any games or points to be made.

We share the silence, aside from the grunts coming from my mate whose back I'm massaging the thousandth knot out of.

"Have you ever heard of a massage?"

A sound between a laugh and a grunt follows the rolling out of a nodule under my thumb.

"Yes. Is this your way of saying you want me to find another masseuse?"

I dig my elbow into his shoulder, and the most adorable, inner childlike cackle comes out of him. My heart swells, and I go back to soothe out the knots.

"I'm kidding. Besides, I've never been big on people touching me."

"How come?"

"My father wasn't a nice guy."

I stop kneading. *What did his father do?*

"Story for another day."

Not wanting to push, I resume massaging him.

I think back to his royal family portraits in the hall. Besides River, who's never home, Dax is all alone.

I, at least, had Jemma, Taya, and the Wallers.

Then it hits me.

Here goes nothing.

"I've been thinking... and I want to visit my old pack."

He nods and groans at my touch. "I'll have guards ready to accompany you."

I blink rapidly, having expected a fight. Gritting my teeth, I brace myself for my next question.

"Will you come with me?" I chew on my bottom lip, uncomfortable with the vulnerability.

Dax faces me, his eyebrow raised. He searches my face for the punchline, then clears his throat. "You sure?"

My hands in my lap, I pick at my fingers, avoiding his gaze. "Yeah, you can see where I grew up, Jemma, and..."

Dax takes my hands.

I peer up at him.

A boyish grin replaces the puzzled look from before. My heart flutters at how something so simple could make him beam the way he is right now.

I lie back against the sheets as Dax crawls on top of me.

"Is my mate asking if I'll go with her to meet her family and see her hometown?"

I cover my face with my palms.

Laughing softly, he pulls my hands from my face. "I'd be happy to."

My wolf soars.

"Get ready. We leave in an hour."

* * *

After hours of running in wolf form, we finally arrive at my old pack. Dax's wolf's fur ripples with the wind. The air permeates rain and honeysuckle.

I'm home.

Dax's large wolf towers over the pack members guarding the borders. They step in front of him, not recognizing their king. Dax lets his dominant aura radiate from him, and security recognize his identity immediately. Liaisons are often sent in Dax's stead, so they wouldn't have known, just like I didn't when he hunted me that first time. At the realization, the guards lower their heads, stepping aside, baring their necks in submission. The royal treatment has my cheeks hot.

My paws pound on the moist soil of my old pack grounds as my wolf takes off past the guards. The bright green trees towering over the lands are a blur from the sides of my vision. It's a familiar sight, one that reminds me of childhood as I race home to Jemma and to a life I've fought for weeks to return to.

Scurrying animals along the forest floor are more hurried than I recall, the quiet patter of their feet now a soundtrack to our pursuit. The king's aura threatens the wild, unsettling all creatures dare to cross the same path as his thundering footfalls beside me.

Dax searches for danger and sends out his power and strength before us as a warning, his protective instincts daring even the smallest of insects to challenge him.

Dax's watchfulness and defense increase with each step, and my own diminishes as we near home and deeper into the forest. I bask in rain and honeysuckle, my shackles dropping, my wolf soothed by the native essence.

My pace slows to a stroll, and my paws come to a stop as we reach the field outside of Jemma's cabin.

Dax walks ahead of me, taking in our surroundings.

The view of my childhood home has always been stunning, but Dax's form in it added something. My painter's eye longs to portray his sharp, masculine features against the soft deep greens and intricate flowers I've painted.

I could never recreate such a masterpiece like Dax.

With a sigh of longing that perks Dax's ears, I shift, baring myself to Dax in the soft grass. He grins, deviousness flashing in his orbs, his fur transforming to flesh in quick speed. My wolf catalogs his naked form contrasting against the field.

I reach for my clothing, which was left by the pack when they heard of our arrival. We both put on clothes, becoming presentable houseguests.

My wolf sends a boost of confidence my way. Taking his hand, I lead him through the winding garden path, careful not to step on the precious flowers, herbs, and plants Jemma must've tilled that morning, judging from the unearthed dirt sinking beneath the weight of our steps.

Small footprints I know all too well greet me on the trail, my pace quickening as I near Jemma's. Tension I didn't realize I've been holding releases from my body, the comfort of my surroundings settling around my heart.

Behind me, I can practically feel Dax's gaze as he scans unfamiliar surroundings for threats. His back is rigid and tense, his shoulders squared for a fight. The only softness to his stature are the fingers curled around my own. It's hard for him to settle if he's constantly assessing for danger, planning evacuation strategies, and radiating suspicious energy toward the towering sunflowers.

A cardinal lands on a nearby branch. Rustling leaves has Dax tensing and darting behind himself. A laugh rolls out of my lungs on its own accord at his cautious but overprotective nature. His inability to relax deepens as his brows furrow at the noise escaping my lips.

His heart is beating normally, but he's anxious, but why? Surely, he's visited other packs before.

Mate doesn't know these grounds as well. Mate doesn't like the disadvantage. Mate is protective over us.

The attacks have been so random the only pattern is they're getting closer to Crescent. Knowing Dax, when he's in this state, all it would take is someone to startle him accidentally and he would hurt them—*or worse.*

Placing my hand on his chest, sparks from our bond crackle like the Pop Rocks I ate as a kid. Under my palm, his muscles relax.

"Hey, look at me."

Dax's eyes meet mine.

The man who is never told no or given a command doesn't hesitate when I tell him what to do. There's something powerful and precious about making power bend.

As his eyes soften, panic dissipates at my touch as my thumb rubs his chest.

"We're safe here."

Taking a deep breath, he nods.

I drop my hand and knock on Jemma's door.

"Who is it?" Jemma's sweet voice sings from the other side.

"'Laina," I say, in my best impression of Jemma's accent.

Dax snaps his head my way.

"What was that?"

I snicker.

Feet shuffle inside as they make their way to the door.

Jemma opens it, the purple gardening hat and gloves I'd gifted her for her birthday falling from her hands and landing beside her.

Jemma likes to stay busy this time of year. It's nice to see some things haven't changed since my departure—much like the graying strands of her hair to her exaggerated display of glee through her crow's feet.

A broad smile forms on my lips as startled shouts of joy escape her own. She clasps her hands in front of her mouth, the movement is a habit she developed to hide the wrinkles she earned from a life well lived. Excitement and happy tears fill her eyes at our reunion. She embraces me in a big hug, squeezing me.

I relish her flowery perfume.

Jemma looks at Dax and takes in his size as her eyes trail up to him. "Who do we have here?"

Dax's hands are behind his back, his feet shoulder-width apart, as he politely smiles at Jemma.

"This is Dax. And, according to the Moon Goddess, he's my mate."

Jemma raises her eyebrows and blinks rapidly.

But I'm not fooled. Jemma probably cornered Caleb as soon as he returned without me and made him tell her everything he knew. Jemma's been too quiet and kept her distance throughout all of this. She would've shown up at the castle herself if she didn't already know about my whereabouts. *That much, I'm certain.*

Dax ignores my downplay and gives a toothy smile to Jemma as he regards her with a nod. "It's a pleasure to finally meet you."

"Well, come on in. I was just about to make some supper." She ushers us in, and Dax follows me, ducking under the doorframe.

I fill Jemma in about pretty much everything regarding the Hunt, how Dax found me, marked me, the castle, and his beta, Sam.

Jemma moves my hair away, then walks over to Dax and gestures to have Dax expose his neck.

I stare as Dax allows Jemma to tell him what to do and does what she says without a thought.

Seems I'm not the only one who can bend powerful men to her will.

When Jemma notices he's without a mark, she purses her lips and furrows her brows, then turns to me.

"'Laina, honey, why haven't you marked him yet?"

The vexation in her question is received as a whine. Jemma always wanted me to find my mate, mark him, and have lots of pups for her to spoil and yell at for straying too far away from the yard.

"Yeah, 'Laina, why?" Dax echoes with a smug look.

I narrow my eyes at him, smiling. *I'll have to remember to thank him later for the hell Jemma is about to put me through.*

"I'm just not ready yet."

She huffs. "The Moon Goddess has sent him to you for a reason. Does he treat you right?"

If right is chasing me through the woods, putting a shock collar on me, and restraining me, then...

"Yes, but—"

"Then, honey, quite frankly, I don't see the problem. Now, I raised you better than to go against the Moon Goddess. I swear, sometimes, you're just as stubborn as your mother was." She looks at Dax. "Is she this stubborn for you?"

"All the time," Dax snorts as he takes another bite of her homemade bread. Leaning back in his chair, he smiles, with his leg resting on his other, enjoying the interrogation.

"She was always like this, you know. Couldn't get this one to do anything she didn't want to do. She could argue forever."

"I do not!"

"See?" Jemma hits Dax's shoulder with the back of her hand playfully.

I exhale my frustration as I let my head drop on the wooden back of the chair.

To my horror, Dax and Jemma get along with ease, never running out of things to talk about, but mostly, they chat about me.

They swap stories of how stubborn and argumentative I can be—like the time she'd tell me to hold on to her so I wouldn't tumble down the stairs. Instead of listening, I'd stick up my nose, cross my arms, and one step later, I'm tumbling down the wooden steps, crying my heart out.

Jemma rants about her love for gardening and what plants she has growing, then brings up my paintings, and I still.

"Jemma, he doesn't want to see those."

"I'd love to see them, Ms.—"

"Oh, please, call me Jemma. You're practically family."

What the hell is happening? Mr. Doesn't Like To Say Please is being charming and polite. *He's letting Jemma touch him and tell him what to do?* Jemma is allowing Dax to call her by her first name—and must really like Dax because she wouldn't even let Caleb, her future alpha, address her as Jemma, and she *liked* Caleb. Having her approve of Dax means she won't ever let me let him go. I'll never hear the end of it.

You don't want to let him go. I mentally kick myself.

I'm trying to decide if Jemma liking him is my worst nightmare or everything I could want when Jemma's words pull me out of my thoughts.

"Oh, you stay here. I'll go get them." Jemma pats Dax's thighs and gets up.

"No, no, no, no," I go to chase Jemma down, but she dodges my grasp.

Dax wraps his arms around my waist and pulls me onto his lap. He exhales a hearty laugh as I wiggle on him, trying to get free.

"Keep it up, and I'll make sure you're immobilized completely," he playfully whisper-growls in my ear.

I still and realize I've made him hard in the process of rubbing my ass on his lap. Not wanting to rattle the beast more, I ignore the goose bumps on my arms.

"So much for loyalty!" I yell to Jemma, who's rummaging through my room by now. *What if he doesn't like them?*

Ignoring me, she yells from my childhood bedroom, "Found it!"

Jemma returns, carrying three canvases. She lines them up on the dining room table, leaning them against the wall.

Dax peers over my shoulder to look at them. "You made these?" He looks at me incredulously.

I nod, cheeks warming, as he continues to praise the details.

"What's this one?" He points to the last painting of my mother.

Her blue eyes are rounded like mine, her full lips spread into a smile, her auburn hair flowing around her wildly as she looks behind her.

I painted her running freely, something I had wished her and I got to do together.

"That's my mother. At least what I think she'd look like. She died when I was born. I don't have any pictures of her."

Dax holds me tighter. "She's wearing your necklace."

I fiddle with the stone. "It was hers."

It wasn't long after I painted the necklace on all the paintings I made of her.

Dax inspects the stone. The way he takes such interest in the things that matter to me . . . I wonder if family is something that matters to him and if this is something I'd be lucky enough to give us one day.

Danger! Baby fever.

I shake the thought from my mind and avert my attention back to the picture.

"My mother used to go to this spot all the time. I can—I can take you to it i-if you want?"

My stuttering exposes my inexperience with sharing myself with him or anybody.

The man in front of me has so much of the world on his shoulders, and now I'm asking him to entertain something insignificant to anyone else like my stories as a parentless child. Something that I perceive to be so minimal in comparison to everything else.

I don't know why I chose now to show him. I've shut him out time and time again, and he's still here looking at me with such possession, interest, letting the words I speak sink in. You would think with how he hangs onto every word I say and the way he's gawking at me that I was the Moon Goddess Herself.

Maybe I'm not as important as the Moon Goddess, but Dax worships me.

He perks up at my offer to show him my favorite spot, and I briefly feel his elation and surprise directed toward my proposition to share a part of myself. Surely, he is taken aback by my walls tumbling, as my vulnerability hasn't been voluntarily offered up until I asked him to come with me to visit my old pack. I guess I could understand his shock, since this is the first time I'm letting him into something that isn't my panties. I felt what I could've sworn was doubt before he shut off his feelings completely.

What would he have to doubt? Could it be that he's doubting whether it's safe to go to a place he's not familiar with? Is he worried about the possibility of an attack?

That would make sense. Dax chooses overkill when it comes to protection.

Despite what he might be feeling regarding our safety, he accepts my offer.

Jemma gives Dax another order to help her with the dishes, explaining that if you don't cook, you clean. He scrambles because he can't follow her commands fast enough.

I smile, finding it humorous that this force of nature is taking orders from a woman twice his age, a third of his size, and who hasn't shown her wolf in years, all because he's worried about her approval.

All for me.

She gives me another tight hug and kisses Dax on the cheek before she embraces him. Dax reassures her that we'll be back to visit. Jemma closes the door but not before she tells me to make sure I'm "nice" to Dax. I can't help but scrunch my nose at that.

"Think she likes me?" he asks rhetorically, wearing a smug look.

Of course he knows Jemma liked him; she's always been sweet and respectful toward others. But Dax received a completely different kind of welcome. She loved him.

"I think you've been replaced as the favorite child," Dax says, walking in the wrong direction.

COME FOR ME

More confused than ever, I look at him. I don't recognize the man in front of me who is doing dishes, taking orders, making plans to visit, and wanting to appease others.

Now he's making jokes? Who is he? Where is the man that would kill any challenge to his rule? Had people for everything?

After his and Jemma's interactions today, I realize I don't really know Dax behind closed doors when he's just Dax and not king to all. *If things were different between us, would he be this carefree and pleasant?*

"It's this way, Your Highness," I say, knowing the acknowledgment would irritate him.

He growls. "Dax."

"*King* Dax . . . right?" I smile and tilt my head in question as I walk backward.

We laugh, and he chases me, and I break from his grasp, shifting. He follows suit. His wolf nips at my tail whenever he gets closer. He doesn't surpass me but is careful to make sure he's never too far behind, watching me run freely with my wolf.

Bliss rolls through me as I run through the forest of my old pack with my mate.

I never thought I would have this—sharing mine and my mother's favorite place.

Tossing the clothes we carried in our mouths, I shift. Dax towers over me, taking in my naked form. His wolf looks at me up and down with a low growl of approval.

I roll my eyes, smiling, and throw my tank top and shorts on. Dax does the same with his clothes after shifting.

We keep running until I approach the bushes and brush that block my haven.

I push the bushes out of the way, separating their leaves so we can see behind them.

Dax steps onto the grassy cliff my mother used to frequent. There's nothing surrounding it but a huge tree that twists and angles itself until its long branch overlooks the rest of the forest.

"We're here," I say.

Dax watches as I walk toward the tree in the clearing perched on the cliff.

It's an old but sturdy tree. I graze my hands over and around the tree trunk and position myself on its branch that hovers close to the edge.

Dax climbs and sits on the branch with me. I tell him how my mother would come here, sit in this exact spot, and look out.

You can see what you would think is the entire kingdom from here. It's quiet and mesmerizing. Pack members said she would stay perched on this tree for hours when she was pregnant with me, just enjoying the view and rubbing her belly, talking to me.

Dax watches me and listens as I retell stories other pack members have told me. Most of what I had to share was about how she often stayed to herself.

"I don't know much else about her."

"That makes sense, considering she was a rogue. She probably didn't want to bring much attention to herself."

What is he talking about? My mother was a rogue? How would he know that?

Dax registers my confusion. "As soon as I knew you existed, I had my men track down everything about you, including your parents. There wasn't much, but the pack records indicate—"

"Pack records? You have them? How?!"

Now Dax looks confused. It's like he doesn't understand why I don't know this already or why I would be looking to him to ask for information about my parents.

He lets out a hearty laugh and smiles. "I'm king, Alaina. I have access to everything."

Duh.

"Tell me everything."

"Your mother's name was Emilia, and she wasn't always a rogue. She became one after her pack was overrun by rogues and vampires. Then she met, who I assume was, your father. She doesn't say much about him in her interviews, just that she had to leave when she did. This is just what she said in the written transcripts. But there's no video or anything else. I'm sorry."

"Was my father mentioned?"

"There wasn't a name or anything."

His speech softens.

I continue to stare, urging him to go on.

"In the interview, they asked about him. They wanted to prepare for whoever might come looking for her. She refused to give a name. All she said was that he was powerful but not a threat. She reassured them no one would be coming after her, not even him. That he didn't know about you and wanted to keep it that way."

I'm reeling. All this time, I assumed my father was dead and that's why my mother was here. But if he's powerful, maybe he survived.

Dax didn't know that I didn't know this information. Otherwise, he would've told me. I never thought to ask him, either.

"May I see them? The records?" I ask, even though part of me doesn't feel like I can ask him for anything after all we've been through. All I've put him through.

"Alaina, you will never have to want for anything as long as I'm alive." He kisses my forehead.

That familiar guilt creeps in. He's doing everything to get to know me, yet all I've done is try to push him away without first getting to know him. I think back to earlier when I felt his doubt after asking him to visit my mother's most treasured spot. He wasn't questioning the safety of the area. Otherwise, he would have instructed pack warriors to come with us. The doubt was because he wasn't sure if it was safe to be happy that I'd asked him to join me, that I wanted him near me, to share an intimate part of me. A part of me I haven't shared with anyone before.

The whole reason I closed myself off to him was out of fear that I could never get close to who I was, who my mother was, and who my father might still be. My inner self climbs and peeks over the hypothetical walls I've built between us. And decide to do something I haven't done since I've met him. Try to love him.

"What about your parents?"

Silent, he stills, and the vibe changes.

For a moment, I think I've overstepped. But then he looks at me.

"Do you want to know *about* them or what *happened* to them?"

CHAPTER TWENTY-FIVE

8-year-old Dax

Standing in the doorway leading to the courtyard, my father is talking to the alpha of the Midnight pack at the conclusion of another meeting where I don't understand anything.

The sound of a ball pounding against concrete catches my attention. Quietly backing away from the conversation, I spot a boy with blonde hair, who's dribbling a rubber ball. The other male pups try to take it from him. He passes it, instructing his teammates where to stand.

Though I've never met him, I recognize his voice. It's the same voice I've overheard sweet talking the kitchen staff into an extra snack and pleading to my father's beta to stay up past his bedtime.

One of his teammates passes the ball back to him but misses as it rolls in front of me, then stops at my feet.

I check if my father can tell I'm not paying attention to find he's too busy in his conversation to notice. I don't want him to see. He might get mad. My father says toys are a waste of time.

"Hey, pass it here!" the sandy-haired boy hollers, jogging over to me, holding his hands out.

I pick up the ball and chuck it to the boy like it might burn me. The boy makes an *oof* sound but manages to catch it. I wince, hoping I didn't hurt him.

To my surprise, the boy reveals he's missing his top two front teeth, laughing at the impact. Even more shocking, he throws it back with just as much force.

I smile at the only boy who isn't afraid of me because of my father.

I throw it back to him as hard as I can this time. Only, he ducks, accidentally hitting a guard.

I gasp, grabbing the boy by the arm to pull him into the entryway, with our backs against the wall.

I'm convinced this boy won't ever be my friend now if it means hiding all the time, but the boy's giggling. *Does he want to get us in trouble?*

"Shh," I say, but I'm trying not to laugh. "What's your name?"

"Sam."

* * *

13-year-old Dax

"Do it now!"

Clutching the knife, I'm careful not to show any hint of emotion unless I want a beating.

I've tortured men by my father's orders plenty of times before. Though I hate it, it's the only time my father is proud of me, and he says it's important for me to learn. He wants me to be a strong king, and strong kings don't cry, but they will make others shed tears if need be.

I'm not strong enough yet. My father says I'll need lots of practice. I want to vomit. He'll beat me for embarrassing him if I do.

There's no way out of this. No one is safe from him.

My father told me this man before me is guilty of raping someone, which helps.

I swallow my bile and eat my sins, killing my first man.

* * *

20-year-old Dax

I've killed many since my first. What's worse is I've developed a taste for it.

My father lied to me about my first kill—that man didn't rape anyone. The only crime he committed was stealing food for his family. Unfortunately, he stole from the crown, and my father took this as a personal attack.

I've tried to stand up to him, refusing to kill another soul, reclaiming my power as the only male heir to his throne, knowing my mother couldn't have more children. *The worst he can do is beat me into oblivion.*

I was prepared for it, and he knew, which is why he hit my mother once he realized pummeling me wasn't effective for my compliance anymore.

Since then, I've become his obedient killing machine, completely desensitized to murder, finding purpose and justification to it: protection.

COME FOR ME

It wasn't until my father had a head injury that things escalated from just a smack across my mother's face to a deadly beating. My father is paranoid, and he thinks everyone is against him. Partly because of the brain injury, the other because they were. My father is feared, not loved. Many people want him dead.

My mother, sister, and I function like zombies, void of our own thoughts and plans, afraid he'll sense them and use it against us.

At dinnertime, Mother is serving us food, and a knife falls from a plate she was holding and knicks Dad's arm. The chair flips behind him as he stands and throws her against the wall.

After taking River upstairs, I hide her in the closet. *She's only nine. She can't keep seeing this crap.* This time, I don't stay with her but instruct her to cover her ears and not come out until I came to get her.

When I return downstairs, my mother is already gone. I see red, and none of my next moves are calculated. I don't intend to kill him. I don't *know* what I intended to do.

I just did.

Unfortunately for my father, he had turned me into a machine. The very monster who could kill without giving it a thought.

* * *

I don't tell Alaina everything, just enough that she can fill in the rest. It's easy to piece together what happened, as I became king next and gained his power of seeing people's intentions. Word has spread of the power-hungry heir, wanting the throne bad enough he'd kill his own father for it. Some even believe I killed my mother.

I don't like to talk about the past, but when I do, she doesn't look away from me, just listens. She realizes we both have lost our mothers. She sees me now as the boy who lost someone, not the man who killed for power.

She kisses me, the first kiss I didn't have to seduce out of her or steal from her. It's soft, loving, and meant to comfort. I've made peace with my past long ago. Nothing else matters anymore but her. But I let her comfort me anyway.

The kiss ends, and our foreheads rest against each other. Our breathing syncs, and we don't speak. At this moment, Alaina doesn't hate me or wish I was someone else or for her to be anywhere else. For now, she's here.

Ruffling leaves comes from the forest. Instantly, I guard Alaina behind me and look around.

Like my father discovered when I ended him, unless you can see them, you can't know their intentions. I stay still, waiting for whatever it is to show itself.

I growl, a warning to rethink whatever attack they might be planning before I end them.

The pounding of Alaina's heart reaches my ears as she picks up on the same thing I have.

A vampiric presence emits great power. The familiar putrid smell tells me he or she is not alone, and the hissing and snarling grows louder.

I mindlink Sam and my guards for backup, but it'll be awhile before they get to us.

"*Get ready,*" I mindlink to Alaina.

Her eyes glow violet, canines forming.

My darling queen looks like a bloodthirsty demon. I note when we aren't in danger to do whatever sexual thing I can to get her to look at me *exactly* that way again.

They emerge from the brush. Rogues foaming at the mouth, saliva dripping as they lick their canines. Vampires jump from trees, hissing and baring their fangs.

"Do you see what they want?"

I nod. "To kill me."

"Why?"

I roll out my neck and call on my wolf.

"Because it's the only way they're ever taking you."

Scanning the horde, I know the powerful vampire isn't among the visible but lurking somewhere around us. Whoever it is, they won't show themselves.

More vampires and rogues file in behind the rest.

"Dax, there's too many of them," Alaina panics.

She's right. Even with both of us, we'd have to take on ten at once to have a shot. The ledge behind us is too far a drop, unless we were able to shift. Even then, it's too risky.

I look for weak spots among them and notice rogues with chunks ripped out of their ears and others missing fur from being bitten previously. This tells me they're survivors of previous battles, but they've slipped up, causing those battle wounds.

The vampires are new, making them eager, impulsive, and less strategic but quicker, which leaves minimal recovery time and little to no room for error.

Clumps of them gather in front of us, each with varying ratios of vampires to rogues than the other. Her best chance is the one with more rogues.

"You take the left. Watch for fangs."

Even though they aren't planning to kill her, that could change at a drop of a hat. Especially rogues, who've been without order and law for so long. After not having to control their anger for fear of repercussions, they forget how to rein it back in.

The faster I kill all my enemies, the sooner I can assist her and get her to safety. Until then, she can hold her own.

They charge in all at once, leaving no space for us to shift, so we fight in our human form. The first vampire lunges and misses, allowing me to throw him off the side of the ledge. A rogue fails to nip at my leg. I protrude my claws and rip its heart out.

Two more charges at me, and I kick one in the face while biting into the other. I peer over at Alaina, who's on the back of some rogue, taking her claws, reaching in front of it to slice its neck. A growl of approval leaves my throat.

A vampire creeps behind her, its intent to jump and pull her off the rogue bleeding out beneath her.

"Alaina, behind you!"

She snatches the vampire, falling off the rogue's back, and rolling until she's on top of him. With the help of her wolf, her canines elongate, and she bites the shit out of the side of the vampire's neck, then claws at its chest until she reaches its heart and chomps into it. Destroying the vampire's lifeline completely.

Her canines are out, eyes glowing violently, blood dripping down the sides of her face, her chest and neck.

My deranged queen.

Appreciating the savagery of my mate, I forget my surroundings, allowing a vampire to jump on me. We fall, with his hand gripping my throat. Half my upper body is hanging off the ledge, hovering over the fluffy trees covering the rocky depths below.

With better leverage and full access to my wolf, I could easily buck him off of me, hurdling him over the cliff, but I'd topple with him at this angle, killing us both. I settle for what I can, digging my claws in his hand and clawing at his eyes with the other. My talons leave marks across his veined face, but it's not enough to get him to relent.

I'm fighting consciousness when waves of anger hit me, but these emotions aren't mine. The vampire is tossed over my head, disappearing into the depths below. The loss of his grasp around my windpipe has me coughing.

Alaina kneels next to me, checking me over. "Are you okay?"

"You shouldn't have done that."

"What're you talking about? I saved your life."

I laugh. "Exactly. Hard to deny you care for me moving forward after you've prevented my death."

She rolls her eyes playfully.

I brush the hair out of her face, cupping her cheek. "Am I wearing you down, little one?"

Staring into the violet swirls of my guardian angel, I sense something different from the usual regretful lust wafting off of her. Like her eyes, they're hypnotic, easy to get lost in.

Before I can name the feeling, a rogue bites her leg, throwing my precious darling like a rag doll into a tree trunk. Tree bark crushes from her impact.

She thuds to the ground, pressing a hand onto her injured leg. Judging by the twisted angle of her limb, it's not broken, but it'll take a day or two to heal completely. Her whimpers and cries call forth this unhinged wolf, red taking over my vision.

Whipping my head to the rogue who dared to hurt my girl, I pounce on the scum, calling forth the strength of my wolf to my human form, hurling him at the vampires trying to creep up on me from behind, tearing out a chunk of his throat in the process.

"Dax!" Alaina screams.

Rogues and vampires lurk toward Alaina, who's struggling to stand.

I barrel through the mob, planting my body firmly in front of her, snarling at the filth plotting to get their hands on my queen. Ready to kill whoever dares try to take her from me, I fling any rogue or vampire off the edge who's dumb enough to get too close.

But there's still too many, and without my formidable queen able to fight by my side, I'm forced to take them on alone in only half of my wolf form. We need backup—and fast.

"*Where are you?!*" I bark into the mindlink at Sam.

"We're still miles away," Sam replies.

I growl.

A wolf prowls forward, and I pin him to the growl with the help of my wolf, tearing his head apart from his body by his ear until his yelping stops.

"Dax, what do we do?"

I glance back at my mate, desperate to get her out of here. Our only option is for me to hold them off until Sam and the rest can get to us.

I take out another vampire, ripping him to shreds.

"Who can get to us first?" I ask Sam.

"Caleb, he's leading the way. He's almost to you now."

I curse the Moon Goddess for Her cruel sense of humor. Unfamiliar with these grounds, my men couldn't pinpoint where we were faster than a native. As much as I don't like it, he's our best chance.

The mutt arrives in wolf form, jumping over the mob, snapping a vampire in half with his mouth and tossing him to the trees. Shifting into his human form, he dives and rolls, then lands beside me to keep Alaina out of harm's way.

"Your Majesty." He nods.

Normally, I detest him and his care for my mate. In this instance, his attentiveness for her is something I can tolerate and even use. *As long as he's willing to lay down his life for my queen, he and I are on the same page.*

Even with him here, I don't let up but neither do the vermin attacking us. With the three of us fighting, we might've had a chance. But with Alaina injured, the others being too far away, I know we can't hold them off much longer.

We need a new strategy, but at least one of us dies in every plan I can come up with. While every fiber of my being would rather it be the mutt, the rogues and vamps aren't focusing on him. If I ran with her, they would just chase us, leaving this mutt to go after the crowd behind, wasting necessary energy.

In such a scenario, we both die.

There's only one way Alaina makes it out of this safely, and I despise the plan entirely.

The mutt and I lock eyes, and he nods, coming to the same conclusion.

Why does he also have to be naked? Dammit. He better not fuck this up.

"You will protect her."

It isn't a question or show of good faith. He will protect her or he'll meet a monster that makes any other version of me seem like child's play, his screams will carry over into hell.

"You know I will."

The heavy pause between us speaks louder than the vermin snapping at us.

I grind my teeth, my jaw flexing. Taking another look at my mate, whose wide eyes burn my soul, I force myself out of her violet trance before I change my mind.

"Take her and go," I reluctantly bark.

My wolf is destroying my insides, hating the idea of being separated from our mate and relying on another to keep her safe. I don't know if I'll make it out of this alive, but I sure as hell won't let them take her from me.

A vampire pounces on me when he thinks I'm not paying attention, and I snatch its throat. I ignore the bloodsucker desperately snapping its jaws at me. His dirty nails scrape at my flesh, stinging me. The smell of my own blood being spilled fuels the darkness in me further. But it also stirs the vampires.

"No way. I'm staying," she protests.

Her words fill me with dread.

"What?!" I whip my head to look back at her. *She's unbelievable.* "Not a chance in hell. You stay here, you get killed."

Part of me wants to kiss her for being so brave, the other part trying to rack my brain to understand. *Why does she defy me at every turn when I try to keep her safe?* She's spent so long trying to run from me, to run away with him. Now, when I tell her to do just that, she refuses.

I should've had the power to read minds so I can understand how to make my mate happy.

I inhale, turning my attention to the mutt, silently communicating what we both already know.

She's going to make this as difficult as possible.

"Please, don't do this."

My chest tightens as her arm posted at her side shakes in ... fear? That can't be right.

What is she scared of? Is she worried this plan won't work? She can't stay here. Why won't she leave? She always tries to leave me. What's changed?

What's her intention?

Looking back at her, I call on my powers, and my mouth parts, my brows furrowing as her intentions play out for me.

Alaina stands on our bedroom balcony in nothing but one of my button downs and a robe in the middle of winter, gazing out at our kingdom, rubbing her swollen belly. The blazing cold is no match to her pregnant wolf's hot flashes. At two and a half months, she's almost made it to the full three-month term. I wrap my arms around her, kissing the raised scar tissue from my mark.

My lips part, and my eyes bug.

She's planning a life with me.

Searching her face for any sign of deception, I'm not sure I can believe what I saw wasn't just wishful thinking and not my powers at all.

By avoiding my gaze, she gives me my answer.

My heart skips a beat.

"I want to stay with you. Please don't make me leave you."

Words I never thought I'd hear.

My wolf howls, and a sound I've never made before leaves me. The time she actually wants me, I have to let her go, knowing there's a strong chance I won't make it back to her.

My heart twists from its reacquaintance to despair.

Something inside of me that's solidified into ice threatens to thaw for the first time in years. As it does, liquid fills my eyes.

My father's harsh words echo in my mind. *Don't start crying like a little bitch. Men shouldn't cry. Show your enemies you're indestructible. Get. Mad.*

Despite his distorted thinking, it's effective.

If I'm going to make it out of this alive, the tears blurring my vision won't help.

COME FOR ME

Directing my rage at our impossible predicament toward the cause of it, I rip the vampire's face in two like paper, his face tearing jaggedly down the center. Both halves of his head are in either of my hands.

The display doesn't stop them. Instead, they up the ante. Three more vampires step up, intending to take me on all at once, their hissing reaching ear piercing decibels.

They're getting impatient.

They want her, and they know they won't get her without taking me out first.

Fuck!

Remembering to put logic over emotion, I come to my senses. "I can't lose you. I'm sorry."

I can't let them take her. They won't have her. She's mine.

I snarl at the mutt, annoyed he hasn't moved at his king's order.

He reaches for her, saving me from my selfish desire to let her stay.

She swats at his hands. "Don't you touch me, Caleb."

Retreating, he looks at me, unsure whether to listen to his queen or king.

Losing focus, I barely dodge a vampire. He nicks the side of my arm.

I look to her, to the mutt, and back to the horde. They're about to attack all at once. *Fuck, there's no time.*

"Take her, *now!*"

Subdued by my high alpha command, the mutt scoops her up in his arms, not allowing himself to be fazed when Alaina tries to fight.

Tears run down her face as she cusses at me and the mutt. He covers her with his body as he charges through the sea of filth before he finally breaks away and sprints with her in his arms.

Away from me.

I try to get in as many glances as possible of her in the midst of fighting the vampires and rogues. With every glimpse of her, I see she's looking right at me. I return my attention to the battle in front of me.

A gut-wrenching howl leaves my mate. When I look back to set eyes on her again, she's disappeared from my view.

A few rogues break from the crowd to follow them, but I force myself to focus on the problem at hand and not risk my life and theirs by running after them. With our separation, their attention is divided, and going after her would mean they'd all of them chasing us.

I'll just have to trust my men will cross their paths soon to take them out, giving the mutt and Alaina their best chance.

What seems like hours later, Sam and several others arrive to aid me, breaking through the crowd, then encircle us.

"Alaina?" I ask Sam, needing to know if I have to add killing the mutt to my to-do list if I survive.

"Taken care of."

I nod at Sam, relief washing over me. A half smile forms on my face, holding back a snarling rogue. My wolf and I come together in full force, as we're able to fully focus on the task at hand now that our mate is finally okay.

But just in case . . .

"Section twenty-eight," I yell to Sam.

"What?"

"If I don't make it out of this, section twenty-eight." I jerk my arm, trying to pull the vampire's heart out in my grasp.

"It's not going to come to that," Sam yells back.

There, I think to myself, finally tearing its heart out, throwing it to the ground and kicking its body out of the way.

"She needs to know. Promise me."

"Tell her yourself." Sam grunts.

I hope I can.

We take out several, but even then, there are too many, and from where I'm standing, I can see up ahead.

There's more pouring in.

My men, no matter how well trained, can't do this forever. There's no backup for me to mindlink to in this territory, so I order my men to fall back.

Just as I do, the breath is knocked out of me while rogues and vampires cling to me. Stumbling backward, I try to fight them off.

Their snapping traps are the last things I see before I topple over the cliff behind me.

AUTHOR'S NOTE

I hope you enjoyed reading this as much as I did writing it. If you did, I would truly appreciate a review on Amazon, Goodreads, or your favorite book website.

ACKNOWLEDGMENTS

To my readers. Your support means more to me than you know. Thank you for taking a chance on me and giving my book purpose. In return, I hope I was able to fulfill the purpose you had for reading it, whether that is an escape or inspiration. Regardless, please remember to take care of your mental health.

To my first editor, Immie Jayne. I've written more than thousands of words, and I can confidently say there still aren't enough words to express how much your support means to me, so I can only hope you find weight in leaving me speechless. Dax, Alaina, Sam, and I are eternally grateful to you.

To my sixth-grade teacher and my classmate in 2007. Thank you to my teacher for the short story assignment, which led me to write my first romantic tragedy. Thank you to my classmate and first ever reader, for your reactions and kind words are what sparked this dream and gave me the courage to make it a reality.

To my copy editor, August Hays, developmental editor, Caryn Pine, line editor, Allison Buehner, proofreader, Samantha Pico, and my first beta reader, Yashira Estrella. As you all said, books are like our babies, and it was difficult trusting people as a first-time book mom. But as the saying goes, it takes a village to raise a child—or in this case—a book. Thank you to my village for putting up with this helicopter of a book parent. Most importantly, thank you for giving my novel—and me—the love, care, and patience it needed.

Other important acknowledgments:

My family and supportive partner.

None of this would have been possible without any of you. Thank you for the role you played. I am incredibly lucky to have such a supportive team to help me leave a lasting legacy.

—C.J. Sweet

ABOUT THE AUTHOR

C.J. Sweet lives in Virginia, where she is a full-time mental health professional devoted to making this world a little more tolerable for the resilient. When C.J. is not listening to people divulge their trauma, she is losing herself in books—a favorite coping skill. C.J. strives to be as relatable as an author as she is a reader, as she, too, found disappointment when she turned eighteen, and nothing magical or paranormal happened.

Learn more about C.J. Sweet on brokenspinepublishing.com. Follow her on TikTok, Instagram, and Goodreads.

Printed in Great Britain
by Amazon